CIVILIANS IN PEACE

A Novel of the War On Terror

Gary T.,

Thank you for your
service to our nation!
I feel lucky that we
ended up in the same seminar.

Paul Craft

COLONEL PAUL A. CRAFT

ISBN: 978-0-9815789-0-3

Printed in the United States by Morris Publishing
3212 East Highway 30
Kearney, NE 68847
1-800-650-7888

Civilians in Peace,
Soldiers in War.

We are the Guard!

- Motto of the National Guard.

Dedicated to my beautiful wife, Laura,
and my wonderful kids, Jack and Kelly

They also serve who wait and worry.

- Anonymous

www.civiliansinpeace.com

Acknowledgements

This novel, a work of fiction, would not have been possible without the very real characters that I have been so lucky to know in my life. It is dedicated to the soldiers with whom I've served, especially Alan Rogers, Matt Kambic, Dana McDaniel, Greg Wayt, Dave Powell, Dave Rhoads, Rufus Smith, Lloyd Austin, Dave Bethel and so many, many others too numerous to mention. In fact, I probably should not have even started trying to list my fellow soldiers by name since I will leave out so many who have meant so very much. Many of you, my fellow soldiers, may see some of yourselves in the positive attributes of the characters in this book. Any negative aspects are based on someone else! Thank you all for your comradeship. I owe you so much for your support, your hard work and your self-sacrifice.

To my fellow teachers and administrators in the Upper Arlington City Schools, this book and my military service have both been possible due to the steady base you have represented. To my family, your support, sacrifice, understanding, and prayers have sustained me through twenty-five years of service.

I am especially thankful to those who have contributed in ways both small and large to this novel, especially Marlene and Warren Orloff, Jeff Weaver, Debi Binkley, Doris and Charles Solt, Jim Farrell, Bob Hestand, Jim Buffer, Mary Anne Nyeste and Ray Kline. Every person who touched this novel left a mark for the better.

"And let's remember that those charged with protecting us from attack have to be right 100 percent of the time. To inflict devastation on a massive scale, the terrorists only have to succeed once."

       - Secretary of State Condoleeza Rice in testimony before the 9-11 Commission.

Prologue One

South Boston
May 11, 4:45 pm EST (2145 GMT)

Normally, a fender bender would be a major challenge for someone who had overstayed his student visa. Today, of all days, it would be the ruination of his young life's purpose. With this in mind, Sayeed Maliki carefully merged left into the center-most lane as he completed the transition from I-90 West to I-93 North just south of downtown Boston. Driving the 24-foot U-Haul truck was never easy, but he had practiced a great deal. The Chelsea U-Haul dealer considered Sayeed to be his best customer since the young man had been renting a truck several times a week for the last couple of years. His public reason for doing so was quite legitimate. He and his friend Nabeel had been running a fairly successful cut-rate moving and delivery business in the area surrounding Cambridge University. Flyers and word of mouth had led to a steady flow of clients. Most were graduating students or young professionals moving from campus dorms to their first small apartments or from those same small apartments to better apartments, or for the most successful of them, to small condos or to houses in the suburbs. Over the last few months several small local businesses had called for one-time or occasional jobs. Sayeed explained to Sam, owner of the U-Haul dealership, that he could not yet afford his own truck but that someday, perhaps soon, Sam would lose him as a customer.

The private reason for the frequent rentals, and indeed for the business plan in general, was much less benign. The business provided the cover, the means, and the skills to conduct what would, he was sure, be considered the most glorious assault ever on the country that Sayeed hated.

He had begun to truly hate America, not just to loath it as he and all of his friends had grown up doing, in April of 2003, when the first images of the deaths of Muslims in Iraq had been broadcast on al Jazeera. That network carried story after story about the deaths of women and children. His feelings had only solidified in his three years in this strange but immoral country.

Sayeed had, grudgingly, grown to admire some of what he found during his time in America. The general friendliness of the people, the law abiding manner in which people drove, the green and well kept lawns and parks, even the way the people talked openly about the weaknesses or poor decisions of their elected leaders. Actually, that last was both admirable yet somehow disturbing. He still struggled to understand how leaders could be effective when every decision they made was debated and questioned so.

Some of what he had found had been very different from what he expected. He had often been told of the manner in which the white majority in America held down its minorities. He had actually seen very little of that, nor experienced it personally. In truth, only on the Haj to Mecca had he seen people of so many races interact without apparent individual or structural prejudice. His own home country of Syria was a hodgepodge of tribes and ethnic groups who barely tolerated one another. He had indeed seen the economic differences that did exist in American society, but to an outsider - something he was sure that he would consider himself even if he would have lived in this country to the end of his natural life - the differences in economic or educational success seemed more a function of choices than of prejudice. The African-American community, in particular, did not seem to yet realize that some of the attitudes within that community were very likely larger barriers to success than anything the rest of society was doing to them.

Despite the admirable or surprising aspects he had discovered about American society, one fact had not changed: Sayeed still hated this place, this country. This country had been founded by men of the book, believers in the same God, the God of Abraham, that he himself worshipped – misguided; yet believers still. However, America had become the embodiment of evil.

An amoral, secular society such as Turkey was distressing enough to Sayeed. This country, however, with all of the advantages it possessed, had actually become an immoral force in the world. Its music, its movies, its television shows, its advertising, and even its leaders exhibited immorality at every turn. Not only did its women not properly cover their hair or skin; they often didn't cover much of anything. Sex, or at least the glamorization of sex, was everywhere. Divorce, abortion and out-of-wedlock births were at unbelievable levels. The society wasn't even logical in its hypocrisy. If he had chosen to, Sayeed could have spent last night - his last night - drinking a beer and watching a naked woman gyrate around a pole. However, if he had lit a cigarette while doing those things, he would have been thrown out of the establishment and subject to criminal prosecution. Only to Americans did this make sense. This society allowed for the killing of unborn innocents by the millions, but the execution of a convicted multiple rapist-murderer led to protests and years of hand wringing, trials and appeals. Only to Americans did this make sense. This society allowed teenage girls to dress and act like whores yet condemned his own society for insisting on modesty and tradition. Only to Americans did this make sense.

Not content to merely wallow in its own depravity, America now routinely exported its depravity to the rest of the world. Hollywood movies, decadent music videos, unwholesome food, Coca Cola; all of these things were overwhelming the culture of the rest of the world. Unless the process stopped, Sayeed believed that the end result would be a world with only one sick culture, a culture that was abhorrent to everyone who followed the Prophet.

All of those thoughts passed quickly through Sayeed's mind as the truck slowly moved closer and closer to downtown Boston. The sun was starting its descent toward the western horizon, with the buildings of downtown beginning to shadow the harbor, which seemed bereft of any large boat traffic that late afternoon. Sayeed briefly concentrated fully on the traffic ahead, but soon found his thoughts wandering again. With so little time left to work, his brain seemed to be in high gear. He stole a quick glance at the passenger next to him. Abdul, the only name Sayeed knew for the man, stared intensely straight ahead. If his mind was racing as Sayeed's was, he showed no outward sign of it.

He had recognized the older man the moment he had appeared at his front door. Sayeed had seen the man several times during his four months at the training camp in the Bekka Valley of Lebanon three years ago. The man had often appeared suddenly to observe some aspect of their training and would disappear just as suddenly. He would occasionally ask questions of the students, always in English, and he expected a reply in that same language. Sayeed had experienced only one short personal interaction with the man and remembered that Abdul had seemed pleased by his answer, no doubt helped by Sayeed's command of English, acquired during his three years in Britain as a youngster when his father worked as a representative for an import/export consortium. No one ever said exactly why Abdul was important, but the instructors, and thus the students, always seemed to stiffen slightly and to become more formal in their interactions when this man was around. Sayeed knew that the man was important, in fact, the rumor among the students was that the man was a confidant of Sheik al Raqman, but at the time he did not know why he was so interested in what Sayeed and his fellow trainees were doing. Now he knew.

Abdul had appeared without warning at Sayeed's door three weeks ago and stayed only a few minutes that first day. After that, he appeared regularly to check on Sayeed's progress on gathering the last of the materials they needed and to make further coordination. Finally, during the last several days they had spent every minute together.

Sayeed had called Nabeel and told him that he needed to return to Damascus because his mother was sick. He told Nabeel that he would be gone for at least a month and that he would call him when he returned. He wondered what the Americans would do to Nabeel after this event was over. He felt a twinge of guilt because Nabeel knew nothing of the plot – Nabeel truly believed that they had been working toward the development of a full-fledged moving company in pursuit of the American dream.

Sayeed and Abdul had assembled the materials, then slowly and meticulously constructed a device similar to the one that Timothy McVeigh had made famous. Sayeed had actually been accumulating many of the raw materials over the last year. He had never purchased more than two bags of fertilizer at a time and had accumulated diesel a gallon or two at a time. However, he had also rarely missed a day of buying at least one bag of nitrogen heavy fertilizer. He had maintained a small vegetable garden in his back yard in case anyone ever questioned his small purchases. His basement was nearly full by the time Abdul had appeared at his door.

Their fertilizer and diesel combination device, contained in containers in the back of the U-Haul, was different from McVeigh's in three key ways: First, there were many more containers than McVeigh had used in downing the Murrah Federal Building in Oklahoma City. Secondly, the initiation devices that Abdul had appeared with, smuggled through Mexico along the drug routes, were much more sophisticated and therefore would lead to a much more complete and rapid oxidation of the fuel. However, the last difference had nothing to do with the explosive power of the bomb.

Sayeed did not know for sure how or where Abdul had acquired the large quantity of Cobalt-60. Created as part of the normal functioning of a commercial or research nuclear reactor, Co-60, harvested from the control rods used to moderate the fission inside the core, had one extra neutron compared to the number normally found in the nucleus of a Cobalt atom. This extra neutron made Co-60 one of the more dangerous radioactive elements created by man. Researchers the world around used it to study the effects of radiation on various materials and organisms and Co-60 was becoming increasingly popular for irradiating meats and vegetables to safely and effectively kill contaminating bacteria and thus increase the shelf life and safety of those foods. Abdul had not said, but Sayeed had inferred, that the Iranian "peaceful" nuclear program had been the source of the material. If so, Sayeed hoped that fact would never be proven. He also knew, because Abdul had told him, that although the shielding container did a nice job of stopping the beta particles emitted by the several hundred grams of material, it was not nearly as effective in terms or what it did, or didn't do, to stop the gamma rays. Sayeed now understood that he was slowly accumulating a life-threatening dose of radiation. He also knew that it would not be important because he would not live long enough for it to matter. Abdul had indicated that he had also brought the material in through Mexico; then across the southern border. Money had been the only obstacle, and Abdul seemed to have plenty of that.

Ahead, Sayeed saw that they were nearing the beginning of the construction project known as the Big Dig. The Big Dig was more than just one project or tunnel; it was a massive redesign of the freeway system that passed through Boston and over and under its waterways. Its name was appropriate. A super highway now ran under downtown Boston. Sayeed had hopes that what they were doing would bring down much of the tunnel structure. Abdul was much better versed in these things and thus likely much more realistic. He expressed hope only for the terror and the economic damage it would bring. The explosion in the tunnel would kill hundreds – with some luck even thousands – but more importantly it would disrupt one of the economic lifelines of New England for months, if not years. The several hundred grams of Co-60 would make the cleanup much more complicated and would increase the terror one hundred fold.

Only on the drive that afternoon had Abdul shared that theirs was not the only truck out this afternoon, although Abdul's presence showed that it was considered by far the most important. Three others were headed for an electrical substation, a nuclear power plant and a water pumping station. Abdul had said, "If the Americans thought that the attacks on September 11, 2001 were challenging, let them deal with a similar situation with no lights, no phones and no water."

Even the time of day was important. The late afternoon meant that only a few hours of daylight remained. Luck had provided the warmest day of the spring so far and hundreds of thousands of air conditioning units were cranked up for the first time, stretching an electrical system that had been running at fairly low capacity for most of the winter months. The destruction of the electrical substation should be enough to cause the entire northeast electrical grid to fail, not unlike it had done on its own in the fall of 2003. Finally, the late rush hour traffic would add to the carnage, the confusion and the death toll.

The one thing Abdul had expressed regrets about was their failure to get detailed "as built" diagrams of the tunnel project. Those drawings would have allowed them to select a spot most vulnerable to damage. Failing that, Abdul said he would let Allah help him to decide when the time was right. He would choose the point where traffic seemed at its worst or perhaps the point that seemed to be the lowest in the tunnel system. Regardless, Abdul assured Sayeed that they would not die in vain. Paradise would await them and their colleagues, but precious few of the others who would die that day.

Ahead, the tunnel began a gentle turn to the left and a slight ascent. Traffic moved slowly, but steadily. Abdul reached over and touched Sayeed on the hand. "I will detonate the device where the tunnel roof opens ahead. I want to disperse the material as much as I can. You have done well, my son. I will see you today in paradise."

Sayeed nodded his understanding. He continued to drive, maintaining spacing with traffic. In the car ahead, Sayeed saw two children, a boy and a girl, craning their necks around to look at the tunnel and the other vehicles. For a moment, the little girl's eyes locked onto Sayeed's. She smiled a shy smile and looked away. Sayeed heard Abdul shifting his position. Ahead, he saw rays of sunshine shifting down through an opening high above. Abdul said, "It is time. Allahu Akbar." Sayeed turned just in time to see Abdul push on the trigger. An impossibly bright light was the last thing his brain registered, for the briefest of moments.

"There are no committees, no conferences, no meetings of experts. Only Kim. Kim alone decides what must be done and then he issues the orders"
 – North Korean defector Park Gap Dong

Prologue Two

Pyongyang, North Korea, People's Army Headquarters
May 12, 8:35 p.m. (1135 GMT)

Major Li Hwang walked out of the 2nd People's Army command bunker and felt a shiver run through him. To any outside observer, the shiver might have been a natural reaction to the chill in the late spring air. He knew that it was a much more chilling thought that his body was responding to.

I can't believe that he's really going to do it, he thought to himself. As the operations officer of a tank Brigade, he had spent a great deal of time thinking about and, on the rare occasions when fuel and ammo stocks permitted, training for just such a scenario. Had the so-called Republic of South Korea and its American masters ever attacked into the North, he was confident that the artillery formations would blunt the attacks and that his tank brigade, along with others, would be able to launch counterattacks that would drive the imperialists from the soil of the North and perhaps far down the peninsula. However, what he had just heard proposed was different. Kim Jong-Il had decided that the armies of the North would be headed south without provocation. This was the madness of 1950 all over again, although Li had been taught that even that assault had been justified by the events of the times. But this, this was predicated on only one thought – if we don't do it now we will never again have the military or economic means to do so. If not now, the group had been told, starvation and privations the likes of which could only be imagined loomed due to the abandonment of North Korea first by the Soviets and now by the Chinese. Since North Korea had known incredible hunger over the last several years, Major Li hated to think what a worsening of that condition could mean to his countrymen. One of the reasons he had remained in the military was to ensure that he would not have to worry about hunger. Even so, as a junior officer, he and his men had worked the fields to help feed themselves. Any worsening of conditions in the North could mean only one thing. Surrender to the South, officially what his leaders called "reconciliation on terms not favorable," would be the only option.

However, the leadership was convinced that if the economic powerhouse that is Seoul could be seized and held, if even for a short period, the North would be in a position to sue for reconciliation with the South on its terms.

But at what cost? Li wondered to himself. *Weren't they all countrymen, artificially separated by the arrogant Americans and the uncouth Russians at the conclusion of what the West called World War II? Wouldn't the operation he just heard described kill untold tens of thousands of Koreans yet precious few of the real enemy?*

Wouldn't the Americans rush in reinforcements and supplies and wouldn't they use their technological advantages to great effect against the North's formations?

Actually, a Colonel from one of Li's sister brigades had asked that last question and had received an answer that seemed to indicate that the Americans would be too busy. Li had no idea what that response meant. The tightly held media of the country

14

had not yet published the news of what had transpired in America earlier the day before.

He had doubts about the ultimate success of the mission, but he had no doubts that he and his brigade would reach their objectives. Or they would die trying.

"I don't know whether war is an interlude during peace, or peace is an interlude during war."
  - Georges Clemenceau

CHAPTER ONE

Arlington Heights, OH
May 23, 5:05 pm (2205 GMT)

Tony Cooper blinked as he walked out of the relatively dim foyer of Arlington Heights High School into the bright late afternoon sunlight. His office had no windows and he often found himself surprised at the weather he encountered at the end of a long day. He glanced again at his watch and saw that it was just after 5:00 p.m. Since taking the Assistant Principal position his days had gotten longer but to make up for it he enjoyed his work less, he thought wryly. From "The Breakfast Club" to "Ferris Bueller's Day Off" and countless movies in between the job of high school principal, or even worse assistant principal, was stereotyped as being filled by power-hungry, incompetent, despotic losers. While he didn't think of himself that way, there were days when he was sure that some students, and their parents, certainly did. Such was the nature of the job. At many schools, including at his own, the head principal could afford to be a little more detached from the day-to-day discipline activities and could therefore focus on being part politician, part educational leader and part cheerleader. If often fell to the assistant principals to be the heavies. Tony thought about the difference in his job since he left the classroom, where he had taught Advanced Placement

16

Physics. Back then, he had spent his time with bright, articulate, motivated students. Now, much of his day was spent dealing with the mean, the lazy, the mentally challenged, the doped up, the troubled and the outright insane – and that list often just described the parents, he again thought wryly.

He was in a cynical mood and more tired than normal at the end of the workday, although that was not uncommon following a weekend drill. His Friday evening and all day Saturday and Sunday had been filled with Army training. After 22 years in the Ohio Army National Guard, he was accustomed to the after effects that a long weekend of training had on his ever-aging body and mind. It was not that the weekends were as physically demanding as they sometimes used to be. As a Major, soon to be Lieutenant Colonel, his duties now ran more toward paperwork than squad assault drills. It was just that having a drill weekend resulted in working twelve days in a row without a day off. Not to mention the missed birthdays, anniversaries, football games and other key events in the lives of his wife and two kids.

This weekend had been dedicated to Civil Disturbance Training at the Ravenna Arsenal Training and Logistics Site. RTLS, as it was known in an organization prone to acronyms, was an interesting place. It was an old, mothballed ammunition production and storage site in Northeast Ohio, complete with bunkers still full of old explosives too dangerous to move and ground contaminated with chemicals that would make any employee of the Occupational Health and Safety Administration or the Environmental Protection Agency shake in his boots. RTLS did, however, offer some excellent old buildings for doing training on fighting in an urban environment. House to house fighting, officially known as Military Operations in Urban Terrain, was what the four hundred members of the battalion had actually trained on this weekend. While the weekend, on paper, was still listed as being dedicated to learning how to deal with civil disturbances, normally consisting of crowd control and riot busting, it had ended up looking a lot like training for war. That change reflected the belief of Tony's boss, Lt. Col. Dana Maguire, that the greatest threat facing the 112th Engineer Bn (Combat) was that they would be called up for the upcoming campaign into Lebanon.

No one had officially announced that such an operation was coming, of course, but given the terrorist attacks on Boston and the northeast power grid, the subsequent identification of several of the terrorists, and the announcement that the CIA believed that the terrorists had trained in the Bekka Valley of Lebanon in camps supported by both Syria and Iran, it was a reasonable assumption to make. The videotape of the leader of the terrorists, Sheik al Raqman, had been only the final proof needed. Now, the question was what President Clark would do about it.

Clark, a young, charismatic one-term Senator, had narrowly defeated Ben McCutcheon, in part due to his relentless criticism of Bush's attack into, and subsequent occupation of, Iraq and McCutcheon's support thereof. Now Clark found himself in a very similar situation early in his presidency. The jury was still out as to the exact form that the response would take, but no one could envision that the U.S. would idly stand by after a series of truck bombs, including the dirty bomb in Boston, had undone an economic recovery well into its sixth year, killed several thousand Americans and tore a gaping hole in the road network, and indeed the skyline, of the preeminent city in New England.

The cleanup was barely begun, but clearly the Boston attackers had been very precise, or very lucky, in where they had chosen to detonate their fertilizer/fuel/cobalt mixture. The blast had breached the watertight envelope keeping the Charles River and Boston Harbor from flooding the underground portions of the Big Dig, with the power off and Geiger counters screaming, the water had saturated into the rubble of the Big Dig for days. What the explosion could not do the water did. The Big Dig, and the section of Boston above it, was now a sinkhole measured in acres, not square feet or meters. Thank goodness that the attack on the nuclear power plant had failed completely, with the driver shot and the bomb fizzling, although still powerful enough to kill the hero security guard who brought down the driver with several well placed pistol rounds. Tony agreed with the expert analysis that even had the attack gone as planned the reactor vessel, in its massive protective concrete and steel containment structure, would have been undamaged. *That hadn't stopped the environmental nuts from demanding that every nuclear power plant in the country be shut down immediately,* he thought to himself. The attack on the electrical substation had proven more problematic, but power had been restored to almost the entire grid within days. Finally, the attack on the water pumping station had proven to be very minor. A backup system had regenerated the pressure to the city within minutes.

Tony, along with all of his colleagues, was sure that Clark would have to respond. Already, the President was getting pressure from polls showing that a Clintonian missile strike or two would not be enough. The public, so quick to turn on both Bush the Senior and Bush the Junior after their military campaigns, was now clamoring for Clark to take action and to seek revenge. The scuttlebutt through the Ohio National Guard headquarters building was that several units had shown up as "units of interest" on a potential activation list. Tony had noted, but not yet shared with Rachel, his wife of almost 21 years, that the rumors had not only placed his unit on the list but also the unit of his newly promoted PFC son, John. John had joined the Ohio National Guard's only infantry battalion right out of high school and even delayed his start of college by a quarter to finish his initial training. Now, with the Guard picking up all of his tuition, John was working toward an engineering degree and the day when he could accept a commission as a Second Lieutenant. Tony had followed a very similar path and was very proud to see his son doing the same. He worried, however, about the effect their potential activation would have on Rachel. She had struggled during his year in Afghanistan back in 2003, including a near breakdown late in his deployment, and that was when she only had him in harm's way to worry about. He worried that she might end up in the nuthouse if both he and John were deployed. Being at home with a 15-year-old daughter – their daughter Julie had just reached that milestone last month - was not exactly the most relaxing thing either, even in the best of times. The insanity inherent to that age, along with the built in conflict between mother and daughter, would not exactly work to counteract the stress of having both of her men away.

The 112th Engineer Battalion, in large part due to the hard work of Lt. Col. Maguire, Tony and the rest of the staff, was currently listed as number one on the Order of Merit List that ranked all similar battalions throughout the Army National Guard structure across the country. They had all been proud of that accomplishment when it was announced a few months ago, but now the reality of what it might mean made Tony wonder if perhaps some of their time might have been spent less effectively.

Thus, the change in emphasis to urban combat training, something that their operations officer, known as the S-3, Major Joe Bortello, an Army Ranger in addition to being a combat engineer, was eager to do anyway. Tony was not sure that he had ever served with a better officer than Joe. When Tony moved up to the Brigade staff next month into a Lt. Col. position, Joe would move up to take his place as the Executive Officer (XO) for the Battalion. Tony was sure that Joe would proceed to do a better job as the XO than Tony himself had done, since Joe had already done the same thing when he had moved into the S3 role Tony had held previously. Admitting that to himself bruised Tony's ego somewhat, since he thought of himself as being pretty good, but the truth sometimes hurts. The sad part is that while Joe might currently be the best officer in the whole Brigade, there were still limits to the speed of his advancement; limits imposed by both the informal good-old-boy system and the formal U.S. Army Reserve Officer Personnel Management System.

Deep down, Tony still found it hard to believe that his unit could be called up. However, the Active Army's cupboard was pretty bare given the seemingly never ending troop commitments in Afghanistan, Iraq, Bosnia, Kosovo and several other hot spots around the world. With what looked to be a looming large-scale operation in the Middle East, Tony had to admit to himself that the possibility of his unit being activated was very real. Despite the recent mobilizations experienced by many of the Guard units for service in Iraq and Afghanistan, a majority of the troops with whom he now served had never carried a live round with the thought that they might need to shoot a person as opposed to a target. The one exception to this for many of the troops was their response to the Mansfield prison riot.

Then, the potential enemy consisted of poorly armed convicts. Felons, but fellow Ohioans. After 16 days, the convicts had seen the light and surrendered. The prisoners' one request had been that no guardsman be involved in the surrender. The sounds of the previous two weeks had unnerved them. Guard helicopters, one of Tony's "Alpha" Company dozers moving into position to bust through a wall and the constant sound of shotguns on a hastily improvised range just out of sight, but not out of earshot, of the prison, had convinced the rioters that perhaps they didn't really need all of their demands met. They were right to give up. Tony knew enough about the details of the assault plan to know that the prisoners would not have liked the outcome.

But now the thought of taking their combat engineer battalion into battle seemed much different. The National Guard had long reminded Tony of a football team that practices for years but rarely, if ever, has a game scheduled. When suddenly a game appears on the horizon, how will the team respond? He hoped to God, as much for his wife and kids as for himself, that he wouldn't find out. He couldn't imagine again leaving his wife of over 20 years ("twenty down, one to go" as he announced every anniversary, much to his wife's chagrin), his fifteen year old daughter struggling with the transition from girl to woman, his job, his friends, even his students. All would suffer in ways small and large, as would he if he lost their company. The thought of his son being deployed as well was an added worry, especially because he had all but pushed John into the decision to join.

As he got into his beat up but still reliable, if one discounted the transmission, which was beginning to slip more and more, 1996 Ford Taurus, he realized that he had not talked to his full time counterpart for a couple of days. Captain Dan Porter was what was known as an AGR soldier. The AGR program is designed to have a small number of full-time National Guard soldiers in each unit to take care of many of the administrative and coordination issues during the time between weekend drills. The idea was that this would allow the "weekend warriors" to more fully focus on training during the limited time they were all together. Conceptually, this program was very good. Practically, it meant that each unit was very dependent on its full-timers. If the full-timers were good, the unit tended to be good and commanders were able to be successful. If the full-timers were not so good, it meant that for the unit to be good the commander and his staff would have to be excellent and also put in a lot of time between weekend drills. This time was unpaid; usually referred to as "God and Country" time.

Captain Porter was fairly new in his role as the senior full-timer in the battalion, but so far he was a welcome change. His predecessor, Captain Grant, had gone ROAD – Retired On Active

Duty. Grant did a fine job on weekends and was loved by any troops with whom he worked, but he might as well have been a part-time soldier because his 'during the month' performance was nil. One of the weaknesses of the AGR program seemed to be a great difficulty in dealing with soldiers who did not perform to standards. They were so influential that any part-time commander who attempted to take them on found his life to be even more miserable than it was before.

Dan had done more for the battalion during his one month in the role than his predecessor had done in the previous year. Knowing Dan's work ethic, Tony took the chance and decided to give him a call. Normally, full-timers worked a 7:00 a.m. -4:30 p.m. shift but he suspected Dan would still be there. After pulling out of the parking lot into the residential streets surrounding the suburban high school he thought of as "his," Tony dialed Dan's number in hopes of catching the young captain. "Captain Dan Porter, 112th Engr Bn. Can I help you?" came the answer before the second ring.

"Don't you ever go home?" Tony asked in reply.

"No Sir, not the day before the Quarterly Unit Status Report is due," Dan said.

"How's it look?"

"Pretty good, really. We actually moved up in three sub-areas and pretty much held steady in the others. Maintenance got a little dicey with the 10KW generator going down but it wasn't enough to make that whole area a "two." It should keep us at or near the top of the Order of Merit List."

"Given the world situation today, Dan, I wonder if that should continue to be our goal," Tony laughed. "Do you think we might someday live to regret that ranking we've spent so much time working toward and bragging about?" Tony heard Dan chuckling on the other end, but the chuckling ended abruptly.

"Actually, Sir, that may not be that funny. The maintenance chief in Lima got a call from the State logistics office telling him that he should drop all other priorities and focus on getting all of our equipment to a category one status," Dan reported. "They do that sometimes when they know an inspection is coming but now that you mention it I wonder if it might mean something else."

"That is strange. We're not scheduled for a unit reinspection, are we?"

"No sir, nothing scheduled; not for at least three months. Oh, and another strange thing. I just got a call from Mike Hinton at Brigade to say that the meeting this Friday to discuss the August computer driven training exercise had been cancelled."

"Did they not get their operations order and briefing completed over the weekend like they were supposed to?" Tony asked.

"Mike wouldn't say what was going on, only that 'something had come up'."

"Dan, are you thinking what I'm thinking?"

"I was trying not to, but as I've verbalized it I can't really think of any way those two events taken together can be good news."

"Anything else going on?"

"No Sir, that's it," Dan said by way of ending what had essentially become his normal near-daily update brief over the course of the last month.

"Dan, I'm going to make some calls and see if I can't find out anything."

"Sir, if you find out anything, please give me a call."

"I will. Thanks, Dan. Have fun finishing the USR," Tony said and hung up the phone.

He decided that his next call would be to Lt. Col. Mark Hendricks, his friend and predecessor in the Battalion XO position. Mark had been assigned as the 16th Brigade Executive Officer position, along with the promotion to Lt. Col., and the headaches, that came with that assignment. The 16th Brigade was the 112th Engineer Battalion's next higher headquarters, tasked with overseeing the training and readiness of the 112th Engineer Battalion and two other battalions. Mark had a reputation for always knowing what was going on. In the civilian world, he was an executive vice president for a large regional restaurant chain.

"Mark Hendricks's office," Mark's secretary, Tiffany, said in her throaty, sultry voice. Tony had never met Tiffany but talked to her often. His mental picture of her went with the name and the voice, although Mark's description of her could most charitably be described as matronly and least charitably as horrific. Tony had convinced himself that Mark was covering up for something, mostly so he could continue to enjoy his mental image.

"Hi there, sexy voice," Tony began. "This is Tony Cooper. Is Mark available? Or you for that matter?"

"Not for dirty minded teasing flirts like you, he isn't," Tiffany laughed.

"Who says that I'm only teasing?" Tony replied.

"Your wife and two kids, to name three people," Tiffany rejoined.

Momentarily bested in their usual verbal sparing match, Tony found himself with no reply. Laughing, Tiffany said "I'll transfer you right in."

"Mark Hendricks," came the next moment.

"Mark, Tony Cooper. How are you sir?"

"Don't you sir me, you bastard. To what do I owe the pleasure of this call? Do you need more advice from your elder and superior?"

"I'll agree to the elder part, but I don't yield the superior part quite as easily. Actually, I just had a somewhat worrisome conversation with Dan Porter. Have you heard anything regarding the 112th being called up?"

"No, I haven't heard a thing other than the "Unit of Interest" stuff," Mark replied. "Why? What have you heard?"

"Two things," answered Tony. "First, our maintenance guys just got a priority mission to bring our stuff up to category one. Second, our exercise brief for the upcoming computer exercise this Friday just got cancelled without a ready explanation."

"Huh. That's not a slam dunk but if I were a betting man I'd have my affairs in order if I were you," Mark opined.

"That's my read on it, too, but as the battalion executive officer it would be nice to know for sure."

"Yeah, but you know Dana McQuire. If he knows something but has been instructed not to divulge it, then even his wife wouldn't know."

"Yeah, I've tried to break him of his Boy Scout ways but I haven't been very successful," Tony said.

"Who are you going to call next?" Mark asked.

"Oh, I'll probably just not worry about it and let what happens, happen," Tony said in a decent rendition of Mahatma Gandhi's voice.

"Bullshit. That's not in your nature."

"Well, I'll probably call Mike Hinton and ask him why the BCST brief has been cancelled."

"You should be able to make him squirm. Just remind him of that 'full-figured' girl from the Red Barn Saloon in Grayling," Mark laughed, recalling an annual training at Camp Grayling, Michigan when they were all younger and thinner.

"Do you realize that you, me and Dana Maguire may be the only three members of the Ohio National Guard who nobody can blackmail with a story like that?"

Mark laughed, "That's only because we have the toughest wives in the group!"

"Probably so," Tony admitted, chuckling. "By the way, you owe me for telling Tiffany that I'm married with children!"

"Just trying to save you some time and heartbreak when you finally meet her. Although, I must admit that she has been keeping the hair on her moles trimmed shorter so they don't distract as much from her lazy eye."

"The gentleman doth protest too much, methinks," Tony said, this time in a not-at-all-convincing English accent. Dropping the attempt, he continued, "Admit it, you dirty old man. She's young and hot, isn't she?"

"If you don't have a problem with overweight older women then maybe you could describe her that way."

Laughing, Tony said, "Thank you for nothing, you jerk. Take care of yourself."

"If you find out anything, please give me a call," Tony heard as he closed his cell phone to end the call.

His next act was to scroll through the cell phone's memory to find Captain Mike Hinton's number. He pulled up in front of his house as he heard the phone start to ring. After four rings he heard Mike's voice mail pick up. At the end of his away message Mike listed his cell phone with the disclaimer that it should be used if the matter was urgent. Tony decided that this matter was certainly urgent in his mind. He dialed the number quickly before he forgot it. He had never been particularly good at remembering strings of numbers. He continued to sit in his car in front of his house - he and Rachel had managed to buy a house located in the one spot in the entire town where cell phone coverage seemed to die as you walked in the front door.

A mechanical voice told him to "Please wait while the Nextel subscriber you are trying to reach is located." Finally, he heard the call ring through.

"Hello?" he heard Mike say.

"Mike, it's Tony Cooper. How the heck are you?"

"I'm doing fine, Sir. How about you? To what do I owe the pleasure of this call?

"I heard that our coordination meeting for this Friday was cancelled," Tony said. "I was wondering if you could fill me in on that?"

The phone remained silent as Mike struggled for a reply. Finally, he said, "Well, the General made that call. Something came up."

"What does that mean?" Tony asked, with an undercurrent of irritation in his voice.

"The powers that be decided that we should hold off," Mike equivocated.

"And why do you think they decided that?" Tony asked.

"I don't know all of the reasons," Mike responded, again after a short delay.

"Mike, you may be one of the worst liars I have ever known. How have you managed to stay married all these years? What do you say when your wife asks if she looks like she's gained weight?" Tony asked.

"I always have trouble with that one," Mike laughed.

"Seriously, Mike. You have to let me know what in the hell's going on. As long as we've been friends, as many times as I've covered your ass and you've covered mine, you're going to hold out on me now? Do you think I would do that if you were in the same situation?" Tony pressed. He felt bad for laying on the guilt so thick, although he really did feel that there was truth to what he was saying.

Again, there was a pause on the other end. Finally, Mike replied, "Tell me what you know so far."

"I know that our maintenance shop got a call to bring our equipment up to category one. I know that you cancelled our Friday briefing with no good reason cited. I know that the world is crazy after the attack in Boston. I know that any reasonable man would come to the conclusion that the 112th is getting called up and sent somewhere we wouldn't pick for a vacation. I know that you are trying to not tell me something you know. I know that if you don't come clean and I find out that you know more than you admit to I will track you down and kill you. That's about all I know."

"All right, Tony. You win. I don't know it formally, but the rumor here at Brigade is that you guys are being activated almost immediately and that you shouldn't plan on a long time at the mobilization station, wherever that turns out to be. You didn't hear that from me," Mike added. "This is supposed to be 'close hold' information."

"Yeah. Heaven forbid that the guys most affected should find out," Tony groused. "Any word where?"

"Rumor is that you are bound for the ancient civilizations of the Middle East."

"Iraq or Afghanistan?"

"Nobody seems to know," said Mike

"Normally that word comes down at the same time," Tony mused. "I wonder why that information would be held so tightly. The MP unit had found out they were going to Tikrit right away. The same was true of the 416th when they were notified of their all-expense paid trip to Afghanistan. Maybe the answer is neither?"

"Sir, may I remind you that we are on a non-secure line."

"You're right, Mike. Thanks for the info. I owe you one. Have a good evening."

"If you find out anything solid, please give me a call," Mike said.

"I sure will."

While Tony was contemplating his next move, the phone rang in his hand. The caller ID screen showed "Restricted" which told him nothing. He flipped it open and pressed the green button to answer the call. He thought for the twentieth time that he needed to get his phone set up to answer when he opened it.

"Hello?"

"Tony, it's Dana Maguire."

"Sir, I was just getting ready to call you. I've had some interesting conversations in the last hour."

"If they've been too interesting then people need to learn to keep their mouth shut. What do you know?"

"I would not be surprised if you are calling me to tell me that we are being activated for duty in the Middle East. I suspect that you are calling to tell me that we are leaving pretty quickly but are not sure exactly where we will go once we deploy or what we will do when we get there. I suspect that you called me on my cell phone because you are horrified at the prospect of talking to Rachel because you know how she is going to take this. That's all I know, or suspect, for now."

After a moment Lt. Col. Maguire said, "Just once, it would be nice to be able to break something to you that you haven't heard already, Tony. You seem to have all of the broad strokes down. I do have a few more details. We are mobilizing one week from today. We'll be in Cleveland for two days of briefings, paperwork and an activation ceremony before heading to our mobilization station, which will be Ft. Dix, New Jersey."

For the second time in an hour, Tony found himself uncharacteristically at a loss for words. After a long pause, Dana asked, "Are you still there, Tony?"

"Shit. Even having a little warning doesn't prepare one to hear it for real."

"I know. Still hard to believe it myself and I've known for a couple of days. I just got the final word to proceed with the mobilization. We need to initiate our phone chain to spread the details of what we know. I am emailing those details to your military account now. Have that script with you when you do your calls so that we make sure we are getting all of the same information out to our people. Let me know when you have called everyone in your chain or if you have any problems. I'll give you a call tomorrow regardless to start making further coordination."

"Damn, Dana. Are we ready for this?"

"I suspect we are as ready as most and more ready than some. Everyone has that same thought before going off to war, I'm sure."

"Probably so. Say, have you heard anything about the infantry battalion?"

"Tony, I don't have anything official on that – not in my chain – but the word on the street is that they are being called up as well. You might want to break that to Rachel another time."

"Maybe so, but it might just be best to rip the scab off all at once."

"Your wife, your call."

"How did Lisa and the girls take it?"

"I haven't told them yet. In fact, I only just got the authorization to tell anyone a few minutes ago."

"You are kidding me. Lt. Col. Dana Maguire, you are amazing. Will Lisa be pissed that you knew but didn't tell her? Or that you told me before her?"

"Why would she be pissed? She knows that an order is an order."

"We are married to different women. Ok, Sir. I'll get started on my calls to the staff. Good luck telling the company commanders."

Tony flipped the phone closed and waited a moment before turning toward the house. As he approached the front door he was reminded of what Lee had said as he prepared to leave for

Appomattox Court House to surrender to Grant – "I would rather face a thousand deaths…"

The scene Tony found inside the house was almost disturbing in its normalcy, given what he had just learned. Rachel was in the kitchen putting the finishing touches on dinner, which looked to be spaghetti, a dish that Julie and John loved but that Tony didn't care for. John was home, flopped on the couch, watching a DVR'd version of last week's "24" episode. The family tried to get together for dinner a couple of times a week and since John couldn't seem to learn how to do his own laundry and lived in a dorm room only ten minutes away, getting him home on Monday and Thursday evenings was never too hard. Julie was no doubt in the computer room multi-tasking - doing homework, IM'ing friends and surfing the web. Misty, their incredibly loving, incredibly hairy, incredibly shedding dog ran up to greet him. Tony gave her a brief rub on the head before heading into the kitchen to see Rachel. His wife moved around the kitchen with small, efficient movements, attending to several dishes at once. Her auburn hair, which showed not a trace of gray, unlike his, was still as beautiful and well kept as when they first married. Her face showed a few lines and she had gained a few pounds, but she still looked great and was often mistaken for being much younger than Tony, even though she was actually slightly older, a fact he never let her forget. All in all, she was aging well, as his pre-nuptial evaluation of his future mother in law had indicated that she would.

He gave her a hug and a peck on the cheek as she started into a story about how Julie had smarted off to her when she picked her up from school. He tried to listen and make appropriate agreement noises at appropriate times, but his mind was going a thousand miles a minute as he figured out how to break the news.

He finally decided to wait until after dinner. He told her that he had a couple of "Guard" calls to make and that he would be back down in about fifteen minutes. Apparently sensing that he really needed to do this, she said "O.K." and turned back to the preparations for dinner. As he made his way up to the bedroom, he called down to Julie and told her to go set the table. She acknowledged, in that borderline insubordinate voice that drove parents crazy but didn't really rise to a level that warranted action.

He made his calls quickly, trying to be calm and reassuring while he talked the members of his staff through the activation order. The calls went well, probably because the staff was made up of senior, experienced leaders. He remembered having had to call a couple of young soldiers during the lead up to the Iraq War, covering for a buddy of his who wasn't available. He especially remembered one female soldier who had cried on the phone and a young male soldier who had actually handed the phone to his mother so that Tony could explain to her what he had just told the young man. Compared to those calls, these five calls were easy, at least in relative terms. These calls were tough enough. He was proud of the way his staff handled the news. Only afterward did he remember that he was supposed to read from the script that Lt. Col. Maguire had said he would email him. Oh well. He felt confident that he had passed everything along correctly.

Just as he finished his last call Rachel called up that dinner was ready. He quickly changed out of his work shirt and tie so as not to splash spaghetti sauce on them, in hopes of maybe getting a second wear out of the shirt before sending it to the dry cleaners, and headed down. On the way down it occurred to him that he wasn't going to need to wear a shirt and tie much in the near future.

At the table, John and Julie made some small talk, mostly about what teachers had done what and who was dating whom.

Even with the several years between them, the teachers hadn't changed much and many of Julie's classmates were younger siblings of John's classmates. Rachel paid close attention, not only because she wanted to know what was up in her kids' lives but also because she loved to be in on the scoop. Tony continued to make appropriate sounds when necessary but stayed out of the conversation for the most part. Toward the end of dinner, Julie said, "Hey, Dad. Remember when you would make us do high-point/low-point?" Tony realized that it had been since John graduated and went off to boot camp that they had done the conversation starter he had begun with them when they were younger. He always suspected that the kids secretly liked it, even when they groused about it.

"I do. Do you want to do a round of it tonight?"

"Sure, I guess," she said

"You go first."

"Okay," she said. "My high point was that I got a 96% on the science test that I thought I had bombed. Mr. Orloff curved it because the class did so bad. My low point is that I got a 93% on the history test that I thought I had aced."

"Dork," said John. "A 93 % is still an A."

"I know," said Julie, "but it lowered my average in that class to a 96%!"

"Dork!" John repeated.

"How about you go, John?" said Rachel.

"No thanks, not right now."

"Why not?" asked Rachel.

"My low point and high point are the same thing but I'm not sure how you will take it, Mom," John said, glancing over at his father.

"What does that mean?" asked Rachel, with a twinge of worry in her voice.

"I think I should tell you later," said John.

An uncomfortable silence hung over the table

"John, can I see you in the living room for a second?" Tony asked, pushing himself back from the table.

"Sure," said John, doing the same.

"No way," said Rachel. "No way you two are going to tell secrets behind my back. I deserve to know what he is talking about."

"Rachel, trust me. I just need to talk to him for a second. We'll be right back and we'll tell you everything."

"If you are going to tell me everything then talk right in front of me." After looking at them for a second while they sat in silence, she said, "Fine. You two go do what you have to do but if you don't tell me what is going on there will be hell to pay."

Tony and John moved out to the family room and stood close to one another. Tony asked "Did you get a call today?"

John nodded.

"And?"

"My battalion is being called up next week. We expect to head to Korea. Word is that we are going to replace an active duty battalion to free them up for duty in the Middle East. How about you, Dad?"

"I got a call today as well. The 112th is activating in three days for duty in the Middle East. We don't know where yet."

"Mom is going to shit. This will kill her."

"Make up your mind, Private. Is she going to shit or is she going to die?" Tony asked jokingly, trying to break the tension.

"She's going to shit, then she's going to die," John said, unwittingly completing a nearly identical sequence to one from a classic comedy movie from Tony's youth.

"Well, the cat is out of the bag now. We might as well go in and break the news. Let me do the talking."

"Gladly." John said.

They made their way back into the kitchen where Julie and Rachel watched them without saying a word. Tony took a long drink from his water before beginning to speak.

"Rachel, Julie... both John and I got activation calls today. John and his battalion are headed for a safe place. They are being sent to Korea to backfill an active duty battalion that is being sent to the Middle East. My unit is headed to Ft. Dix. We don't know where we are headed after that. I wouldn't be surprised if we ended up replacing an active duty unit somewhere as well so they can head to the Middle East." He knew the last statement probably wasn't true, but he felt it was a white lie worth telling to attempt to soften the blow.

All three of the others watched Rachel as she processed the news. Her expression oscillated back and forth between crying and anger. She settled on both. Through tears, she turned to Tony and angrily screamed out, "I told you to get out when you got your twenty in! I told you not to encourage John to join up! God damnit, I knew this would happen. They can't take both of you. There must be some rule against that! I can't take it. You know I can't take it!" She turned to John. "You're not going. That's it. There's no way they can make you go. You have classes. They talked you into joining by saying they would pay for your college. They can't pull you out in the middle of a quarter!" She then started to cry more openly, under her breath repeating very unladylike, and very uncharacteristic phrases like "Those bastards" and "Those sons of bitches." Julie looked like she didn't know whether to cry, flee the room or go to hug her mother. John looked like he wanted to bolt. Tony scooted his chair closer to Rachel and put his arm around her shoulders. Rachel flung his arm off and said, "Don't touch me. This is all your damned fault."

Tony moved his chair back and said, "Rachel, we knew this might happen. John and I both signed up knowing that we could be called. And quite frankly, after Boston, I want to go."

"You want to go! And leave me here? Fine! But John isn't going."

"Rachel, you know that he has to go."

"Mom, I have to go. I *want* to go," John added.

"You are as brainwashed as your father. I can't believe either one of you. You make me sick. Marching off wherever they send you. No thinking for yourself." She stood up and headed up the stairs to the bathroom. They could hear the water running, no doubt washing away the tears that continued to flow freely.

"Well, that went about like I thought it would," John opined.

Julie said, "I can't believe you guys are leaving me alone with Mom. She's going to freak out."

"She'll be fine. So will you. But, she's going to need a lot of help. I need you to grow up quickly, Julie. You have to start taking some more responsibility around here and also keep from adding any more stress on Mom. This is going to be a tough time for all of us," Tony added.

"When do you guys leave?

"We both leave in a week," said John.

"A lot to do between now and then. Julie, can you clear the table and do the dishes? John, you better get home and start getting ready. Plan on contacting your professors early on to see about what you can do to get credit for the courses you are in this quarter. I'm heading up to face more of the music."

*   *   *   *

As John drove home he thought about the things he needed to get done. He would try to see all of his professors tomorrow. There were only three weeks left in the quarter, so he thought he had a strong case for asking them to grant him credit with the grade he currently had in their course. He felt pretty good about Sykes in Physics – he had an A in there thanks to his father's tutoring in high school. Wilkins in Psych should be OK. His ROTC class was a no brainer.

Harris in English might be a problem. A modern day hippie, Harris was no fan of the military. John was sure that his grades on a couple of writing assignments had been lower than they might otherwise have been if only he had parroted the liberal line they were fed everyday in class. Unfortunately, he had let his own pro-military feelings come out in one of his first papers. He had felt he had been fighting an uphill battle ever since. He would give it a shot, but he wouldn't be surprised if Harris refused to grant him credit.

Packing wouldn't take long; he hadn't accumulated much in his short time away from home. That thought made him think of his mother. She had been so stressed out that he hadn't really had a chance to talk to her. He wished there was some way he could figure out how to convince her that this was something he wanted to do; something that he needed to do. He decided to text her. His generation's answer to intimacy, as his father liked to call it. As he drove, he quickly typed "hi mom hope u r ok dont worry ill b fine. tlk tmrw. luv J." He pressed the send button, hoping that the long note would help calm her nerves.

As soon as he got into his room, he logged onto AIM and IM'd his entire "Friends" address book with the news. He had held off letting everyone know until he had told his parents; he hadn't wanted the word to get back to his mother through the grapevine. Moments after he sent out the message he got several replies, most of which consisted of condolences and promises of a going away party that would rock the campus. John smiled at the thought.

"Only in the agony of parting do we look into the depths of love."

  - George Eliot

Chapter Two

Cleveland, OH
May 30, 5:30 pm (2230 GMT)

The crowd rose as the soldiers of the Headquarters Company of the 112th Engineer Battalion marched into, and made their way to the front two rows of, the hotel ballroom. Tony led half of the company's troops up one aisle and Dana Maguire led the other half of the company up the other. On the stage was a mixed group of general officers and local and state politicians. The ceremony proceeded with a predictable mix of speeches and recognitions. The largest round of applause was reserved for Lieutenant Colonel Maguire after his short speech about selfless service, duty and country. The ceremony also reminded Tony that the U.S. military was one of the few organizations left where a chaplain could still open and close a ceremony with a prayer. He remembered the old saying that "there are no atheists in a foxhole" and realized that it was probably that fact that explained why the military was still allowed to get away with public prayer.

 At the end of the ceremony the troops were released to mingle and gather in an informal reception. Tony quickly found Rachel and Julie standing with Dave Rosen and his wife. Captain Rosen, the assistant operations officer, had finally managed to impregnate his wife of several years and she was expecting in less than a month. On top of that, he had also just received a promotion at work; a promotion that was now going to a co-worker of his since the Army had activated him for what their orders said was "An indefinite period not to exceed twelve months."

Dave's wife had not taken the deployment any better than Rachel had. Dave was obviously nervous, unsure how to handle his young wife's stress. The two wives quickly fell into conversation about the unfairness of the situation. Dave and Tony gathered to talk about the details of the next morning's trip to Ft. Dix. Just as they started, Tony saw Mark Hendricks approaching with a beautiful blonde woman who appeared to be in her mid-twenties. Tony knew Mark well enough to know that this woman was too old to be Mark's daughter and too young to be his wife. He was more than a little curious as he and Dave turned to face the oncoming pair.

"Tony, Dave, I wanted to make sure I caught both of you before you got away. You guys will be in our thoughts and prayers," Mark said, shaking their hands. "And Tony, I know you two haven't officially met, but Tiffany asked that I bring her along so she could see you guys off. At one time or another she has talked to almost all of you guys."

Tony smiled slightly, extended his hand and said, "Tiffany, it is a pleasure to finally put a face to the voice. I must say that you are exactly how I pictured you, although Mark's description of you was not completely accurate."

Tiffany, along with the others, looked puzzled but decided not to ask. Instead, she said, "Tony, I'm so sorry that you are being sent over. I'm just so glad that Mark doesn't have to go. I can't imagine how bad this is for you guys."

Tony wasn't sure how to answer that initially, so he took the moment as a chance to introduce the rest of the small group. Gathering his thoughts, he replied, "It's not bad at all – we signed up for this. When the first images from Boston came across the television screen we all knew that this day might come. Quite frankly, if it wasn't for Rachel and the kids, I wouldn't have any second thoughts. In fact, I think what we are going to do is easier than what the ones left back here are facing. At least we have each other, all going through the same thing. On active duty posts, there are lots of other families going through the same thing at the same time. For Guard families, they're spread out across the whole state and they really have to work hard to stay in touch or to get together even once in a while."

Dave added, "Well put, although I'm sure it's tough on the active duty wives as well."

Rachel said, "Yeah, but the active duty wives knew what they were getting into. I was married to Tony for 15 years without him being gone for more than a few weeks at a time. Now, for the second time he's being pulled away from his family and his job."

Mark, apparently realizing that this debate could go on for a while, made his leave by stating that he needed to "make the rounds." Tony gave Mark a look that said "I knew you were lying" as he left.

After the reception wound down the troops were free to spend the evening with their families. The only rules were that they could not travel more than 15 miles away from the hotel and that they were to report to board the buses at 4:30 a.m. Rachel, Julie and Tony had a quiet dinner before retiring upstairs – Julie to her room and Rachel and Tony to theirs. They called John on his cell phone; John was in Toledo for the going away ceremony for his unit. Rachel and Julie were heading over there first thing the next morning – or at least first thing in civilian terms. Tony's last words to John were "Keep your head down. Listen to your officers and NCOs, but think for yourself as well. Do what comes natural and what feels right – it usually *is* right.

Tony was disappointed that the final night didn't include some last chance love making, but Rachel wasn't in the mood for much more than stressing, cuddling and talking. He figured, at this point in their marriage, that was enough, and it was what she needed.

*   *   *   *

Cleveland, OH
May 31, 4:00 am (0900 GMT)

Tony gave Rachel a hug and a kiss as she lay in bed and then knocked on Julie's door until she woke up enough to open the door and accept a hug and a kiss as well. Rachel and Julie were headed to Toledo later that day for John's going away ceremony, but it was only a couple of hours drive away and didn't start until 4:00 p.m. He was glad that his two ladies could sleep in a little before making that drive.

He then went down to the lobby, finding it already half full even though the report time wasn't for another twenty minutes. Evidently he wasn't the only one who had experienced trouble sleeping through the night. . He saw a couple of young soldiers standing with wives or girlfriends, getting every last minute together that they could.

By the allotted time, only one soldier had not reported. The hotel shift manager let the First Sergeant and a couple of his cronies into that unfortunate soldier's room and he was roughly pulled from his bed with what looked to be a monumental hangover. The men and women of the Headquarters Company, quiet, sleepy and apprehensive, loaded the buses and settled in for the 12-hour drive that would take them to the next stage in their lives.

*   *   *   *

Toledo, OH

May 31, 3:05 pm (2005 GMT)

John followed the soldier in front of him, keeping in step with the aid of the Sousa march blasting from the Owens Community College Auditorium speakers. The line of troops ahead of him snaked down the aisle and into the front two rows. The crowd, filled mostly with parents and other family members, stood and clapped as the members of Bravo Company, 143rd Infantry Battalion, made their way to their seats.

The briefings and training over the last two days had clarified their mission. They would be taking over responsibility for a section of the DMZ north of Seoul. They would not be right on the border; the South Koreans had that duty. They were to be a few miles back, tasked with rear security and with supporting the South Koreans as needed. The area was quiet and had been for almost thirty years. Pretty easy duty, although potentially very dull in John's opinion. He wished that their orders were for the Middle East. *That's where the fight is*, he thought. *Not in the mountains of Korea.*

He tried to listen to the words being spoken from the stage, but they all seemed to be variations on the same theme. Service, duty, honor, dangerous world, global war on terror. All the right words spoken by all of the right individuals; all predictable. Finally, the speeches were over and the troops were released. John found his mom and sister, and they exchanged hugs. He worried that his mom might embarrass him by crying or not letting him go when they hugged, but she seemed to sense his need to keep face with his peers and gave him an appropriate hug and a smile. "We are so proud of you, John. Your Dad would love to be here, but he's on the bus to Dix. He asked me to give you a hug from him." She proceeded to give him another hug.

"I would have loved to have seen him off, too." John said. "We are flying out tomorrow morning with a stop in Alaska for fuel and then straight to Seoul. We will have a couple of days of orientation training and then straight to our positions. I'll email you once we get into country, Mom."

"You better, or I'll come over there and visit you myself."

John laughed, "You just might do that! I'll email, I promise."

Out of the corner of his eye, John saw his squad leader approach. Turning, he said, "Mom, Julie, I want you to meet Sergeant Cody. He's my squad leader."

"Pleased to meet you, Ma'am. You've got a good son here; he's one of our best. He'll make a good Sergeant someday if we can talk him out of going over to the dark side and becoming an officer."

"I'm afraid his dad got to him in terms of brainwashing before you, by about 19 years," smiled Rachel. "It's nice to meet you, Sergeant. Take good care of him over there."

"I will, Ma'am." To John, he said, "Coach, we're getting together in room 205 in about ten minutes to go over some last minute details."

"I'll be there, Sergeant."

Sergeant Cody exchanged goodbyes and headed off in hunt of other squad members. John turned back to his mother and sister and said "Mom, I better get going. I'll walk you guys to your car."

"Why did he call you Coach?" Julie asked.

John shook his head ruefully and said, "Remember the coach at Ohio State before Tressel? A couple of the guys started calling me that and it kinda stuck."

Julie laughed, "I love it. I'm going to start using it."

"Only if you want a black eye," John laughed, playfully messing up Julie's hair. She squealed and skipped a few steps away.

They made their way to the parking lot. Only at the car did Rachel break down. She hung onto John and cried gently. "Be careful. I don't know what I would do if anything happened to you."

"I'll be fine, Mom. You take care of yourself. Don't worry about us. We'll be fine." Hugging Julie, he said, "Twerp, be good. Help Mom out."

"I will. I love you, John. I mean Coach!"

John pretended to swing at her and then turned the motion into another hug. "Me too, but I'll deny it if you tell anyone."

He straightened his beret, gave them a last wave and a smile, and then headed to room 205. As his drill instructor had beaten into him, to be early is to be on time.

*   *   *   *

Atlanta, Georgia
May 31   3:45 pm (2045 GMT)

Linda Rogers walked out of her boss's office in the CNN tower, unsure whether to be excited or apprehensive. She had just been handed what had the potential to be a fascinating, career enhancing making assignment; the chance to be imbedded with U.S. forces as they began their operations in response to the terrorist attacks of May 11. However, she was not comfortable with the ground rules her boss had just handed her.

She didn't trust the military to begin with. They had always seemed too controlled, too secretive. The agreement in place for this assignment merely added to her sense of that. She would not be able to file her report until the operation was over, and only then with the military's go ahead. Further, she did not know where they were headed. Her boss had agreed with the ridiculous statement that she could be jailed if she failed to abide by the agreement she had signed. She was sure, based on the Major

Palmer she had just met, that her opinion of military men would only be reinforced. The Major had seemed flippant and evasive. His assistant, some young captain, might as well have been a mute.

On the other hand, the chance to be a part of an ongoing operation, to see it first hand, was exciting. She had, quite frankly, had great luck in her career so far. She was honest enough with herself to realize that. Of course, having good luck is one thing. Being able to seize on the opportunities as they arise was another, and she had so far been able to do exactly that. She hoped that this would become another such opportunity. She was to depart for Kuwait in one week. She was to report to the CNN Bureau Chief in Kuwait City where she was to receive further details. She was told to pack for an austere environment and to expect a deployment of several weeks. All of those things put together told her next to nothing.

Oh well, she thought. The good news is that her boss had authorized her to load up on any equipment she felt she needed using her CNN credit card. She intended to hit several outfitters so that she could deploy with the best gear available.

She reminded herself that she would, again, need to find someone to watch her cat.

"Arriving at one point is the starting point to another."
    - John Dewey

CHAPTER THREE

Fort Dix, NJ
June 8, 2:45 pm (1945 GMT)

Tony felt sweat pouring down his forehead as he plopped down behind a small bush and aimed his empty 9mm pistol in the general direction of the simulated "enemy" position on the hill to his left front. Even loaded, the pistol would have been of very little use from this distance unless his only goal was to call attention to his position. He thought to himself that he was getting too old, and frankly too damned fat by Army standards, to be practicing 3 to 5 second rushes like he had when he was an 18-year old enlisted Marine at Camp Pendleton, CA.

Matt Giardi plopped down behind the next bush over. Matt looked more effective and less winded than Tony felt. He was sure that had as much to do with the eight fewer years and thirty fewer pounds Matt carried than the Ranger training symbolized by the arched patch on Matt's left arm. Tony felt that his enlisted Marine training was nearly the equivalent of Ranger school, although he wouldn't have wanted to prove that by going through either of the courses again. Matt was assigned to a position that would have been the very last he would have selected for himself. He was the S1 – the personnel officer – for the battalion and as such was in charge of a small section tasked with keeping the paperwork of the battalion correct and up to date. He also arranged ceremonies, processed awards and planned social events. As much as he may have hated the assignment, Matt handled it well and it actually matched his skill set much better than he would have admitted. On the down side, Matt could be annoying and some troops did not respond well to his cutting, and sometimes downright cruel, sense of humor. The S1 position had the saving grace that it helped to fill out his resume and thus he had accepted it at the end of a successful, although at times rocky, company command. Matt had expected to become the S3 and get promoted to Major within the next few months as Tony moved on and Joe B. moved up, but the activation looked to have locked all of them into the places they had held when the activation order came.

Tony realized that he had been behind this particular bush long enough and scanned for another spot within a few seconds' run. He spotted a fallen log not far ahead, jumped up as nimbly as he could and ran, crouched at the waist, toward it as fast as he could, hoping he wouldn't break a hip on his next flop to the ground. Again, the thought that he was too old for this came to mind.

Fort Dix, located in southern New Jersey, was an old army post with a long and fairly mundane history. It was kept alive mostly as a caretaker post now; only truly springing to life when it was time to send more troops into harm's way. When called, it was one of the locations that National Guardsmen and Reservists used as their mobilization station. They came from around the country and stayed at Ft. Dix while they completed the myriad tasks involved in turning citizen-soldiers into just plain soldiers. At the mobilization station, soldiers were prodded, poked and groped by medical personnel, filled out countless documents, were provided with all of the equipment they would need for their deployment – or at least as much as the Supply Officer types could put their hands on – and finally trained and tested to ensure that they could do their basic jobs, could hit a target with their assigned weapon at least two out of three times, and could move, shoot and communicate as a cohesive unit.

During the first and second Gulf wars, that process had taken many weeks or months. This time, Tony and the 112th had been there for just over a week and were told to expect their departure within the next week. The post commander was required to validate the unit, which means he needed to sign off on a statement that said, essentially, that they were not all that likely to kill themselves if sent overseas and that they might even have a chance of killing the bad guys. The actual wording was more mundane, something like "The 112th Engr Bn has completed the TCERT training required for deployment to the CENTCOM TOA and is hereby certified as ready for onward movement," but everyone knew what it meant.

The 112th had actually made good progress toward that goal; much better than Tony might have guessed. The final training event, due to start at the beginning of the next week, was a three-day field problem that was a combination of tactical training and a command and control exercise. Tony saw this as a formality. His staff – technically Lt. Col. Maguire's staff but every executive officer saw the staff as secretly belonging to him – was as good as the Ohio Army National Guard had to offer. In fact, Tony would have held it up against any active duty battalion staff. There were individual weaknesses and idiosyncrasies, of course, but most of these people were successful, hard charging leaders in their civilian jobs and that competence, along with an incredibly broad range of skills, carried over into their military work.

The S4 - the supply officer, Captain Steve Fleischer, was a real character and projected an image, with hair that was perpetually slightly longer than standard and a little bit of a pot belly, that would never land him on a recruiting poster. However, he was a heck of a scrounger and problem solver. Of course, sometimes it was best not to know how or from where he came up with some of the equipment and supplies.

The S3 – operations officer – Major Joe Bortello, continued to impress. Tony again thought that it was good that he had a few years on Joe because he would hate to compete for promotions and assignments with Joe on a level playing field. Besides being competent, Joe would have made a decent recruiting poster save for his rapidly receding hairline. He was thin, good looking, could run like a deer and lifted weights regularly. He had a reputation for being a party animal, but his wife had very recently given birth to their first child and Joe was already going through the domestication process that most men go through at some point in their lives. Matt Giardi as the S1 and Captain Scott Johnson as the S2- the intelligence officer – rounded out the primary staff. Scott was a good officer, although the Intel officer for an engineer Bn was not always the busiest man in the world. Coupled with himself as the executive officer and Lt. Col. Maguire as the old man, Tony could not think of any better group with whom to be deployed. Of course, he could have gone a lifetime without actually finding out.

A flare blazed up into the sky, pulling Tony out of his thought process. He looked around and realized that he was now very near the back of the platoon size element. The controllers had popped the star cluster to announce the end of the exercise as the lead members of the platoon closed within the engagement limit of the bad guys. The Headquarters/Headquarters Company (HHC) First Sergeant pumped his first and indicated a rally point off to the left. Tony hoisted himself up and trotted the fifty or so yards with his equipment jangling all around him. As they gathered, he noticed a HMMV pulling up. The HHC clerk climbed out and jogged up to Lt. Col. Maguire, who was similarly making his way to the rally point. After listening for a moment, Maguire nodded and turned to point at Tony, Joe, and Vic Riley, the BN Command Sergeant Major (CSM), the senior enlisted man in the Battalion. They quickly made their way to the HMMV where their boss indicated that they should climb in. As the clerk started the vehicle into motion, none too smoothly, Tony reflected on the first vehicle he had driven in the Army. That ¼-ton Jeep had as much similarity to this vehicle as a horse did to the Jeep. This behemoth could go almost anywhere, carry almost its own weight and could run on four shot out tires if needed. It also could gulp down an incredible amount of diesel, something that stressed their supply officer constantly.

"We've been called to the Post HQ," Dana announced. "Evidently they have some new information for us."

"I sure hope that info includes when we leave and where we are going. They seem to be in a hurry to get us somewhere. It would be nice to know where that is," Tony opined.

"I suspect that is exactly what we are going to find out," Lt. Col. Maguire replied in a tone that indicated that he wasn't particularly interested in talking any more. The rest of the trip to the HQ passed in silence, each man alone with his thoughts.

At the main entrance to the HQ building, they were met by a young captain who Tony recognized as some sort of assistant to the base commander. The junior officer asked the group to follow him and led them to a conference room where they had sat through a welcoming brief when they first arrived on post and had visited again for a progress briefing a few days ago. The difference this time was that an armed guard stood outside the entrance to the room. The guard, who had no nametags, unit patch or rank on his gray, digital pattern Army Combat Uniform (ACU), checked their I.D.s and returned them. Before opening the door he said, "Gentlemen, this room is temporarily designated as a secret facility. You may see classified documents out in the open. You are to take nothing from this room that is not contained in a specially designated folder that you may or may not be provided with." Without asking if they had any questions, he opened the door, watched them go through, followed them into the room, and then closed and locked the door behind him.

Inside, the room looked much the same as it did every week. The difference only became apparent after the post commander asked them to find their seats and switched on the projector. A large "TOP SECRET, NO FOREIGN DISTRIBUTION" slide came up. Normally, a "Confidential, For Official Use Only" slide was the first one displayed. The post commander, a large, gray-haired Infantry Colonel, welcomed them and then turned the podium over to a younger man wearing an ACU uniform. Like the guard who had checked their IDs, his uniform also had no nametags, rank or patches on his shoulders. He made a point of introducing himself as "Mark" with no rank or last name. Mark looked to be in his mid thirties. He had hair that seemed just on the edge of being too long for him to be a soldier but perhaps too short for him to be an average civilian. Tony guessed that he must be either Special Forces or perhaps even CIA; both groups who were famous for anonymity.

"Mark" began, "Gentlemen, I am here to read you into your battalion's role in "Operation Righteous Justice." Your battalion will be assigned to the 18th Airborne Corps as a Corps asset. You will have a key role in what is going to be a fast, precise and overwhelming mission. Here are the broad strokes of the operation." He paused and seemed to realize that the post commander was still in the room along with the post operations officer. He turned and said "Colonel, thank you for your assistance. I can handle the briefing alone from here."

The post commander was obviously taken aback. He paused, then seemed to realize that he really had no argument to make. The 112th was nominally under his command because it was on his post. However, he and his operations officer had no part in whatever operation was to be discussed and therefore had no need-to-know about the details of any upcoming operation. His overwhelming curiosity was not reason enough for him to argue that he should be allowed to stay. All of these thoughts played out across his face over the course of a few seconds. Evidently deciding that discretion was the better part of valor, he retreated from the room with his operations officer in tow.

Once the door had closed, "Mark" turned back as if the incident hadn't even occurred. He repeated the phrase "Here are the broad strokes of the operation." The next slide showed a map of southern Turkey, Syria, western Iraq, Lebanon and northern Israel. There were arrows representing a ground axis of advance north from Israel toward the Bekka Valley, an air assault axis of advance from western Iraq also into the Bekka Valley and an amphibious assault apparently aimed for the Beirut airport. Further, reserve forces were designated in western Iraq and southern Turkey. After giving the team a short time to peruse the slide, he said, "This next slide shows the broad strokes of the fires plan." Air corridors were shown coming into the area from several directions, including air strikes from what must have been a carrier group in the Mediterranean and strikes from airbases in Iraq, Turkey and Israel. Most interesting were the designated targets. Not only were targets in Lebanon shown, but also many, many in Iran.

Switching back to the first slide, Mark said, "Your part is with this air assault. We will assault into a large terrorist training base here in the Bekka Valley. Your engineers, organized as small dismounted teams, will be on the second round of helicopters. The job of the first troops in, soldiers from a battalion of the 101st Airborne, is to kill people and to secure the perimeter of the facility. Your job is to clear any buildings they don't clear and to set the demolitions that will blow up whatever we find that we don't want the enemy to have access to. We are not going to hold onto these facilities. There's really nothing strategically important about the buildings or this camp other than the people we want to kill and the material we find there. However, we learned in Iraq that you can't leave large caches of weapons lying around or someone is going to wander over, pick them up and use them against you. As soon as you get your job done we are getting back onto the helicopters and heading for the next objective. We aren't sure what that objective will be. Even if I did know, I wouldn't tell you."

"Your first step in your planning is to break your battalion into eighteen survey/demolition teams of eight soldiers each. This is basically an EOD (Explosive Ordnance Demolition) mission, but there aren't enough EOD teams to go around so we are turning to you engineers. Your teams should be filled with combat ready light engineers; what the English have always called Sappers. For every six Sapper teams you can have a command cell of three people – I assume you will use your company commanders for that. Your battalion can have a command cell of six people to include two medics. You will also designate a separate logistics team of six people to resupply any of the Sapper teams that run through their generous allotment of C-4 and initiation systems. Everyone else will be left behind at the assembly area. In other words, out of the 450 troops in your battalion, you need to have your best 160 ready to go and everybody else in the battalion ready to support them. You will have all of the demolition you could ever want to train with for the next two days. We may or may not have another day or two in western Iraq to do the same. Are there any questions?" He asked it in a way that indicated that he did not really want to answer any questions.

Nevertheless, Lt. Col. Maguire asked, "How long of a deployment should we plan for?"

"You should pack for a two week deployment and plan on an eighteen month deployment. We will need to travel light. We are not sure how long this will take, that's up to the politicians. Right now you know that you will be acting as pure Sappers in eight man teams. Your job is to have those teams ready to go."

"What can we take with us to help in our planning?" Tony asked.

"You can take what you have in your heads and nothing else. The post commander will be back here in a moment to give you some administrative information. You are to share none of the details of what you have learned here with anyone. Lives, your lives and many others, depend on this being kept a secret. If it comes out that you have leaked anything you will be imprisoned and I personally will work to make sure you are charged with treason." Again, he didn't look like he desired to answer any more questions. This time the men obliged him.

By way of dismissal, he said, "Welcome aboard, gentlemen. You have an important role. I will be around post until we leave and I will fly over with you. Sergeant Major, your job is to make sure that the men take only the bare necessities. No creature comforts, no coffee pots, no books, no electronics. Mission critical equipment only. We will arrange for shipping containers for them to pack up all of their non-mission essential items and we will ensure that they get shipped to you as soon as you get settled into something semi-permanent over there. Should only be a few weeks, give or take a few months. Lt. Col. Maguire, you will be receiving two satellite connected combat laptops with secure connections when we fly out. They will contain the full plans for the operation. I'll provide those to you as soon as we are wheels up. Lt. Col. Cooper, I mean Major Cooper, you will be provided with one as well. We need to talk later about your part in this." With that, he gathered up his computer, disconnected the cords and exited the room. The guard walked in, looked around and said, "The facility is no longer secure." With that, he walked out of the door. They could hear him trotting down the hall, apparently in an attempt to catch up with the briefer.

The men sat wordlessly, each thinking about what to say. After only a moment the post commander hurried in and said "Lt. Col. Maguire, here is the folder containing your departure information, your TCERT certification and some personnel actions. Your unit is certified ready to deploy and released to the 18th Airborne Corps. We have cleared the range 40 demolition complex for you for the rest of your time here. Your S4 can coordinate with mine to get whatever you need for your training. I have instructions to open the bunkers and our motor pool to you. Whatever your battalion reasonably needs, you get. I must say that I have never seen a reserve unit given such carte blanche. Use it wisely." Looking like he wanted to say more, or more likely longed to ask a question or two, he paused. The pause turned into a silence. Finally, he said "Good luck, Gentlemen," turned on his heals and headed out the door.

The group sat quietly as Lt. Col. Mac slowly looked through the folder. He passed around the first paper after he looked it over. It showed the unit departing from Dover Air Force base, a two-hour bus ride away, in the evening, the day after tomorrow. He looked over the second and also passed it around. It was an official memorandum from the post commander stating that the 112th Engr Bn was certified as ready to deploy to the Centcom Theater of Operations. Similarly, the third piece of paper was passed around. It was covered by a sheet that proclaimed "Secret: No Foreign Distribution." It contained one short paragraph on Department of the Army letterhead assigning the 112th Engr Bn to the 18th Airborne Corps. On the last paper his eyes went a little wider. This seemed to be the first thing that surprised him, although that surprise was tempered by the trace of a small smile at the corner of his mouth. He gathered up the first three sheets as they completed their circuit around the table and put them back into the folder without offering to hand the last paper around. He stood up and said, "Let's get to it." As they walked out, he continued, "Tony and Joe, get together with Matt Giardi, Steve Fleischer, and Scott Johnson and come up with a training plan. CSM, let's you and I get together with our commanders and first sergeants and start designating teams and developing a very light packing list. Joe, make sure Matt is fully read into the operational side – we can't have him focusing only on personnel stuff right now. I'll explain why later."

*   *   *   *

Near the village of Chigyong-dong, South Korea
15 miles south of the DMZ
June 9, 10:15 am (0115 GMT)

John looked up and down the valley, amazed at the steepness of the mountainsides and the work that must have gone into the carving of the terraces on which the rice paddies of the narrow valley grew in their beds of water. He wondered how a tank battle could possible be waged in such terrain. *Not a lot of question as to where the enemy tanks will go. Shouldn't be hard to hit them*, he thought. *On the other hand, not much question as to where the defenders would be either.* He hated to think of a battle fought in this terrain.

His squad was assigned to overwatch a bridge and a crossroads. It seemed more of a Military Police mission than an infantry mission, except for the requirement to blow up the bridge if need arose, which seemed more like a Combat Engineer mission. Therefore, in perfect Army logic, the mission went to an Infantry squad. They had gone over the bridge demolition scenario several times, with the various squad members playing different roles each time so that they could fill in for one another if one of them were not available for whatever reason. John felt

57

comfortable with his role. His Bravo team was to provide forward security for Alpha team who would actually remove the safety devices. Sergeant Cody would actually trigger the charges.

After the first few hectic days, the squad had settled into an easy routine. The only real surprise for John was that he was selected to act as the Bravo team leader. The corporal assigned to that role had not made it through mobilization station; they had discovered that he had diabetes and sent him back home. They had assigned a new private, Root, fresh from boot camp and the infantry school, to the team. Suddenly, John found himself the senior PFC. Given that he had less than a year in service, this was surprising. Even more surprising was the fact that Alpha Team had two PFCs with more time than he. For whatever reason, Sergeant Cody had decided not to move one of those men over to Bravo Team but had instead decided to have John run the four-man team. John was excited for the opportunity, but nervous as well.

His team manned its outpost twenty-four/seven. Two men slept back in the small tent that was their squad quarters while two men manned the bunker. In the bunker, only one man was required to be awake at a time, which meant that theoretically, one could sleep a total of eighteen hours a day. Some of the guys seemed to be trying to do exactly that, but John found he couldn't sleep that much. He had taken to reading everything he could get his hands on. Unfortunately, that wasn't much. He had read the two novels he had brought with him. None of his fellow team members were readers, excepting the motor mags that Campbell had with him. John had even found himself reading a copy of the Army Field Manual "The Platoon in the Defense" that Sergeant Cody had brought with him. He actually gleaned a couple of things from that reading that he had incorporated into his team's bunker design and layout.

Now, a week into the duty and with another week before he could count on a trip to the PX, he was reduced to reading the technical manuals for the charges and detonators for the bridge. He found that his high school and college Physics courses had given him enough knowledge that he could follow the circuit diagrams. He had played around with the circuit tester and had taken on the task of testing the circuits and the other specified daily checks. On the first day, he found a problem on the east circuit and was able to isolate the problem. He called over Sergeant Cody, who looked at the fault and said, "I'll call it in."

"I can fix it, Sergeant."

"I bet you can, college boy, but the procedure says to call it in and the engineers will come out and fix it."

"Tell you what, Sergeant. How about you go ahead and call it in but I go ahead and try to fix it. When the engineers come, they can check my work."

"Tell you what, Private. How about you keep your hands off it before you blow us all up. You can watch the engineers when they fix it in case the need ever arises and they are not available. Fair enough?"

"O.K., Sergeant. Fair enough."

When the engineers got there, John watched them work. He realized that they knew little more than he did about circuits. They repeated the diagnoses that he had already completed and reached the same conclusion. He was gratified that they did just what he was planning to do before Cody stopped him. After they left, he reported the completion of the repair to the squad leader.

Cody asked, "Were you right in terms of what you wanted to do?"

"Yes, Sergeant. It was a fairly straightforward splice."

"Good to know. Your knowing how to do that might come in handy some day. Nice work, Coach."

"Perpetual peace is a futile dream."
    - General George S. Patton Jr.

CHAPTER FOUR

FT. DIX, NJ
June 9, 7:30 am (1230 GMT)

The battalion colors flapped softly in the light morning breeze, just enough to show off the battle streamers attached above the flag. The streamers carried the names of battles dating back to the Civil War; back to when the unit now known as the 112th Engineer Battalion had been known as the Cleveland Grays. The streamer the men were most proud of was the red one with the words "D-Day" on it. The 112th had gone onto Omaha Beach on Day One – not in the first wave but on the first day nonetheless.

A, B, C and HHC companies were lined up facing the long row of Vietnam era barracks that had been their home for the last couple of weeks. The men were unusually quiet and focused as Lt. Col. Maguire finished telling them a sanitized version of what he had learned the previous evening and what would transpire over the next few days. The staff had worked late into the night - actually early into the morning - to develop as aggressive a two-day training plan as any of them had ever seen. It would commence in 60 minutes, as soon as the Company Commanders and First Sergeants had broken their companies into their demolitions teams - what they would call Sapper teams - and support teams.

"We have two more items of business to take care of before we get to work. Major Cooper and Captain Giardi, front and center!"

he bellowed. Each gave a slight start, not expecting this, and then hurried from their spot with the staff at the back of the formation. They stopped one stride in front of Lt. Col. Maguire and gave a salute. Dana returned the salute and in a quiet voice told them to go to parade rest. In a much louder voice, he addressed the formation. "There is a little known rule that states that when someone is identified for promotion, but is then activated, that they can still be promoted as long as their home state commits to holding an identified higher ranking slot open for them. The State of Ohio, showing exceptional judgment, has decided that it did not want these two fine officers to have their careers put on hold due to our deployment and have indeed committed to holding those slots open."

With that, he called them and the unit to attention. Captain Johnson stepped forward and read the promotion orders as Lt. Col. Maguire stepped in front of each officer and slipped the new rank onto the tab of their ACU Jackets. He gave them each a pin-on rank, and in a voice only they could hear said, "The helmets take too much time for me to mess with them during this ceremony. Here's some rank you can use to fix them up when you get time. Congratulations to both of you. This is well deserved." He shook their hands in turn and then ordered them to do an about face. He then led the formation in a round of applause. He called out for them to "Post" and as they neared the back of the formation he gave the order for the commanders to take charge of their units. As soon as he stepped away, the first sergeants and Command Sergeant Major came forward. Before long, they were bellowing orders and names, attempting to establish a new order out of the old formations.

"Congrats, Tony, or should I say Sir," said Joe while shaking Tony's hand.

"Thanks, Joe. You'll get this same chance before long."

"A couple of years, yet. And then only if we pull this mission off successfully, I suspect."

"We will, Joe."

The rest of the staff gathered around the two newly promoted officers shaking hands and offering their own congratulations. Captain Mike Cristal, the commo officer and resident smartass, proceeded to repeatedly salute Major Giardi. Matt returned the salute the first two or three times before realizing that he was being screwed with, at which time he grabbed Mike in a headlock and proceeded to give him an old fashion noogey on his bald spot.

Lt. Col. Maguire picked that moment to walk up to the group and say, "I take back what I said about this being well deserved, Matt. If you can't act your age, try acting your new rank." The words came out harsh but the hint of a smile behind his eyes showed that he was only a little annoyed.

"We have a lot to do and not much time to do it. We need these teams to be sharp. Scott, make sure that Post knows that we are going to exceed the maximum pounds of demolitions that the ranges are rated for. Steve, keep working with the post supply guy to get those artillery and mortar shells. I want to be able to use realistic items to make caches for our guys to destroy. It looks like we got all of the C-4 and initiation systems we asked for – my desire is that we have none left over to turn in."

He paused to make sure that everyone was still tuned in. He then said, "Guys, we are going to go through a little reorganization. Tony, you are being called over to building 102 to meet with Mark or whoever the hell he is. Take my HMMV, I'll ride with the CSM. My understanding is that we are going to lose you at some point; they have something else in mind for you. Joe, I'm moving you into the XO slot and Matt, you are now the S3. Your S1 NCO will have to pick up the slack – I don't have anyone to backfill you with. Let's push these teams long and hard. Let's go." He walked toward where his commanders were conferring as their squad leaders and NCOs continued to work to bring the new structure into place. By far the largest group of enlisted men was gathered around the HHC First Sergeant, whose company of support troops had grown to nearly three hundred overnight.

Tony caught up to his commander and asked, "Any idea what's up with me?"

"I really don't know. I suspect some sort of liaison role. Doesn't make sense to have two Light Colonels in a battalion, I guess. You have a pretty good record based on what you did in Afghanistan. I suspect it will be something interesting. Mark, or whoever he is, wanted you over there half an hour ago. Let me know what he has to say."

"I will. Thanks, Dana." Using Dana's first name felt strange after so many years of "Sir or Colonel." He and Dana had briefly been the same rank as captains and had been on a first name basis then, so it could have been worse. Still, it would take some getting used to. He walked over to the HMMV, started it up, and headed for Building 102. He wondered what he would learn there.

The drive to the center of post took only a few minutes, but it was long enough to remind himself that anyone who actually plopped down money to buy a civilian version of a HUMMER was crazy. The huge vehicle had a horrible ride, was so loud during operation that conversations could only be held by yelling, and offered surprisingly little in the way of seating space or cargo room. He wondered how much someone would need to be compensating for something to make driving one of these on an everyday basis desirable.

Ten minutes after leaving the 112th area, Tony walked into the post headquarters building and was greeted by a young Corporal who looked barely old enough to shave. In response to Tony's question, the Corporal gave directions to the pair of offices that had been turned over to "Mark." Tony resigned himself to perhaps never knowing Mark's real name and decided to drop the mental quotation marks he had been using up until that point. He knocked on the door to the office indicated and heard footsteps followed by the sound of locks, at least two of them by the sound, being released. The door opened to reveal the soldier, at least Tony assumed he was a soldier, who had guarded the briefing room the previous day.

"If we are going to keep running into each other we might as well be on speaking terms. I'm Lt. Col. Tony Cooper." As he said it, he realized that he had thought about this promotion long enough that he could mentally adjust to the rank change quickly enough.

"Yes, I know. Congratulations on the promotion. My name is Robert."

Again, Tony wondered if they were even soldiers. This young man was obviously not old enough to be the same rank as he, yet he showed no hesitation about not appending "Sir" to his response and showed no discomfort in using his own first name. Tony decided that he had to ask the question. "What unit are you with, Robert?"

"There are things you need to know right now, but there are also some things you don't need to know," Mark said, walking in from the other office. "Thanks for coming over. I take it the formation took a little longer than I had hoped. Congratulations on the promotion."

"Thank you. Actually, with everything we had to accomplish, it did take a while, although I don't think we wasted any time. It wouldn't surprise me if you are hearing many 'booms,' and big ones, by noon."

"I hope so. Your troops were not exactly our first choice, but they were available and for a National Guard battalion seem to be pretty good."

"Mark, or whatever your name is, this battalion may not be able to march with, run with, or compete in a swim suit competition with their active duty counterparts. But don't worry. When it comes to getting something done I wouldn't trade them for anyone."

Tony paused, looking at Mark and seeing no reaction, continued, " However, it does strike me as strange that a National Guard unit is assigned to this mission. You yourself admit that we weren't your first choice. Any idea why they assigned us to this?"

Mark smiled and said, "That's a good question. First, there just aren't that many Engineer Battalions available. Secondly, this air assault is a very, very tightly held secret. The world will be focused on the build-up of troops in Northern Israel. Your battalion being sent to western Iraq will not raise eyebrows or make anyone think that something big is going on. If we sent a high profile active duty Combat Engineer battalion to a quiet spot in the Iraqi desert, questions might be asked."

Tony processed that for a moment. Nodding, he said, "That makes some sense. But don't worry about the 112th. This battalion will be fine."

"I hope you are right, Colonel."

Tony decided now was the time to ask some more questions. "Now, Mark. You seem to know a lot about us, including about upcoming personnel actions even before we do. It would seem that it's only fair that I know a couple of things about you and Robert. Who exactly are you? And how do I even know that we work for, or with, you? If we are being attached to the 18th Airborne Corps or the 101st Airborne, why haven't I seen anybody with those patches stopping by? All I get are you two; with no patches, no ranks, nothing. The only thing we have to go on is that the Post Commander deferred to you. What do you have in writing that I can see to verify that we should even be listening to you?"

Robert looked to the older man. Mark looked like he was taking his time deciding how to handle this. Reaching a conclusion, he went to his desk drawer, searched briefly for a file, found it and pulled out a piece of paper. He handed that over to Tony. Tony scanned it and saw that it was on 101st Airborne Division letterhead. It was signed at the bottom by the commanding general, MG Ken Robinson and countersigned below that by LTG Lloyd Austin, commander of the 18th Airborne Corps. The body of the text was brief. It stated in part that:

"All personnel of Ft. Dix, NJ are to cooperate fully with the agent bearing this letter in matters pertaining to the attachment, training and deployment of the 112th Combat Engineer Battalion." and further stated that:

"By Department of the Army order HQ09124-16, the 112th Combat Engineer Battalion, OH Army National Guard, is attached to the 101st Airborne Division effective 8 June, 2007.

It went on to give a contact number for any questions. Tony took a small, green notebook from his side cargo pocket and jotted that number down. Mark made no move to intervene.

"I notice, Mark, that it refers to you as an agent. What does that mean, exactly?"

"Colonel, I am employed by the C.I.A. but detailed to the Department of the Army. It is a program put into place based on the lessons of the Afghan and Iraq conflicts. We realize that we needed to have real time coordination and real time integration of our operational and intelligence functions. I have been involved with the planning of the operation as an augmentation to the 101st Airborne staff. I have the assimilated rank of Lt. Col., just like you, although my date of rank is designated such that I outrank you and your commander. For times when that isn't enough, General Austin's signature comes in handy."

"His signature, and the fact that he could squash most normal men with his bare hands. I served with him, or rather for him, in Afghanistan," Tony said.

"I know. He claims to have a vague memory of you. His senior rating on your Officer Efficiency Report was certainly kind enough."

"Again, Mark, I feel that you know much more about us than we know about you. I suspect that I am going to have to get used to that feeling." Tony paused, then continued. "I also suspect that if you are here rather than a military type that the mission of the 112th is going to be a little more than what you laid out for us the other day."

Mark smiled and said, "The mission of the 112th is basically what I explained yesterday. They are going to find and blow up any munitions they find laying around the camp that we hit."

"Then why all of the cloak and dagger? This seems like the type of coordination they could send a Major off of staff to do."

"Actually, Robert, as young as he is, does have the assimilated rank of a Major. Life ain't always fair, is it?" Mark laughed. "The first reason we are here is that the 101st Airborne staff is stretched pretty thin and they needed the help to cover this base. The second reason is that I suspect they get nervous having us around and might have welcomed the chance to get us far away from the flagpole. The third reason is you."

Tony was stumped by that last. "Me?" he said, sounding none too intelligent.

"You will notice that the decision by the state of Ohio to go ahead and promote you gave the 112th Battalion one more Lt. Col. than they needed. In some outfits, including active duty outfits, they would have you stay and continue to serve as the XO. Nominally, we are indeed going to have you stay with the 112th. However, in reality we need to grab you for another mission. That mission needs some rank to it for political reasons and having some combat engineer experience won't hurt. I will be heading up that mission but will need to do so in a behind the scenes way. The people we will be dealing with aren't really that trusting of the CIA. When that time comes, you will, to outward appearances, be my boss. We will have military reps of many sorts on this group. Most of them will indeed be what they seem. Robert and I will not. The head of the mission will probably be a full-bird Colonel from the Department of the Army staff."

"Can you tell me what the mission is?"

Mark smiled, "If you are as smart as you think you are, or your testing suggests at least, you should be able to figure it out. For right now, you have some homework to do. I need you to spend the next few days studying up on the history, geography and political structure of Lebanon and Syria."

"Lebanon *and* Syria? Lebanon makes sense, but why Syria?"

"Again, don't ask questions you should be able to figure out for yourself."

Tony realized that he had at least the inkling of what must be going on. The CIA was famous for being good at many things. One of those was the covert overthrow of governments in an attempt to install new governments more friendly to the United States. It seemed likely that they were hoping to do the same thing here. If successful, the new government, or the group hoping to be the new government, would need to cooperate, in official jargon "to liaison," with the current operation. His guess was that he would be a minor part of the team designated to do that. It sounded like an interesting mission. He still liked the idea of leading Sappers into combat to destroy illicit enemy munition caches. However, the mission that suddenly presented itself seemed interesting as well.

Tony noticed that Mark was watching him and seemed to have the sense that Tony had the broad strokes of what was going on figured out. "O.K." Mark said. "For now, Tony, satisfy yourself with getting smarter on the area. Have you ever done a speed reading course?"

"I took a class on it once. I've got some of the techniques down. What resources do you have available?"

Mark walked Tony over to the second desk in the inner office. On that desk were what looked to be about ten volumes. On the top was one that Tony recognized. Thomas Friedman, one of his favorite columnists, had first made a name for himself with his book *"From Beirut to Jerusalem."* Tony was impressed with anyone who would include that on a regional reading list. Looking through the rest of the stack he recognized only the generic white Department of Defense "Country Studies" for the two countries. He had never read these two volumes, but he had read the ones for Korea, Turkey and Afghanistan, so he knew what he would encounter. The rest seemed to run to academic texts by what were, to him, unknown authors. He suspected that they would be dry, but on the other hand he had always dreamed of a job that would pay him for reading. Now, at least for a couple of days, he had found it. He settled in and decided to start with Friedman. He saw that there were yellow legal pads and pens on the desk along with what looked to be a National Geographic map of the Middle East. He loved to look over maps, or better yet Google Earth, as he read non-fiction accounts. He also liked to jot notes and thoughts. He realized that there was no way that Mark could have known both of those things and realized that Mark was, if nothing else, thorough. That was a good sign. After asking Robert the location of the rest room and the nearest chow hall and pop machine, he felt he had everything he needed to get started. He settled in for what looked to be an easy couple of days.

The morning passed quickly. At noon the three of them went to lunch at the small cafeteria that served the post headquarters and adjacent buildings. They talked little, and as outsiders they seemed to attract a few glances. Uncomfortable with the attention, they ate quickly and returned to their little hideout. Tony spent the afternoon skimming through the rest of Friedman's book and started through the country studies. He took some notes out of the "Country Study" books regarding the characteristics of size, population, literacy rates, infant mortality rates, etc. None of these data individually were very helpful, but together they helped to paint a picture of two countries very much in crisis. They were ancient, yet something seemed to hold them down in a perpetual quagmire of war, famine and disaster. At separate times, Mark and Robert made their way in and out of the room, with little explanation of where they were going. Tony grabbed dinner on a to-go tray and brought it back to the office. Mark let him in and then announced that he was calling it a night. Around 7:00 pm, Robert announced that it was time for him to go as well.

Tony asked, "How should I lock up when I'm ready to go?"

Robert smiled and said, "I'm sorry. I have to learn to be more direct. It's time for both of us to go."

"Oh, so that's how it's going to be," Tony laughed. "You two are really making me feel like part of the team. What time do we start up in the morning?"

"Plan on being here around 8:30 a.m. We don't buy that whole 'we do more by 9:00 a.m. than most people do all day' Madison Avenue crap. You sleep when you can, because there's going to be a time when you can't," Robert smiled.

"Sounds good, Robert. See you tomorrow." Tony made his way out to the parking lot where he saw his, actually Dana Maguire's, HMMV still sitting. Unlocking the chain that wrapped around the steering wheel, he drove himself out to the barracks and found it quiet. Walking through, he saw that the orderly rooms and the supply rooms were occupied with the usual supply and personnel types. A few of the sick, lame and lazy were also about. However, it was obvious that the Sapper types were still out in the field. He had heard faint blasts early in the day but realized that he had not heard them all afternoon. He realized that the sky had cleared and without the echo off the clouds the sound of the explosions must not have been carrying all of the way to main post. He was tired and bleary eyed from reading all day and he decided to take Robert's advice and sleep while he could.

*　　　　　*　　　　　*　　　　　*

Tony was asleep when he heard the others making their way in. He looked at his watch and saw that it was 0130 – 1:30 a.m. in the civilian world. He asked Joe how it went.

"Good, although we have a lot of work to do. Out of 18 teams, 16 didn't meet the time standard we set on the initial course. We've got to break them out of the safety/training mode and into mission mode. The NCOs need to learn to operate without an officer looking over their shoulder. I'm afraid the old maxim that you fight how you train is biting us in the butt. All of the focus on safety for all of these years, as well intentioned as it was, has messed with our ability to do anything quickly."

Tony said, "We've had that discussion over beers a time or two and never figured out how to break the cycle. Those few times there was a small incident, life was impossible and careers were in jeopardy. Remember the kid who lost the pinky toe at Grayling? Hell, that took us forever to get over. What time are you cranking up in the morning?"

"First formation at 0730 – full battle rattle and ready to load the trucks. We're going to nap in the afternoon and then go all night. The next day we'll stand down according to our plan and then load the buses for Dover. What the hell have you been up to all day?"

71

"I sat in an office and read. I could tell you what I read but then Mark says I would have to kill you. I'm only partly joking."

"You always were a scammer – always getting out of the hard stuff. I want to be you when I grow up!" Joe teased. "Now shut up so we real soldiers can get some sleep."

Joe turned off the light and was snoring in less than two minutes.

*   *   *   *

Near the village of Hasuhan, Kangwond-do, North Korea
June 9, 1:30 pm (0430 GMT)

Major Li looked at the long line of tanks as they made their way from the railhead, past the fuelling trucks and south toward the assembly area. Fifteen miles to the south lay the artificial line that had separated the peninsula for over fifty years. With any luck, that border would not be there in another month. Li felt more comfortable now that the Brigade was moving into position. He still wondered at the wisdom of what they were tasked to do, but the manic activity required over the last few days, getting the tanks and other vehicles loaded and moved toward their launching points, had given him little time to fret.

The news of the attacks in America and the realization that the Middle East would soon erupt into war again gave him the hope that maybe the U.S. might indeed be too distracted to react quickly or strongly enough to stop his country's plans. More sobering to him was the idea that his country's leadership must have had some foreknowledge of the attacks – how else would they have known that they could count on a distracted U.S.? This operation had clearly been planned prior to those attacks.

Those worries were above his pay grade, of course. His worry now was more properly limited to helping his commander to get his forces into position. Ahead, he saw that a tank had thrown a track and that the tanks behind it were backing up. Evidently, it didn't occur to the tank commander in the tank behind the broken down tank to go around it – he had been told to follow that tank, after all. *Idiot!* Li dropped down into the interior of his tank, switched the radio to the first company's frequency and yelled for the tank commander to go around and get the line of tanks moving again. He then switched back to the Battalion net and called for maintenance support for the broken down tank. By the time he finished with that call he felt his driver start their tank moving forward again. He raised his upper body back out through the turret to confirm that the line of tanks was indeed moving again. To his relief, he saw that it was.

"They have not wanted Peace at all; they have wanted to be spared war -- as though the absence of war was the same as peace."

- Dorothy Thompson

CHAPTER FIVE

Ft. Dix, NJ
June 10, 6:45 am (1145 GMT)

Tony joined the 112th staff for a morning run; something he used to be able to do with ease when he coached and ran with the Arlington Heights cross-country team for the first ten years of his teaching career. His move to administration had forced him to stop coaching. His laziness had forced him to stop running. Now, even the slow three and a half miles they did taxed his none-too-svelte frame. At breakfast, the talk was all about the training the day before and the training to come. Tony sat at a table with Dana, Joe, Scott and Matt Giardi.

Dana asked what the previous day had consisted of for Tony. Tony told him that it looked like he was being picked up for a liaison role of some sort, working for the 101st Airborne. Right now, he was just doing general reading about the region. He was sure that he would learn more as time went on.

"Did you learn any more about our battalion's role?" Dana asked.

"No. My guess is that it will be basically what was briefed to us."

After breakfast, as they walked back from the chow hall to the parking lot where the battalion's morning formation would be held, Dana pulled Tony aside and asked him what he had learned about Mark and Robert and their role in this whole thing.

Tony said, "He's representing the 101st Airborne Commander. That's all I really know."

"That's it? Who is he? What's his last name? Or Rank? Is he Army?"

"Dana, he doesn't strike me as the type that likes to share a whole lot of intimate details. You might be better off asking him these questions yourself."

Dana nodded and seemed to accept that response. He told Tony that Steve Fleischer had gotten him another HMMV so Tony could keep the one that Dana had loaned him. They walked on, seeing the company first sergeants ahead gathering their troops into formations.

Tony saw Mark and Robert watching the formation. *So much for their not being early risers*, he thought. Mark walked over to Lt. Col. Maguire as the latter prepared to get into position to take over the formation. The pair spoke briefly, with a couple of brief glances in Tony's direction that piqued his interest. Dana then moved into a position to take over the formation and Mark and Robert walked over to a non-descript staff car and drove away. Dana gave a few remarks regarding the successes and challenges of the previous day and reminded everyone of the schedule for the next couple of days. It was still amazing to think that 48 hours from now they would be on a plane heading for the Middle East.

Tony knocked on the locked office door a couple of minutes before 0830 and Robert let him in. Tony made his way to his desk and realized that Mark was looking at him. He returned the look, raising an eyebrow.

Mark smiled and said, "You did good. Dana knows more about what's going on than he has let on. We asked him to ask you a couple of questions this morning to see how much you would share. He said you did well, answering questions in a way that gave answers that were satisfying without actually revealing a whole lot. That's a gift we were hoping you possessed."

Tony stewed for a moment before saying, "Look, Mark. I'm a little too old and have reached a rank where I don't enjoy being kept in the dark. You guys obviously have a use for me or I wouldn't be here. If you feel you can trust me, and I assure you that you can, why not tell me what is going on here?"

"What do you think is going on?"

Again, Tony hesitated, and then figured nothing ventured, nothing gained. He said, "I think that you have a group in either Syria or Lebanon that is ready to take over as soon as we move in. You are going to send them what is ostensibly a military liaison team to coordinate their actions with ours. That probably means that they are military as well. You CIA guys will be the real brains behind the operation, but you don't want them to know that because nobody in the world trusts you."

"Not bad, Tony. Not quite right, but not bad. What about the 112th mission?"

"My guess right now is that it is just what you say it is. Am I wrong?"

"Not really. The 112th will indeed be doing what we say they will. However, we will be with them, looking for an item or items that we don't want blown up. In fact, we want to take it with us, or at least evidence of it, to show the group we are meeting. You're right about that group. They are a group of Syrian officers ready to give up on Assad and align with the west. They have seen the writing on the wall and realize that their country is a backwater and will be for as long as the leadership doesn't change."

"What are we looking for exactly?" Tony asked.

"It's something that terrorists should not have. It should help us to sever the link between Syria and Iran. The Arabs and the Persians have never really trusted each other. Their mutual hatred for Israel and their support for Hamas and Hezbollah have helped them to work together for now. What we hope to pull out of those camps should give that group something they can take to the world and to their people to justify a split with Iran and the overthrow of the government of Syria; as a danger to the people of that country."

"How can they possibly align with us since we are aligned with Israel?"

"Israel will immediately recognize them and offer to give them back the Golan Heights. We have several other countries, including Britain, who will also recognize the new government immediately."

"What's my role in all of this?" asked Tony.

"Basically what I laid out before. The fact that you have a degree in Physics and are a combat engineer helps to add credibility as you explain what we have found in a way that will convince them. Robert will be some help on that. Behind his soldierly appearance is a fairly smart mind. He has a Masters in Nuclear Engineering from Penn Sate."

"No kidding, Robert. I did some summer course work at the Brazzelle Reactor back in the 1990's." As Robert and Mark smiled, Tony realized that there was little he could tell them about his background that they didn't already know.

"I spent a lot of time around that darn little thing myself." Robert laughed. "I think we had a couple of the same professors, even though I was about ten years behind you. They haven't changed much."

"What are we planning on finding – Cobalt 60, I would guess?"

"At a minimum," answered Mark. "We think we may actually find some fissionable material as well."

Tony was stunned, searching for a response. "The Iranians would never go that far. Giving terrorists the makings of an atomic bomb? Are they fucking crazy?"

"Some of them are. There is a real struggle for the soul of Persia and the soul of Islam. On this front, the bad guys have prevailed. Trust me, when this gets out it is entirely possible that Syria's will not be the only government to fall. We just don't have the contacts to do much to help that happen in Iran right now."

"Why will they - by they I mean al-Jazeera and the rest of the Arab street - believe us? Won't they think it is a put-up?"

"Wait 'til you see the makeup of our 'liaison' team. We have included some people who we think will be helpful in getting the truth out."

"Tell me more about that," asked Tony.

"Not yet. Need to know and all that. I've already told you more than I probably should have at this point."

"Why me, by the way? There have to be hundreds of Army officers more qualified for this," Tony asked.

"For a couple of reasons. First, you were available. You kind of fell into our lap and had the credentials we were looking for. Second, having you do this won't rouse suspicion from our side. You are the right rank to serve as a liaison at several levels. The fact that you are just a National Guardsmen means that folks don't expect much out of you and don't expect you to be caught up in anything big."

Tony thought about that for a second. "Just a National Guardsman. You would have thought that after we supplied 30% of the forces to Afghanistan and Iraq that people would have dropped that old prejudice against reservists. Hell, I wouldn't trade most of the active duty guys for my guys. I remember back in Afghanistan when the CSM of the 10th MTN said that Santa Clause must be a Guardsman. He pissed off about one third of his command. I would have liked to have seen him accomplish his mission without us. We may not be as skinny or as fit or march as pretty…." He stopped himself from going further down that road – he fretted about it all too often. "Oh well, I guess some things don't change."

"We obviously don't buy into that "just National Guardsmen" crap completely or else the 112th, or you, wouldn't be here," said Mark. "But we are also not above using that prejudice when it supports our purpose. Thus, welcome to your 'liaison' role."

"Makes sense, I guess. Hell of a way to run a war, though." Tony said as he settled himself in for another day of reading. Mark said he was heading to the SCIF (Secret Compartmentalized Information Facility) and made his way toward the door.

Over his shoulder he said, "Tony, I'll take you over with me tomorrow morning before we get ready to take off. I have some stuff on the secure web I want to show you."

"Sounds good. Have a good day playing spy."

Robert chuckled softly as Mark made his way out the door.

"It is an unfortunate fact that we can secure peace only by preparing for war."
- John F. Kennedy

CHAPTER SIX

South of Hashuhan, North Korea
3 miles North of the DMZ
June 11, 9:45 pm (0045 GMT)

Major Li again found himself in the relatively cool late evening air. The mission brief was complete and the final orders had been given. Three days until kickoff. Again, the leadership talked in positive terms. The formations of the South Koreans and the Americans had not responded to the North's quiet forward deployment of its forces. In fact, the intelligence officer reported that the U.S. had moved some of its best forces to the Middle East, replacing them only partially with reservists deployed from their homeland. The North's artillery batteries, the battering rams that would open up to doors to the south, were almost completely in position. The tanks would move forward to the border, formally violating the armistice agreement, the evening after next. The attack would kick off the next morning, with forces racing forward to secure the bridges. If those bridges were not seized intact, the rush to the south would become a trickle. He had to admit that the plan presented was obtainable. However, he also worried that it depended on an ineffective initial response from the U.S. and South Koreans. He hoped that assumption turned out to be true. The lives of his men, and maybe even himself, depended on it.

*   *   *   *

Kuwait City
June 11, 3:45 pm (1245 GMT)

Linda walked down the street from the Kuwait City CNN
Bureau to travel the two blocks to her hotel. She was unnerved by
the looks she got from the Arab men. They seemed fascinated by
her blonde hair and the legs showing from below what was, for
her, a very conservative skirt. They looked at her with unabashed
curiosity, without any outward sign of shyness or shame. She
reconciled herself to limiting her future outfits to pants and even
decided that a headscarf might not be a bad idea. The men here
were obviously not ready, yet at the same time apparently eager,
for exposure to women who were not covered head to toe.

     The meeting with the local bureau chief had been
frustrating. She had hoped to get detail of her assignment only to
find that he knew less about what was going on than she did. The
only really useful piece of information she had received from him
was that she would be picked up at her hotel the next morning at
nine o'clock local time. She would spend the rest of the day
packing her bags and writing up her notes, preparing herself for
whatever adventure lay ahead.

*   *   *   *

US Route 13, Northern Delaware
June 11, 4:55 PM (2155 GMT)

As he sat on the bus surrounded by the rest of the staff, Tony
thought that the last two days had been a blur. He had learned
much more about the upcoming operation. The Sapper teams had
made great progress, although Joe and Dana still worried about
speed. Tony, too, hoped that they would have a few more days to

get themselves ready when they arrived in country, but he was sure that the teams would be up to the task. He was more worried about his role. He still didn't know exactly what was expected of him or if he could do it once he found out what that was. Not knowing, not being in charge, was something that drove him crazy.

He saw that the buses were turning onto Route One and to the front left saw what looked to be the front gate of Dover Air Force Base. The trip had gone quickly. Sleeping on a bus was a gift he had possessed since he was a kid. The rest of the troops were stirring in the back of the front bus on which he and the rest of the staff rode, and he assumed the same was true on each of the other nine buses in the convoy. Along with the four HMMT Cargo trucks carrying the rest of their personal and unit gear, they must have made for quite a sight driving down through New Jersey and northern Delaware.

They unloaded into what looked like a small airline terminal, but without any of the amenities normally found therein. The troops quickly moved into, and overwhelmed, the terminal. Those few individual travelers, many of whom looked to be retirees flying 'space available,' were shepherded into a small side room so that the soldiers of the 112th could get as comfortable as they could. Their first flight was scheduled to lift off in two hours; that flight would take most of the command staff and the company advanced parties. The first manifest, one hundred soldiers in all, was scheduled onto a C17. Those hundred soldiers, including Tony, Dana and Joe B., were herded out to the back of the terminal, right on the edge of the tarmac, to begin the process of marrying up with their personal gear and weapons.

A C-17 aircraft was pulled up to the next building over. Tony asked a passing airman if that was the plane they would be loading. The airman yelled over his shoulder "I think so, Sir." He, Dana and Joe walked over to get a closer look. What they saw was sobering. One after another, four flag draped coffins, no doubt filled with the bodies of the latest casualties of the still smoldering fights in Iraq and Afghanistan, were brought off the plane as a small honor guard rendered honors. It was an incredibly formal process. The most touching part was that none of this was done for the public or the cameras. The three realized that they were the only witnesses not formally involved with the process. The airmen went through the honors ritual out of respect for the fallen heroes, not for publicity, recognition or any other extrinsic reason. They did what they did because it was the right thing to do, and it was how they would want to be treated if the roles were reversed. Tony recognized the process, having seen it from the front end in Afghanistan, when the fallen soldiers were just beginning their journey home. Dana obviously recognized it as well from his tour in Iraq. Joe, who had only been deployed stateside, seemed most affected.

Without any real coordination, the three of them arranged themselves into a line, came to attention and saluted, dropping that salute only after the final casket was wheeled into the large door of what they realized must be the casualty processing station that Dover Air Force Base was perhaps best known for. Looking out of the corner of his eye, Tony saw Joe finishing a silent prayer and making an unobtrusive sign of the cross. The three of them turned and walked back to the group. Tony silently vowed to do what he could to keep as many of their men from coming back in that manner as possible. He felt sure that the same thought was going through the minds of the other two men as well.

Once back with the group, they realized that the Command Sergeant Major had made sure that their gear was already staged, ready for them to grab it and go. Standing next to the small pile of packs, helmets, webgear, body armor and weapons, keeping an eye on it, was Corporal McCheeny, Dana's driver. Just a few feet away stood Mark and Robert, next to a pile of their gear that all by itself stacked higher than the pile formed by the gear belonging to the CSM, McCheeny, Tony, Joe and Dana.

"Whatever happened to packing light?" asked Tony, peeved but amused.

"Some pigs are more equal than others," Mark smiled. "Come here and we'll even out the piles a little bit." They walked over. Mark handed Tony what appeared to be a standard, although somewhat bulky, laptop computer carrier. Robert handed two identical cases over to Dana. "These are satellite phone modem equipped. They hook into the secure SIPRNET and into the accounts we set up for you. Here are your initial passwords," he said, handing over small cards. "Dana, both are set up for you but you can transfer one to either your XO or S3, they both have been granted temporary Top Secret clearances the same as you and Tony. You can also access the World Wide Web but you won't be able to email except to a .mil account. The uplinks are secured so you can type in the clear. Don't lose these, the paperwork is horrible if you do."

"Can't be that bad, I don't see you asking us to sign a receipt for them," Tony pointed out.

"I meant the paperwork for sending your bodies home. I'll kill you if you lose them!" Mark laughed. "Seriously, it would be very, very bad for those to fall into the wrong hands so take good care of them. There are extra batteries in the bags as well as everything else you need. Windows based, very standard interface. I think you'll both know how to use them. See Robert or me if you have any questions. You can play with them on the flight over – once we are airborne. Tony, you will find a breakdown of our liaison team along with profiles of each member. Spend some time getting to know them. We'll hook up with them as soon as we hit Iraq."

"Si vis pacem, para bellum ("If you want peace, prepare for war!")

      - Favius Vegetius Renatus

CHAPTER SEVEN

Over the North Atlantic
June 11, 8:15 PM (2315 GMT)

The flight over was like all flights in military aircraft – long, loud and uncomfortable. The C-17 was a relatively new aircraft, billed by the Air Force as being able to land and take off from rough combat airstrips. Tony had learned in Afghanistan, however, that while the Air Force had made that claim so that the Army would support their bid to purchase a fleet of the aircraft; the reality was that the Army had trouble getting the Air Force pilots to take the aircraft onto anything other than a paved, long stretch of runway. It might be possible for the plane to land on dirt strip runways, but he had never seen it done.

Tony was sure that he would have the checkered pattern of the web seat imprinted on his rear end when he deplaned. He took the time to get to know the new toy Mark had given him. The computer was not all that different from the one he used at school. It connected easily and quickly to the web and SIPRNET, even in flight. He logged on to his AOL account and saw that he could indeed read his email. He typed out a quick email to Rachel and hit send. An error message came up immediately. He smiled to himself. Didn't hurt to try. He had talked to her and Julie earlier that day, before the bus left Dix. He didn't really have anything to add but wanted to see if what Mark had said was true.

He logged onto his .mil account and saw nothing but routine messages. Only then did he log onto his SIPRNET account to see if there were any messages there. It came up almost immediately and showed two new messages. The first was a standard welcome email from some system administrator. The second was from Mark, with Robert cc'd. He noticed that the email address was as generic as their first names – no clues there. Mark asked that he respond to this test message just to insure that everything was working and to lock their addresses into his address book. Tony did so with no reply message text – he had nothing pertinent to say at that point.

He saw several icons on the desktop that obviously were meant for him. The first one he clicked on was labeled "Liaison Team." What came up was a PowerPoint presentation with the cover slide 'Contingency Liaison Team' with a subtitle that read "Membership and C.V."

He began to make his way through the presentation after first looking to make sure that nobody else could see his screen. He had used his rank to grab a spot against a bulkhead – more noise and vibration but also more support and concealment. As it turned out only Scott Johnson could conceivably see his screen. Scott, showing the ability to sleep in almost any position that so many soldiers possessed, had already dozed off. The first slide, bearing the title "Team Chief," showed a picture of a full-bird Colonel who looked to be tall and about 250 lbs, in the Norman Swartzkopf model of an officer. His name was listed as Colonel Bill S. Hansen, US ARMY, Civil Affairs. The next page showed an abbreviated resume. It indicated that he was an active duty officer and was currently assigned as the G-8 – Civil-Military Affairs Officer – for the 18th Airborne Corps. His resume further indicated that he had not always been a Civil Affairs officer; he had been an infantry officer in his youth to include tours in both the first Gulf War and two tours in Iraq. His awards included the

Bronze Star and the Combat Action Badge. Neither of those told Tony much about him as a soldier – they gave those out fairly regularly, including to Tony for his tour in Afghanistan – but they served to assure him that Colonel Hansen was no chairborne-ranger paper-pusher either.

The second intro slide, entitled "Deputy Team Chief/Senior Engineer Rep" came as a little more of a surprise. On that slide he found a picture of himself, obviously pulled from his electronic personnel file. It showed Tony in his Class A (green) Uniform with a nameplate on the floor in front of him. The photo had obviously been photo shopped in that his rank, which he knew had been Major at the time of the photo, showed the silver oak leaf of a Lt. Col. rather than the gold leaf he knew he had worn. Similarly, the rank on the signboard was listed as Lt. Col. and the date shown was two weeks ago, not the seven months it had actually been. Mark and Robert and their types at work, he mused. The resume page was fairly straightforward, but played up his physics knowledge and engineering expertise to an extent that he would have been uncomfortable doing. However, to someone who only had this slide to go on, he would appear well suited for the mission.

The next intro slide was entitled "Finance and Logistics Liaison" and showed a picture of a not-unattractive female Major named Elizabeth C. Rodriquez. She had dark, Hispanic features but with a hint of something else mixed in. Her resume showed her to be a supply officer. She was currently assigned to the 101st Airborne logistics staff. She had done a tour of duty in Afghanistan as the commander of a personnel services company; in fact her time in country had overlapped with Tony's by a few months but he couldn't remember having seen her before. That was not altogether surprising given that there had been over 7,000 soldiers at Bagram Airbase at that time. The next team member was listed as "Operations Liaison" and had the picture of a stout, fit recruiting-poster style infantry Major named Roger G. Gears. His resume showed him to be assigned to the operations shop of the 101st Airborne Division and to have served as a company commander in Iraq back in 2005. He had done another tour as an operations officer for the 503rd P.I.R. in 2006. His decorations included all of the usual, plus a Purple Heart. Tony expected to be impressed with him when he met him.

The fifth intro slide had "Engineer Representative Assistant Liaison" on it. Where the picture was on the other slides was a text box with the term "Picture Not Available." The name listed was Major Mark Anderson. Tony assumed that this was Mark, although again he would not have bet much money on that being the same name that Mark's mother had given him. His resume listed an engineering degree from Ohio State University and graduation from the same Corps of Engineer schools that Tony had attended.

The sixth slide had "Asst Operations Liaison" as the title with a poor quality but still recognizable picture of Robert. His name and rank were listed as Captain Robert Palmer. His resume showed good engineering and management experience and graduation from the U.S. Army Ordinance Advanced Course.

The seventh slide, entitled "Liaison Team NCOIC" showed an iron-jawed African-American Master Sergeant by the name of Lionel Patterson. He looked like he could chew nails and ask for seconds. His resume showed a good array of troop and staff assignments, including two Iraq tours. Again, Tony's first impression was very good.

The next slide, entitled "Liaison Team Logistics Support Specialist" showed a young, apparently Hispanic Corporal by the name of Manuel Gonzales. His resume showed very little other than his age. At twenty years old, he must have joined the military straight out of high school.

Next, a slide entitled "Security Detail Chief, showed a staff sergeant by the name of Harris. Immediately behind him was a slide showing a Sergeant named Ortiz, identified as "Security Detail Member."

The eleventh slide was a bit of a surprise. Entitled "Embedded Reporter – U.S.," it showed a female reporter that Tony recognized from one of the cable news channels - initially he couldn't remember which one and then remembered that it had been CNN. Her name, Linda Rogers, had become well known over the last couple of years. She happened to be in Cuba on a special visa covering a human-interest story when Fidel Castro had finally died. She handled that opportunity magnificently and was viewed as a rising star in reporter circles. She wasn't as attractive as Tony's all time favorite – Solidad O'Brien – but she wasn't hard on the eyes either.

If the eleventh slide was a bit of a surprise, the twelfth and final slide was a huge shock. Although the name and picture didn't mean much to Tony, Rahib Bratrawi looked to be of Middle Eastern decent and about Tony's age. However, it was the slide title that caught Tony completely off-guard. It said "Embedded Reporter – al Jazeera." Bratrawi's resume showed work doing freelance for CNN and the BBC before joining the Arab news network al Jazeera several years back. Tony realized by looking at the dates that Bratrawi had covered Ramallah back when Ramallah was not an easy place to cover. That meant that he was either very brave, or had enjoyed a relationship with the insurgents that had offered him some protection.

Tony contemplated what the inclusion of the reporters meant in terms of the mission. He realized that what it probably meant was that whatever they expected to find was information that Mark's bosses really wanted to get out to the world. Whatever it was must be damaging to the interests of the bad guys, whoever they were, and helpful in justifying the actions of the U.S. Still, what a risk - to take embedded reporters, especially one from al Jazeera, on a secret mission into an Arab area. Would they be able to control what came out? Could it backfire? Could they count on the reporters to keep operational security? What if the mission goes badly?

Tony couldn't decide if including the reporters was incredibly dumb, incredibly risky, or perhaps the smartest thing he had heard of in a long time. Embedded reporters almost always grew sympathetic to the units to which they were attached; probably something akin to the Stockholm Syndrome, he supposed.

He looked forward to the chance to talk to Mark about the team but saw that now was not the time. Mark was on the other side of the aircraft working his own laptop. He would be hard to get to and they would be surrounded by others bound to hear any conversation they could have on this noisy aircraft, considering that whispering wasn't exactly an option.

He accepted that he would have to wait. He reduced the PowerPoint presentation and looked at the other icons on the desktop. The one labeled "Cobalt-60" caught his eye and he opened it. What he found was a three-page refresher paper on the properties of that substance and how it was isolated and used. It was mostly review, except for the analysis at the end. The analysis included a discussion of how one could determine the origin of a batch of Cobalt-60 by looking at specific isotope ratios.

Tony closed the files he had opened and, wanting some time to process what he had read before looking at the other files, logged off the system. He shut the laptop and put it back into its case. He leaned back against the bulkhead and let the vibration flow through his body. His mind was going a mile a minute, and he remembered actually being surprised when he realized that he was nodding off.

*   *   *   *

Tony awoke with a stiffness in his neck that again reminded him that he was not twenty anymore. Looking around, he realized that nothing seemed to have changed with the exception that even fewer of the passengers seemed to be awake than when he had dozed off. A glance at his watch showed that he had slept for the better part of four hours. The plane must be well over halfway across the Atlantic. It was scheduled for a stop in Germany and then a straight flight into Balad, Iraq. After that, they would be ferried directly out to the forward staging area in the western Iraqi desert. Tony considered getting the computer out to read some more of the files on his desktop. He never managed to get the energy level up and soon dropped off again. The next conscious thought he had was when the plane began its decent into Rhein-Main.

The stop in Germany was routine. They were kept in a side terminal while the plane was serviced and refueled. The most exciting things available to them were a few vending machines. Tony approached Mark but was rebuffed when he wanted to discuss the team. "Not here. Not secure enough. Keep reading," said Mark. "We'll have plenty of time to process once we are in country." Annoyed but accepting, Tony walked over to where he saw Dana, Joe and Matt conversing.

"We're figuring out who to leave at Balad and who to send forward. Mark told us to leave a team of five to help greet the follow-on groups as they come in and to coordinate their movement forward. Here's who we have tentatively listed to stay at Balad," Dana said, handing over a small piece of paper.

Tony studied it. "It looks pretty good, especially Fleischer leading the team. I would replace Evans with Roberts – Evans is a talker and getting him as far as possible into the desert should be a priority. Roberts, on the other hand, wouldn't tell anyone if his clothes were on fire. Fleischer can talk too. We'll have to read all five of them the riot act in terms of keeping quiet. OPSEC is vital on this one."

"No doubt. I agree with switching out Evans. Joe – make it so," Dana ordered. "I'm going to hit a toilet attached to the ground. It looks like they are serious about turning this plane around quickly." The others followed his glance out the large windows and saw that the fuel truck was pulling away. Tony and Joe followed him toward the restroom. The toilet on a C-17 did indeed leave a lot to be desired.

"No battle plan ever survives contact with the enemy."
  - Field Marshal Helmuth von Moltke.

CHAPTER EIGHT

Forward Operating Base Cobra, Anbar Province, Iraq
June 12, 8:35 am (0535 GMT)

The hot air hit Tony like a blast furnace as he stepped from
what he hadn't realized was a partially air-conditioned C-130
airplane interior. He had thought it had been hot enough in there.
Now, in the blazing midday sun with the temperature at 110
degrees, he realized that he had been relatively cool and
comfortable before. *No wonder the people in this part of the
world are so tough to get along with*, he mused to himself.

Forward Operating Base Cobra stretched out before him. It
consisted of a large perimeter lined with wire mesh boxes filled
with dirt – named HESCOs after the company growing rich off of
coming up with the idea. Inside the HESCO walls were perimeter
towers manned by Marine grunts, adobe style (a fancy word for
mud in this case) buildings that must have been original to the site
and what looked to be newly, and hastily, constructed wood and
metal buildings; no doubt built by local Iraqi contractors. Outside
of the perimeter, sun baked desert spread out toward the horizon.
Occasionally, small homes or a few ragged stands of struggling
trees or tilled fields broke the otherwise featureless terrain. The
line of soldiers was waved into a relatively large wooden building

with "Welcome to FOB Cobra" painted over the door. The makeshift terminal was just large enough to fit one C-130's worth of soldiers in it, and as the last one in Tony called for the soldiers to tighten up so that everyone could fit in.

A large Sergeant First Class wearing a 101st Airborne patch on his left shoulder climbed onto a counter and gave a welcoming speech that included a description of the general camp layout and a series of warnings, two of which, not picking up unexploded ordnance and shaking your boots out in the morning to check for spiders and scorpions, both stood out in Tony's mind as being solid advice. After the quick in brief, the soldiers were herded into loose formations and headed off to the locations designated for their teams to unpack, prep their equipment for the next day's training, eat and bed down. The same SFC pointed Tony toward a small building with no sign. Carrying his uncomfortably heavy load of gear, he headed in that direction.

The building seemed nondescript from the outside. He tried the front door and found it locked. He worked his way around and tried the only other door he found, located on the back. It, too, was locked. As he worked his way around the rest of the building perimeter, he found a few clues that this might not be an ordinary building. Partially hidden behind a wall of mini-HESCOs were a satellite uplink and a large, civilian style generator. It was humming quietly, evidently in low-draw mode, but apparently ready to pick up the load at a moment's notice. No windows were open; all were shuttered tight. On the north side of the building were standard air conditioning units, humming away. Actually, looking again, he decided there seemed to be more of the AC units than one would normally find attached to a building of this size.

He completed his circuit of the building and found himself at the front door. He raised his arm to knock and just as he did so, the door opened. A young soldier, at least he wore the standard

ACU uniform of a soldier complete with nametape – "Kline" – and Private First Class Rank, held the door open and said, "Can I see some I.D. please, Sir." Tony produced his military I.D. The soldier examined the I.D. and Tony's face alternatively. He then referenced a clipboard. As the soldier did his thing, Tony looked around the little plywood walled foyer, noticing a monitor that showed various views around the building. He had not seen any cameras outside, so they must be very small. Finally satisfied, the soldier said, "Go on in, sir." He pointed down a short hall.

"Where am I headed?"

"I'm not sure, sir. They told me I would be court-martialed if I got further than an arms length away from the front door or let anyone in who wasn't on my list."

Tony smiled, thinking that Mark must already be there. Mark had left them as soon as they hit Balad, saying that he would see them at the Forward Operating Base (FOB). Tony worked his way down the hall. Two rooms branched off to the left and right - one outfitted as what looked to be a break room and the other as a standard office. As he reached the end of the short hall, he saw that it led to a cross hall that looked to run the length of the long axis of the building. On one end, he saw what looked to be a conference room. On the other, all that was visible was a closed door. Hearing no activity from the conference room, he headed toward the closed door. Offices branched off the hall on either side, each looking fully equipped with computers, secure phones, modems, printers and large monitors. As he reached the door, he reached for the knob, half expecting it to be locked. Rather, it opened easily and quickly. Mark and Robert looked up from where they were huddled around a computer monitor. The room was set up as a multi-media conference/work space. Mark said, "It's about time – I thought you guys got lost. The team is going to start arriving soon."

"Nice to see you, too, Asshole. Time to answer some questions."

"Actually, I was just getting ready to practice my team in-brief. That will answer a lot of your questions."

"Sounds fair enough. Do I get to critique your performance?"

"Absolutely. Maybe your teacher experience will come in handy."

Mark made his way to the podium. Robert called up a presentation with a title slide labeled "Top Secret – AMB/RES." Tony didn't recognize the designation, but the intent was obvious. Mark cleared his throat and launched into his spiel. The first few slides reviewed the current operational picture. Several times, he reminded the members of the non-existent team that secrecy was vital and he made a special point to the also non-existent reporters that any breach of the agreement they had signed would result in their detention for the duration of the upcoming operation and then some. He rolled quickly through the slides, giving specifics about the upcoming operation that were impressive in their detail. The operational diagrams showed the ground assault into the Bekka Valley from the south and an aerial assault into what was labeled "Objective Calf." Mark explained that Objective Calf was a terrorist training and logistics base funded and run by Sheikh al Raqman. The next slide showed a biography of al Raqman, listing the terrorist operations for which he was believed to be responsible. The last operation listed was America - May 11.

"Raqman is one of the key objectives of this operation. With bin Laden dead, or so deep in hiding that he may as well be dead, al Raqman has picked up the slack. His ties to Iran, Syria and Lebanon, along with the fact that he hadn't hit America directly until last month, had given him the freedom to operate more openly. We are very hopeful that we will find him in the camp when we go in. We would love to have him. The terrorists must know that we are massing ground forces in northern Israel. They will know that those ground forces cannot possibly reach the area of the camps for days, maybe even weeks. We hope that this gives al Raqman and his men a false sense of security. We have consciously and conspicuously, not included any large aerial assault capability in the forces being gathered in northern Israel, again to give Raqman a sense of security."

He paused and took a drink from a water bottle he must have placed on the podium prior to Tony coming in. After screwing the cap back on tightly and setting the bottle down carefully – the room was full of electronics after all - he began again. "However, in the grand scheme of things, al Raqman is not that important for what this team is out to do. What we expect to find is radioactive material, perhaps even fissionable material. We have solid evidence that Iran supplied the Cobalt-60 for the Boston attack and further evidence that they have supplied even more. Our primary mission is to find this material, to document its existence, and to prove to the world that Iran was directly, and Syria indirectly, involved in the attack on the United States. We have picked you two reporters because you are seen as professional and objective. We are giving you unprecedented access."

He toggled the slide show forward and showed a closer view of the assault plan. He said, "You have your choice of helicopters to ride in for the first part of the operation. In fact, if you want to ride in with the assault battalion on the first wave, you can. The important thing is that you satisfy yourselves that we are not doing anything underhanded."

Tony interrupted and asked, "Is this in-brief for the team or for the reporters?"

Mark thought for a second and said, "You're right. I thought I could do this for everyone at the same time, but it might not be possible. Maybe I should brief the team prior to briefing the two reporters?"

"It might make good sense. That would also give the team the chance to introduce themselves. Then again, it might give the reporters the sense that we are too staged if we separate the briefs."

Mark pondered for a moment. "You could be right. I'll run it by Colonel Hansen when he gets here. Let me carry on as if I'm finishing the brief for everyone." He took another drink and continued. "This slide shows the assault plan. The second wave in will be teams of combat engineers – Lt. Col. Cooper's battalion – who will destroy any conventional weapons caches and also help in the search for anything less conventional. Lt. Col. Cooper and Captain Palmer will secure, document and transport any material found. Once we have secured and documented the material, we will gather enough of it to show the world what we have found. The rest will be sent back to Iraq for processing by the International Atomic Energy Commission. We will then move into the second phase of the operation. We will be traveling by helicopter to a meeting of Syrian opposition groups just south of Damascus. These groups include high-ranking members of the Syrian military and pro-Western, or at least anti-Assad, dissidents. We will share the evidence we have with them. They will use it in an attempt to effectuate a near bloodless coup. They intend to seize the main government run television station and broadcast their evidence and their call for the resignation of the entire government and the formation of a temporary ruling council. They have committed to holding free elections within twelve months." He paused for another drink of water and said, "This dust is doing a number on my throat." Dropping back into character, he continued, "The dissident group will decide how much they acknowledge our part in securing the evidence. Further, they will decide if they feel the need to keep a small amount of the material. You, as journalists, will be free to stay with them or to travel back with us. My suggestion would be to travel back with us. There is no guarantee that their velvet-covered coup will succeed and being around if it does not would be unpleasant. Either way, you will continue to be bound by your confidentiality agreements for the timelines discussed."

"At the end of the meeting, we will fly back to the objective to rejoin American forces. Once that operation winds down, we will fly back to the forward operating base in Iraq to await further developments. Are there any questions?

He paused and then said, "Give me your questions. Whatever questions you have right now, Tony, are surely similar to what the team or our journalist guests will have."

Tony thought carefully and then began. "The operation makes good sense. I'm curious to know what we will brief the air assault and engineer troops to make sure they recognize what they find, but I assume you have a plan in place for that." He paused just long enough for Mark to nod. "The flight to Syria is worrisome – helicopters are fairly vulnerable, especially if they are spotted fairly far out. Do the military members of the group we are meeting with have enough clout to make sure that the assault forces, not to mention our little two helicopter flight, aren't engaged by their Air Force or Air Defenses?"

"We believe so. The main assault force will fly along the border of Jordan and Syria. Both countries are going to receive last minute calls from the highest levels telling them not to mess with the flights or to face dire consequences. As far as our flight to Syria, the plan is that we will be identified as a military liaison flight from Beirut. We'll use a flight plan that supports that – heading south at low level and then popping up when we reach the imaginary line from Beirut to Damascus before heading east. Anybody who actually sees the helicopters will understand that we are not from Beirut, but on radar there is nothing that will make anyone the wiser."

Tony continued, "We could use a Nuclear Emergency Response Team or Weapons of Mass Destruction Radiological Team on this mission – is there one on the mission profile?"

"No." Mark replied. "For operational security reasons it was decided that including them would tip our hand. We are going to have to do this with what we have available to us. Palmer has been to both of those schools so he will fill the role they would. We have good intel on what the containers look like so we should have an easy time finding them. Robert will do the testing/handling of the material we find. Should not be an issue."

"Easy for you to say," Robert chimed in from behind the projector.

"What about leaving some of this with the Syrians? I assume you mean a very small sample."

"Yes, and also a bunch of photographs and signed statements."

"Why do you need us again? By us I mean the non-CIA members of the team?"

Mark said, "Because this must be seen as a U.S. military initiative. The U.S. Army and the other branches actually have built up an incredible amount of goodwill by the way they have acted in Iraq. Despite the rhetoric and the lapses at Abu Gharib and al Katani, the Muslim street in general and the military of the surrounding countries in particular realize that the American military conducted itself in a remarkable manner – treating bad guys on both sides equally and, with limited exceptions, working to protect the general public. The dealings the Syrian group has had so far have been with people like me – people purporting to be members of the U.S. military. The journalists think the same thing. We absolutely cannot have them suspect otherwise. In fact, only you and the commander will know the details of who Robert and I are. We are going to go into our roles before the rest of the team arrives – which should be in a couple of hours." He said, looking at his watch. "Any other questions as far as the briefing goes?"

"No. However, I'm sure the team will. The first one might be 'How did I get assigned to this damned operation?'"

"A question that is asked often in military circles, I am sure," Mark laughed.

*"In making tactical dispositions, the highest pitch you can attain
is to conceal them."*
   - Sun Tzu

CHAPTER NINE

FOB Cobra, Anbar Province, Iraq
June 13, 9:45 am (0645 GMT)

At a word from Master Sergeant Patterson, the team members
stopped milling around and found seats. Mark, Tony and Colonel
Hansen entered the room and made their way to the front. As
they did so, Robert called "Room, Attenhut!" Colonel Hansen
looked at him disapprovingly and said, "Take your seats. This is
too small of a team to stand on ceremony. Don't anyone call a
room to attention on my account." Robert nodded, looking
chagrined, and took his place behind the projector and laptop.
The Colonel remained standing and said, "I think everyone has
met everyone else. Major Anderson will actually go over the
team members in his slide presentation, so we will skip
introductions. Mark." The Colonel sat down heavily in the front
row seat saved for him.

Mark took his place at the front of the room. He paused and
then said, "I don't need to remind you that what you hear from
this point is classified Top Secret – Pegasus. You military
members have all been granted that clearance, although that fact
is not marked in your personnel files. No one outside of this room
who you will come into contact with has the same clearance. You
reporters are subject to the agreement you signed. As promised, I
think you will find the story you are about to hear and the mission

you are about to have a chance to cover will be worth your time, effort and patience." He then launched into his spiel. As the Colonel had promised, Mark started with a slide for each team member, relating much of the information Tony had read in the CV's provided to him. Mark introduced himself and Robert as if they were ordinary members of the military, complete with ranks and assignment histories to match what they now sported on their uniforms. After finishing going over the background of the last team member, Mark moved into the operational brief Tony had seen yesterday. Observing the others more than watching the brief, he saw that his reaction yesterday was being mirrored by the rest of the group. Disbelief, worry and amazement showed on the various faces. The two reporters looked like they were amazed to have been let into some sort of inner sanctum.

At the end, Mark opened it up for questions. The reporters were the first to raise their hands. Mark motioned toward Rahib and said, "Yes." Rahib, probably from long habit at press conferences, stood up to deliver his question and said, "Rahib Bratawi, al Jazeera." When the rest of the room chuckled, he realized his mistake and looked embarrassed. Nevertheless, he went ahead with his question. "You say we are flying from here to the Bekka Valley. Through whose airspace will we be flying?"

"Good question. We will be, as close as possible, straddling the border between Syria and Jordan on the outbound leg of our journey. Both countries will be given enough warning that the flights are occurring so that they can call off their air defenses, but hopefully not so much that they can get warning to the bad guys. Further, that flight path will give both countries the opportunity to claim that our flight actually went through the other country's airspace."

"Why not fly from Israel?" Rahib asked as a follow-up.

"Again, good question," Mark responded. "The ground build-up in Israel will be the subject of much coverage by the international press. It is not that it is a feint – that assault will have real, long term objectives. However, it will serve to distract the attention of the world – and hopefully of the bad guys. They will expect to have several days to prepare for any potential arrival of coalition forces. One of the things that will not be visible in northern Israel will be any large-scale air assault capability, so they should view the main threat as being a relatively slow moving ground assault. With them having a false sense that they will have a few days to work with once an assault begins, we are hopeful that we will be able to catch them off guard."

"Tell me more about the "bad guys" as you characterize them," asked Linda. Tony watched her as she asked the question and continued to watch her as Mark made his reply. He realized that she had certainly gotten as far as she had, at least in part, based on her looks. She had a girl-next-door, wide smile look that he had loved ever since his boyhood crush on Marie Osmond. However, her eyes showed an intelligence one didn't always find in women with blonde hair and disarming smiles. He shook himself out of his non-productive thought pattern in time to hear Mark continue.

"….in Lebanon for about three years after fleeing the Wuristan area of Pakistan once Musharaf let the U.S. put in ground forces to finally clear out that nest of vipers. Al Raqman is the successor to bin Laden in the ideological arena, with the exception that he has no interest in a Sunni-Shiite rift the way that many of bin Laden's accolates do. He doesn't have the organized network that al Qaeda had, but he has served as an inspiration to small cells around the world. This camp is his most successful, concerted effort to build a more formal network.

"What separates al Raqman from bin Laden is that he is operating in his homeland. He is Lebanese on his mother's side. He speaks the language; he looks like the other people around him. He is able to blend in. He rarely travels in groups larger than three or four. He is known to be a radical, but he has traveled extensively in the western world as well. He has ties to Iran – something that bin Laden never had. These ties have very likely given him access to Iranian, and potentially North Korean, radiological material. All in all, he is a very tough customer. We also believe, with bin Laden seemingly permanently out of sight or perhaps even dead, that al Raqman is the single biggest threat to America and the world. We are hopeful to capture or kill him, to discredit him in the eyes of the world, and to stop his network for good."

Linda followed up with "How firm is your intelligence that he is at the camp?"

"Pretty solid. He is tolerated by the Lebanese government so long as they can ignore him and claim that they don't know where he is. If he were to leave the Bekka Valley, he would break that unwritten agreement. We are virtually certain that he is in the valley. We are extremely hopeful that he is in this camp in particular. Understand, however, that he is somewhat of a secondary objective. The real objective is the radiological or fissionable material. With that, we feel we can help the dissident group in Syria to overthrow their government, isolate the Iranians, and stop al Raqman's ideological appeal around the world. Next to that, his death, as satisfying as it would be, is secondary."

Colonel Hansen said, "Let's talk more about our mission to Syria. Talk to the team about what exactly we hope to accomplish."

Mark thought for a moment and said, "Assad was elected with a 75% majority in the last election. This was odd, since his was the only name on the ballot. He suffered a protest vote, or more clearly an undervote, of 25%. This is unheard of in these mock democratic elections and is one sign of his unpopularity. His meddling in Lebanon, his alliance with Iran, his cooperation with the U.S. in Iraq lately, all have upset one group or another.

However, his security forces, like those of his father, have always been able to keep a lid on any potential trouble. Well, those days look to be over. One of the men we will be meeting with is the second in command of the security forces. Others include high ranking military members, opposition politicians; nominally democratic but only time will tell. However, the feel of the intelligence community, and of the Department of Defense, seems to be that this may be the first serious group capable of taking on Assad. They have agreed, in principle, to try to make the coup bloodless, and have also committed to holding democratic elections within twelve months. As to what we will do, we are to provide them with evidence they can show to their people and the world that Assad and his government have been caught up in some very bad things and have been dealing with some very bad people. This, along with the agreement of several countries to extend recognition almost immediately, should be enough for them to gain a degree of legitimacy while they work to gather the reins of the huge bureaucracy that is Syria."

Rahib interjected by saying "How will you convince the world that the evidence is real and not fabricated?"

Mark smiled and said, "That's where you come in. You are very well trusted in the Muslim world, according to my sources. It is our hope that Ms. Rogers's and your coverage of this operation will help to convince the world that this evidence is real."

"So I am to be a shill for the U.S. government?"

"No. You will report what you believe is truthful and right and the chips will fall where they will. We are only controlling the timing of your report, not the content. You can choose your vantage point, your perspective, and your position on the battlefield. You will see what we see and report what we do. If you feel that we are misleading you, report that. If you feel that we are cruel, dishonest, or inhumane; report that. What I am convinced you will do is to report what you see and what we do and that your honest reporting will be enough to convince the world. You are too smart to believe much of what you hear around the world in terms of how hated we Americans are. What you and I both know is that there is a reservoir of good will out there. We are hopeful that your honest reporting will help us to tap into that reservoir. The world will be a better place with this material out of the hands of terrorists and, God willing, with al Raqman dead."

Rahib sat back in his chair, apparently satisfied yet looking decidedly peeved as well. Mark turned to Robert and said. "Robert will hand out an instruction sheet showing the timeline for the next day or two – to include when we lift off. First assault flight is out of here at 0330 tomorrow night - actually the morning of the next day. We follow wheels up at 0530." Lots to do before then. Colonel?

Colonel Hansen lifted his bulk out of his front row seat and turned to the group. "I want a staff huddle, in this case that means everyone, at 0700 tomorrow morning. Master Sergeant Patterson – please make sure you feel good about the administrative and logistics requirements prior to that time. Mark, Tony, if you could join me in my office."

Linda interjected and said "Sir, can we join you? You promised full access, after all."

Tony watched the Colonel and realized that he was dying to turn to Mark to ask his opinion. Tony turned to Linda and said, "Actually, we have a personnel item to talk about and then we'll come out of executive session and invite you two in. Colonel, is that ok?"

Colonel Hansen said, "My thoughts exactly. I'll send one of these guys out to get you when we are ready."

They retreated into Colonel Hansen's office and he motioned them into chairs. After the door was closed, Hansen said, "This is as strange a situation as I have ever been in. I am supposed to be the acting commander with the emphasis on "acting." I have never been a great thespian, Mark. How are we going to pull this off with me not knowing half of what you know?"

"Hell, Colonel. We are both making this up as we go along. You actually do know most of what I know. The one thing that I have that you don't is a direct communication line into the 101st Airborne Tactical Operations Center and a priority designation higher than their commanding General. What that means is that I can make helicopters, and almost anything else I want, appear when and where I want. Use that. The important thing is that the three of us can convince the journalists and the Syrians that we are what we claim to be – a purely military team on a mission representing the Department of Defense. It's not really that far from the truth."

"Any worries about the team now that you see them?" the Colonel asked, looking at both of them.

"I worry that these reporters are smarter than we give them credit for. They may figure out more than we want them to," Tony opined. "On the other hand, I'm not sure that it will matter all that much if we find what you think we will, Mark."

"Yes, sir. I think you may be right. So long as this is primarily a military mission, some CIA involvement may not be the kiss of death."

"What's with the sir stuff all of a sudden, Mark."

Mark laughed, "Just trying to get into character. I had forgotten how Pavlovian you guys are about those things. I'll be yelling 'Hooah' next thing you know!"

Hansen smiled at that. He then indicated to Tony and said, "Go get our reps from the Fifth Estate lest they believe that we are in here planning deception. When they get in here, let's talk about the site exploitation plan. I want to know where the best place will be for me and Tony to locate and also have the reporters hear it all so they can decide when and where they will fly out and who they will hang out with."

Tony nodded and went out to the hall. He saw the two reporters seated talking with their heads close together. They looked up, saw him wave, and started his way. As they passed him in the narrow hall, Tony caught a whiff of Linda's perfume and thought to himself that there was a smell one didn't always encounter during military operations.

They all gathered around a map board in the Colonel's office and Mark led them through, in his best imitation of an operations officer, the site exploitation plan.

*   *   *   *

Linda walked out of Colonel Hanson's office and followed Rahib to their little two-desk office. They sat, rolled their seats close to one another, and shared impressions about what they had seen and heard.

"What do you think, Rahib? Any chance they will find the nuclear material they think they will?" she asked.

She had been relieved to find that Rahib was almost Western in his attitude toward her, showing none of the reluctance that other Arab men had shown in dealing with her as a woman, especially in close quarters. He leaned in and said, "It's possible. Al Raqman is a psychopath of the first order. There have been rumors about his desire for a dirty bomb for years, and look how that has turned out. There are other rumors that he has more of that material and also that he wants a nuclear bomb. It is possible."

"This is an amazing chance for us," Linda said. "I just wish that we were able to file stories as we go."

Rahib smiled. "Quite frankly, I now know why they had us sign what we did. Word of this getting out would ruin any chances they have."

"I know, but it is still frustrating. What do you think of the team?" Linda asked.

"I worked with the U.S. military a great deal in Iraq. This seems like a good group, all in all. I like Hanson; he seems like a straight shooter. The same with Cooper. Something doesn't seem right about Anderson."

"I'm not sure what you mean?"

Rahib shook his head. "I'm not sure, either. He just seems too smooth. I can't really explain it. We didn't hear much from Gears, but he strikes me as one of those bull headed infantry officers. Can't really tell about Rodriquez. The NCOs seem pretty typical."

"Wow. You *have* spent some time around the U.S. military. Very complete analysis. I agree with you on almost all of it. Hansen does seem like a straight shooter. Cooper doesn't quite seem to fit the mold I expected from Army soldiers. He seems almost like a civilian."

"He is a Reservist or a National Guardsman." stated Rahib.

"How do you know that for sure?" Linda asked. "His resume was vague on his background."

"His shoulder patch is one I've never seen before. I have gotten to know all of the division patches for the active duty units in Iraq. When I see one now I don't recognize, in his case the crossed castles, I know I am dealing with a reservist. He does have the 10th Mountain Division combat patch on his right shoulder so he has had some combat experience. That matches what his resume said about Afghanistan."

"Again, wow. You know our military better than I do. I'm impressed. Well, we'll know soon enough. I'm going to write up my notes." She turned to her laptop, which had been charging while they were in the briefing and follow-on meeting. Rahib turned to do the same.

      *   *   *   *

Near the village of Chigyong-dong, South Korea
June 13, 10:08 pm (1308 GMT)

John walked toward his team's position reflecting on the briefing he had just heard. Evidently, the intel types were passing word down that the North might be massing forces on the border. No one, at least in his chain of command, seemed to be able to answer the big "Why" question. All that had really changed about their existence was that they were required to keep their helmet, body armor and Nuclear, Biological and Chemical protective suits close at hand.

"Let 'em come," Corporal Lott, John's fellow team leader, had shouted at the end of the little brief. John wondered if Lott really realized what that would mean, although there was a part of him that agreed with the sentiment.

"I hate war as only a soldier who has lived it can, only as one who has seen its brutality, its futility, its stupidity."
 - General Dwight D. Eisenhower

CHAPTER TEN

Near Hashung, North Korea
June 14, 5:30 am (June 13, 2030 GMT)

Major Li felt his senses being overwhelmed by the thunderous roar of the rockets and artillery rounds as they flew overhead. He could imagine a solid dome of steel over their heads as almost every gun in the North's inventory opened fire, pointed toward the south. To his immediate front he saw the first tanks of the lead company making their way through the gaps that had been blown into the double row of wire fences marking the DMZ. So far, everything was going just as planned. By this time tomorrow, his Brigade was scheduled to be twenty kilometers south, through the narrow valley and securing the lower end so that the follow on forces could flood onto the plains north of Seoul. Had he retained any of the religion of his ancestors, it occurred to him that this would be as good a time as any to pray.

Speed was key now. He heard his Brigade commander on the command net screaming for the battalions to move, move, move! He knew that if he switched to the battalion or companies frequencies he would hear the same. Eight bridges between them and the mouth of the valley. They had enough engineer equipment to replace only one bridge. That meant they needed to capture at least seven of them intact. Speed was the key to making that happen.

*   *   *   *

Near the village of Chigyong-dong, South Korea
June 14, 5:35 am (June 13, 2035 GMT)

John made his way back from the outhouse that served as their restroom. It reminded him how many things he took for granted back home. At home, a few steps from his bed were a toilet, a sink with running water, and a shower with an unlimited supply of hot water. Here, a hundred meter walk got him to a two-seater port-a-john. The sink was a bottle of hand sanitizer and the shower was a Wet-One rubbed over his body as he changed clothes. It occurred to him that in prior wars even those conveniences would have been luxuries. *Not a lot of Port-a-Johns at Valley Forge*, he mused. *Or heated tents.*

North, he saw what looked to be lightening in the still dark sky. Only in the east was there a hint of dawn. He thought he could make out thunder to the north as well.

He ducked through the door flap of the GP Medium tent and stepped into the pitch-black interior. "That you, Cooper?" asked Sergeant Cody.

"Yes, Sergeant."

"Is it fixing to rain out there? Thought I heard thunder."

"The sky's clear. Look's like a storm is hitting just to our north, though."

At that moment, a strange whistle, or more like a whoosh, sounded above them, followed a minute later by a thunderous explosion just to their south.

"What the hell?" someone yelled in the dark. John stumbled to his cot, his hands reaching in the dark for his helmet and body armor. "Incoming!" someone yelled.

113

The tent was filled with the sounds of several men scrambling at once. "Get to your positions," yelled Cody. "I'll get the platoon on the radio and see what the hell is going on."

John struggled to find his way to the doorway of the tent and through the flap. In just the few minutes he was inside the world had brightened. He could still make out the flashes and thunder to the North, but no longer confused them for anything other than what they were – people trying to kill him and his friends. He ran for his team's Forward Observation Post. The night shift was hunkered down, apparently safe and sound. "Root, Campbell. You guys okay?" he shouted as he ducked into the hole.

"We're fine. Who the hell is shooting at us?"

"Don't know. Sergeant Cody is trying to find out." More rounds, evidently rockets, rained down on the crossroads they were over watching. They could hear shrapnel impacting on the roof of their dugout shelter. "Someone doesn't seem to like us being here," John added.

Campbell, always a smartass, said, "I'm with them. I don't like us being here either!"

John was too tense to laugh. He heard PFC Williams scrambling in. His team was now complete. He was glad to see them all together, safe and sound. The field phone at his feet rang, and he reached to pick it up. "B Team OP, this is PFC Cooper."

"Cooper, Cody. Platoon received word from higher that the north is shelling the whole valley. Rumors are that tanks are headed down. We are to hold position until further notice."

"Roger. Until it stops raining steel, I'm not that interested in moving anyway, Sarge."

"I'm with you on that."

"Any word on blowing the bridge, Sergeant?"

"No, Coop. We have a lot of U.S. and South Korean forces north of us who would need to use that bridge if they have to move south. We don't blow that bridge until we are ordered to."

"Got it. We'll hold here."

"Keep your head down, B Team."

*   *   *   *

FOB Cobra, Anbar Province, Iraq
June 14, 9:30 a.m. (0630 GMT)

Tony and Major Gears walked into the 101st "Jump" TOC (Tactical Operations Center) to take part in the final coordination meeting prior to mission jump off. The "Jump" TOC was manned by most of the assistants to the key staff of the actual 101st Division staff. It was led by the actual Division Operations Officer, a full-bird infantry Colonel by the name of Hankins. Gears was welcomed back like a returning son, exchanging greetings and handshakes form the assorted Captains, Majors and Lieutenant Colonels. Colonel Hankins spotted the pair across the room and motioned them over. He gave Gears a two-handed handshake and said, "How's life on your super-secret mission? What do they have you doing?"

"We're tasked with processing whatever it is that we find in the camp, Sir," he replied. Tony realized that it was actually an artful answer, giving enough information without giving too much. Unfortunately, Gears continued. "The guardsmen are going to be blowing up any normal stuff found. We are going to make sure they don't blow up anything they shouldn't."

Tony again realized that this again wasn't a bad answer, although the tone of voice used, especially how Gears said 'Guardsmen,' grated on his nerves. He realized that Gears wasn't going to get around to introducing him anytime soon. He stepped forward with his hand extended and said, "Colonel Hankins, Lt.

Col. Tony Cooper. I'm the deputy commander of the team to which Major Gears has been assigned. I'm also an ex post facto member of the 112th Engineer Bn – I was recently promoted out of the XO position and assigned to this team."

"Pleased to meet you, Colonel," Hankins said. "Welcome to our Jump TOC. We're going to start the final coordination brief in a few minutes."

"Yes sir. The biggest thing we need is the final movement plan; namely the pickup zone times."

"We'll cover those in detail. Will you be representing the 112th?"

"Not alone. Their S3 will be over as well. Major Girardi."

"O.K. Gears can show you around and introduce you to the key players."

Gears did exactly that, although again the interactions were more about him catching up with and kibitzing with his peers than actually making sure that Tony knew the key players.

Tony had seen this before; in Afghanistan. The active duty types, even when placed under the nominal command of a guardsman or reservist, retained the same rating chain as they had always had. When the reverse happened, the guardsmen and reservist found themselves being rated by their active duty bosses. These ratings, formally presented on an Officer Evaluation Report, became the basis for consideration future promotion boards. As such, the active duty officers assigned under guardsmen often had their first loyalties to their original chain of command.

They had not quite made their away around the TOC when the staff started gathering their materials and heading for the briefing tent. They followed the crowd and made their way to the seats assigned to them. The briefing followed what was called a 2-3-4-1 format, in which the Division S3, serving as the TOC commander, introduced everyone and then turned it over to the staff. The S2, the intelligence officer, gave an update on the latest intelligence about the enemy camp, including some impressive imagery. The S3, the acting operations officer, updated the group on the overall plan. He briefly turned the floor over to a young captain serving as the "S3 Air" who covered, in extensive detail, the plans for who would fly out when. Tony took furious notes. Looking over, he saw that Matt Girardi was doing the same. The S3 turned the floor over to the S4, the logistics officer, who very briefly went over his topics. Finally, the S1, the personnel officer, finished up the formal part of the briefing with a few details. The biggest part of the personnel officer's briefing dealt with how casualties, both wounded and dead, would be handled. It made for a sobering end to the briefing.

After his staff had finished their portions, Colonel Hankins stood up and opened the floor for questions. Several hands went up. Hankins pointed to a Lieutenant Colonel who Tony remembered had been introduced as a fellow engineer officer. The officer, named Johnson, Tony remembered, stood and directed his question to the personnel officer. "What happened to our request to have our own Engineer Battalion assigned to this mission?" he asked.

Many pairs of eyes quickly shifted to Tony to watch for a reaction, then shifted away. Tony felt the eyes on him and worked hard to keep his expression neutral.

The S1 stood and said, "The Corps Commander himself nixed the request. The feel was that it would be too obvious to pull our engineers out of Israel – people would be bound to ask questions."

Nodding, the active duty engineer Lt. Col. started to sit. Obviously realizing that he wanted to say more, he stood back up. He turned to Tony and said, "Lt. Col. Cooper. Any feel for how ready this guard Battalion is?"

Again, Tony felt most of the eyes in the room move to him. He stood, turned to his fellow engineer and said, "They're as ready as they can be. The 112th is the highest ranked National Guard battalion in the country. The staff is strong and the Sapper Teams did very well during the train up. I don't think you need to worry about them – they'll do their job."

The active duty Lt. Col. looked at Tony for a long moment. Realizing that there was nothing more to say on the subject, he nodded and sat down. As he did so, he added, "I hope you are right." Tony could have strangled the man for the dubious look on his face as he said those last words.

The rest of the questions and answers were fairly routine. After only a few minutes, Colonel Hankins brought the meeting to a conclusion, directing the staff to handle any other issues "offline." Tony gathered his stuff together and indicated to Gears that he was going to head over to the 112th with Girardi before heading back to the team's hooch. Gears acknowledged and indicated that he was going to stay around the 101st TOC for a while and would meet Tony later. As Tony made his way to the door, he looked back and saw that Gears had headed straight for the Engineer Lt. Col. who had questioned the inclusion of the 112th Engineer Bn and their readiness. As the tent flaps closed, he saw the pair exchange a warm handshake and a laugh.

"When war does come, my advice is to draw the sword and throw away the scabbard."
-   General Thomas "Stonewall" Jackson

CHAPTER ELEVEN

Objective Calf, Bekka Valley, Lebanon
June 15 9:00 am (0700 GMT)

The helicopters swooped in low over the mountain ridge. Before them, the crew and passengers saw what looked to be the Hollywood set of a war zone. The camp was made up of several buildings, all built as little compounds with low walls around them, surrounded by fields covered by what looked to be obstacle courses and rifle ranges. There was a perimeter fence of barbed wire and several towers. Every tower appeared to be burning and several small blazes were burning inside the perimeter as well. Two attack helicopters were buzzing overhead. As they watched, one unleashed a stream of tracers toward a vehicle that had just crested a small hill west of the camp. The vehicle stopped moving and burst into flames. No one exited the vehicle. *I hope that was some bad guy and not some family out on a picnic*, Tony thought to himself. Tony could see troops scurrying about, but no real front line or major conflict was evident. Over the noise of the rotors, only sporadic small arms firing could be heard. Tony hoped that meant that most of the heavy fighting was finished.

The helicopters landed on what looked to be the rifle range and the passengers, including Tony, Colonel Hansen, Linda and several others from the team, jumped to the ground and ran, bent at the waist, until they were out of the wash of the rotors. They gathered into a loose group and then looked for some sort of direction. Around them, troops from the 112th Engineers were gathering into their teams and gathering their equipment. Robert, trailed by Rahib, jogged up from the direction of the main set of buildings. He approached Colonel Hansen and said, "The troopers have cleared the main compound and the 112th is tasked to begin cataloguing and destroying munitions. Not all of the buildings have been cleared, however. Lt. Col. Maguire will set up in that first building. It looked to be the camp mess hall." Turning to Linda he said, "Ma'am, that might be a good spot for you to be. Colonel Hansen – Major Gears has commandeered an office in there for you and your staff as well."

The group made their way into the building where they saw Dana and his staff setting up. Matt Giardi was on the radio taking reports and Joe was huddled with some of his staff officers telling them what he expected. Dana spotted Tony, nodded over and then turned back to listening to his radio. Tony longed to be part of that operation, but had to admit that they looked to have it handled. Robert pointed the way to the other side of the building where they found Mark also listening to a radio. As they came in, he lowered the radio and said, "Colonel Hansen, the assault went off well. The troopers lost a few men but secured the perimeter. No material has left the site, although surely the word has gotten out about the assault. The 112th teams are starting their survey. No sign of al Raqman or his command group, unfortunately. All for us to do at this point is to stay out of the way. I have our two helicopters standing by in northern Israeli airspace. They are aerially refueling periodically so that they can respond immediately as soon as we call them forward."

"Helicopters can aerially refuel?" Linda asked.

"These can. We borrowed them from Special Forces Command."

Hansen looked around and said, "OK. Let's monitor the situation from here. Tony, take Linda around to wherever she wants to go. Don't get shot."

"Yes sir. An order I will willingly comply with." To Linda, Tony said, "Let's go next door and see where they are starting their sweep."

They made their way back into the 112th's operations center and watched the organized chaos for a moment. They saw Matt making notations on a camp layout and heard him call to Dana that Teams 2 and 4 were starting their sweeps. From the map, Teams 2 and 4 were working a large building just south of their location. Tony looked at Linda with an eyebrow raised. She nodded and they headed for the door. As they exited, he turned to her and checked to make sure her helmet was strapped on and her body armor was secured tightly. It was. She checked his in turn. Satisfied, they made their way at a half-trot toward the large building where they expected to find the teams.

As the east side of the building came into view, they saw a team setting a small charge on what looked to be the front door of the building. The building was probably about the size of a small ranch house. It seemed large enough that it would have some internal structure; things like rooms, halls and the like. It promised to present a complex building clearance target; with lots of places for bad guys to hide.

At a signal, the team members quickly moved about 20 feet away and turned their heads away from the door. Several seconds went by before a small charge, its sound muffled by what must have been a sandbag wrapped behind it, took off the door latch. A member of one of the teams moved forward and kicked the door open. An instant after the door flew inward, a figure ran out of the building screaming what Tony later realized must have been something like "God is Great." Two steps out of the door, just as several team members began firing at the unexpected target, the man disappeared in a flash of light and sound. Forty feet away, Tony and Linda were knocked down by the concussion, their breath gone. Closer in, the effects were devastating. The engineer who had kicked open the door was an unrecognizable mound of flesh, with the top of his head missing. It was recovered 30 yards away by the mortuary affairs team. Two other team members were killed instantly and the team leader, partially protected by distance and the body of another squad member, was seriously wounded. Calls of "Medic!" rang out while the assistant team leader ordered grenades thrown into the door. Tony, still dazed but functional, yelled out "Belay that order!" To the assistant Sapper Team Leader he said, "Remember, we are looking for something both very valuable and very fragile. We need to clear these buildings the old fashioned way – one room at a time."

"Screw that, sir," the assistant team leader said. "Did you see what just happened doing it the old fashioned way?"

Tony recognized the man as being from Wooster but could not remember his name. His body armor covered any nametag. He seemed to remember that the man worked in construction. Putting that aside, he said, "I know, Sergeant. But we need to recover this material intact. Otherwise, those men we just lost will have died for nothing. Gather your team, I'll go in with you." To Linda he said, "Wait out here until you hear the all clear."

Tony walked up to where the sergeant was pulling his men together – some were covered in blood from their first aid efforts – efforts they had turned over to the team of medics who had just arrived from the Battalion headquarters section. "Let's do this," Tony said, pulling his 9mm pistol from its holster. "I'll go in and left. Sergeant, you follow me and go right." Pointing to a young PFC with an M16 he said, "You follow both of us in and respond to our directions. Start out going straight but then listen and watch for cues." The young soldier nodded, looking terrified.

"The rest of you follow when you hear us call "Clear" or when you hear us scream for help."

They worked their way along the wall. As they reached the door, Tony made eye contact with the others and nodded. They nodded back. He closed his eyes for a quick two-second prayer and then leapt through the doorway, diving to the floor to the left of the door, scanning the room as he did so. As he looked around the apparently empty room, he heard the sergeant and then the PFC make their way in. None of them spotted anything of interest in the small room into which the front door opened. Looking around to make sure, Tony then indicated the next doorway, which seemed to lead to a short hallway. Glancing to make sure that the others understood, Tony turned again to face the doorway and the hall beyond. He did so just in time to see a figure enter the hall from a side room and begin running down the hall toward them. Instinctively, he dropped to one knee, fired off two rounds and then dove to his left. The figure fell, but his momentum carried him into their small room. As Tony rolled he saw the Sergeant jumping the opposite direction in a similar fashion to what he had done. More amazingly, he saw the young PFC jump onto the fallen man, apparently in an attempt to shield them with his own body. Tony waited to feel the impact of the explosion, closing his eyes and attempting to burrow into the crack between the wall and the floor. As the crack was less than an eighth of an inch thick, he made little progress. Time stretched out until it finally occurred to him that an explosion might not be coming. He opened his clenched eyes to see the PFC still lying over the man and the Sergeant – Smithson he realized the Sergeant's name was - cringing against the opposite wall. Cautiously, Tony worked his way to his feet and approached the PFC. He realized the young man was reciting what seemed to be the 23rd Psalm. He pulled on the soldier's arm and the soldier opened his eyes, apparently startled to still be alive. "Private, that was either the dumbest or the bravest thing I've ever seen. Either way, don't fucking do it again. Now get up and let's look at what we've got."

As they did so, the rest of the team burst in, weapons ready. "Clear!" Tony yelled out. "Hold fast while we figure this out." He rolled the body over. The man was indeed wearing a suicide vest and his hand was clasped around what appeared to be the detonation cord. In the center of his forehead was a small penetration wound. Only then did Tony see the growing puddle of blood gathering on the floor beneath the man's head.

"Nice shot, Colonel," the PFC opined.

"I'd feel better about it if I hadn't had my eyes closed," Tony said, with little mirth in his voice. "I'd feel better, as well, if that cord was not in his hand."

The PFC looked over the device for a second. Out of the corner of his eye Tony saw the Sergeant gathering himself up and making his way over as well. The PFC calmly reached down to the suicide vest and untwisted a wire. He then removed the man's hand from the detonation cord, unhooked the cord and handed it to Tony. "A souvenir for you, Colonel. You saved our asses."

Tony took it, realizing that his hand was shaking, and said, "What you did was the gutsiest thing I've ever seen. I'll make sure you are recognized for that. What's your name, son?"

"Stafford, sir. Hell, if I had had enough time to think about it I wouldn't have done it. Don't recommend me for anything or I'll have to tell everyone that you hit a target two meters away with only one out of two rounds."

Despite the tension of the moment, Tony chuckled. Turning to the Sergeant, Tony said, "It's not easy, but that's how we have to do it. The troopers have the perimeter but we need to clear these buildings with our own assets while preserving what we find as well. Get to it, Sergeant, and don't forget to call in progress." With that, he walked toward the outer door. As he did so, he saw that Linda had been watching the entire exchange. She started to say something but he shook his head and walked around the side of the building. He sat down heavily with his back to the wall and reached for his canteen. She came around the building and watched him struggle with the canteen cap with shaking hands. She crouched down, took the canteen from him, opened it and handed it back. He nodded his thanks and took a long drink. "That was impressive," Linda said.

He shook his head and said, "I almost pissed myself. I thought I was dead back there. So much for heroics."

"You *were* almost dead – along with several others. However, you saved lives, including your own. Not bad for a school teacher."

He looked up at her and smiled. "Coming from a pansy assed reporter, I guess that's high praise."

He sat, breathing heavily, until he felt his hands stop shaking and thought his legs would hold him. Linda crouched next to him, thankfully not saying anything but being supportive just by being there. Feeling more in control, he looked up, a look of appreciation in his eyes and said, "Let's get back to battalion and see what else is going on."

As they walked back through the door they heard Major Giardi yell, "Quiet in the TOC! Lt. Col. Maguire. Team Six seems to have found something unusual. They think it might be what we are looking for."

Dana said, "Roger that." He walked quickly down the hall and told Colonel Hansen. Hansen yelled for Robert and Tony and said, "You two are my subject matter experts. Get over there and check it out. Reporters, probably worth you going as well."

Tony looked at the situation board and map to see where Team Six was. Major Gears spotted the team six icon first and pointed it out. The team appeared to be in a small, non-descript building a couple of hundred meters away. He nodded to Linda, Rahib, and Robert and the four of them headed out the front door and turned left. With Robert leading and Tony trailing, they made their way at a light jog – not that any jog is light in 25 pounds of gear. By the time they were halfway there, Tony was again reminded that he was old and fat. Robert seemed to sense that the others were struggling and slowed his pace somewhat. Linda and Rahib both seemed to appreciate the slower pace as well. The small group arrived to find soldiers forming a small perimeter around the building and the team leader, a young sergeant named Collins that Tony knew to be pretty good, waiting for them. "What do you have Collins?" he asked the younger man.

"Sir, we have several containers we don't recognize. They appear to be very heavy and well shielded. Further, we have a smaller container with a lock on it. The Geiger counter is going nuts in here."

"Dangerous levels of radiation?" Tony asked.

"High, but tolerable according to the chart they gave us. Wouldn't want to live in here."

"Alright," said Tony. "Show us what you got."

Collins led them into the dark interior. It took a second for their eyes to adjust. Once they did, the saw what looked to be a workroom; Tony recognized many of the tools as being similar to those found at the metal shop at his school. Collins walked them to a room like a large walk-in closet where he pointed out the containers.

" Do you recognize any of the markings, Rahib?" Tony asked.

"Those are in Persian," he said, pointing at some large containers. At some others, he pointed and said, "Those look to be Cyrillic, probably Russian." On the small container he pointed and said, "This is obviously Asian; maybe Chinese?" Tony thought back to his time in Afghanistan, where they had an attached Korean engineer battalion under his Engineer Group and said, "I think it looks Korean –a little too blocky of lettering for Chinese or Japanese."

Robert pulled a sophisticated looking and surprisingly small Geiger counter out of his side pocket and worked the controls. He held it to the containers that looked to be Persian and then examined the readout. "Looks to be Cobalt-60," he announced. Next, he held it to the containers presumed to be Russian. "No reading at all, no radioactivity present," he announced. Finally, he held it to what they believed to be the Korean case and again looked at the display. He looked surprised and worried. He adjusted the instrument and again held it to the case. He looked at it again. He turned to Tony and Linda and said, "This appears to be weapons grade Plutonium. I would estimate several kilograms, enough for a nuclear weapon as powerful as those used on Nagasaki or Hiroshima."

"Holy shit," Tony said, immediately chagrined that he could come up with nothing more intelligent than that.

Linda looked like she had been hit and said, "Plutonium from North Korea? If that turns out to be true, that's grounds for war."

Rahib nodded and said, "al Raqman must have been crazy. He can't have believed that he would get away with this. You would surely have been able to trace this back to the host countries."

Robert shook his head and said, "These isotopes are likely from reactors that have not been monitored. Their radiological signatures are probably unknown. We could have deep suspicions like we did in the Boston bombing, but no proof based solely on the material. Now, with both the containers and the material, we do. I suggest you two get whatever pictures and video you want." To Tony he said, "Sir, can you find a soldier to serve as their cameraman if they want one? I'm going to take a bunch of still photos before we move anything."

Tony walked back out into the sunlight. He spotted a young Spec-4 he recognized and called out "Morris! Come make some history. Is that okay Sergeant Collins?" Sergeant Collins waved over his acceptance while he made his way around the perimeter checking on his men. "These reporters have handheld minicams. Do you think you can run one?"

"Absolutely, sir. The only classes I got A's in during high school were multi-media courses. What are we filming?"

"Morris, if you had told me your favorite class was Physics I would have answered that question. For now, you are going to have to figure it out for yourself."

*   *   *   *

Near the village of Chigyong-dong, South Korea
June 15, 2:30 pm (0530 GMT)

John made his way to Sergeant Cody's position and worked his way into the bunker. The squad leader nodded and said, "Cooper. Thanks for coming over. I wanted to let you and Lott know that the word is that the North Koreans have crossed the border and might be heading this way. Company Headquarters is trying to get orders from Battalion, but evidently Battalion got hit hard by the artillery strike. We are to stay here and watch the bridge and the intersection. They told us to check the demolition circuits following the artillery strike. Evidently the demolition on the first couple of bridges wasn't successful and they think that the circuits might have been damaged.

"I'll check them, Sergeant," said John.

"Good. I think you know the system as well as anyone. Let me know what you find. Lott, have one of your guys trail behind him watching what he does. Your position is actually closer to the bridge so it would be good to have someone from your team know what they're doing as well."

"No problem." To John, Corporal Lott said, "I'll send Pho. He's pretty good on technical stuff.

John nodded to Lott and said, "He'll do well. I'll stop by and pick him up after I come back from reading my guys into the word on the Koreans."

Sergeant Cody dismissed them by saying, "Sounds good, thanks for coming over. I'll be in touch."

"The higher level of grand strategy (is) that of conducting war with a far-sighted regard to the state of the peace that will follow."
-   Sir Basil H. Liddel-Hart

CHAPTER TWELVE

In Flight, Southern Bekka Valley, Lebanon
June 15, 1:00 pm (1100 GMT)

The noise in the Pave Low helicopter was deafening, but the breeze felt good after their hours on the ground in the sun-baked Bekka Valley camp. Tony was on the second helicopter as it flew in trail, echeloned slightly to the left, of the lead chopper. Around him in the back were Linda Rogers, Master Sergeant Patterson, Corporal Gonzales, Major Gears and Robert. On the lead chopper were Colonel Hansen, Mark, Rahib, Staff Sergeant Harris, Major Rodriquez, and Sergeant Ortiz. The choppers were flying nap of the earth, which made for a wild ride. Tony found the sensation unnerving, especially because his rearward facing seat position only allowed him to see the terrain they had already passed, not what they were headed toward. According to the flight profile Mark had briefed, as soon as they were on the line from Damascus to Beirut they would rise up and fly level. Tony found himself looking forward to that.

The Bekka Valley had proven to be a surprise to him. His experience in the Middle east had been one of desolate landscapes with some minor exceptions in the narrow river valleys of Afghanistan. The Bekka, however, was nearly as green as the valleys in California, with neat fields planted with crops. The mountains to the East were snow capped and, while not as majestic as the Rockies of Tony's home state of Montana or the Hindu Kush Mountains of Afghanistan, would put the Appalachians to shame. There was still a hint of dryness and poverty in anyplace that wasn't irrigated, but in the valley floor itself Lebanon was as beautiful a place as any he had ever seen.

Around him the others looked tired, worried or, in Corporal Gonzales's case, bored. Similarly, the door gunner from the helicopter crew looked relaxed to the point of nodding off, while still managing to keep an eye on things. Tony, as the senior passenger, had been given a set of headphones and he could hear the pilot and copilot talking as if this was the most routine of trips. Perhaps for the Special Forces Command it was, but for Tony and most of the rest of the team, this was the adventure of a lifetime. Flying into enemy territory, carrying evidence that would shake the world, meeting with Syrian dissidents, these were things of fantasy, not of his world. Nevertheless, there he was.

Right on time, the helicopters slowed, steadied and rose up over the ridgelines they had been flying below. Through his headphones, Tony heard a beeping noise start immediately. The pilot said "Radar signature, acquisition strength acknowledged." With that, the beeping cut off. The rest of the flight was as much like a training flight as it could be.

Even the arrival was routine, almost anti-climatic. The helicopters were guided in by a smoke grenade and a soldier wearing a dress uniform. "A dress uniform in this heat!" Tony thought to himself. The helicopters set down and the passengers, rather than rushing off as they had before, sat and waited for the blades to stop spinning. They then gathered themselves and their gear and gathered around Colonel Hansen to the front and right of the lead helicopter. As they organized themselves, they saw a similar size group forming in front of what looked to be either a large house or a small headquarters building. Colonel Hansen led them over to the other group. He stopped several paces in front of the other group, rendered a hand salute and said "Colonel Robert Hansen and a group of American officers to meet with you, Sir." The senior ranking member of the other party, who seemed to be wearing a Syrian Air Force uniform, returned the salute and then stepped forward to shake Colonel Hansen's hand. In heavily accented, but very proper, English he said, "Please join us inside out of the sun and heat. We will have some tea."

They gathered in a large conference room. Much time was consumed in the serving of tea and cookies. Their host introduced himself as Lieutenant General Aziz Assad Barat, the deputy chief of staff for the air force. He introduced several of the other members of his group, which included a member of parliament, an army Major General and another General - Tony missed what grade of General he was - with the security ministry.

Colonel Hansen said, "Sir, we have just come from the camp of al Raqman and have gathered evidence from that location that we would like to share with you. We understand that some of you, and many of your countrymen, may be reluctant to believe some of what we will tell you and show you. We have brought with us two independent observers. We have a reporter from CNN and one from al Jazeera." He motioned to Linda and Rahib, who stood in turn and introduced themselves. "They have agreed to testify honestly in terms of what they have seen in exchange for the right to publish the story to the world when the time comes. I believe that you may know the work of both of these reporters. Further, I would like to introduce other members of my team." Each member introduced him or her self and then sat back down. Only Harris and Ortiz were absent. They had stayed out front to keep an eye on things.

"I'm going to allow my deputy, Lt. Col. Cooper, to proceed with an overview of what we found. Lt. Col. Cooper."

Tony made his way forward while Robert cranked up his portable computer and - Tony had never seen one before - its integrated projector. He pointed it the nearest blank wall and Tony began. "Gentlemen, I am going to begin by setting the stage for you. We had intelligence going in that we would find radiological material at the al Raqman camp. We were not sure what kind or how much, but we expected to find some. Quite frankly, what we found, with the evidence we found with it, is shocking. First slide, please. On this slide, you see a series of three lead lined canisters with Persian markings. Our Geiger counters indicated that these were strong Gamma ray emitters. Our Persian expert says that the markings indicate that these possess a radiological danger and indicate that they contain rods of Cobalt -60. We believe that the analysis will show that this Cobalt – 60 is from the same sources as that used in the Boston attack. The canisters and associated paperwork found on site seem to indicate that the source of this material is the Araybi reactor in Iran. There was enough material for four more attacks on the scale of Boston. Evidence collected on site indicates that Istanbul, London, Washington D.C. and Paris were all potential targets. We have brought a sample of this material for your analysis." He motioned to Corporal Gonzales who brought forward a small, lead-lined container and placed it heavily on the table. "This quantity, in this container, is not hazardous to be around for short periods, but it should only be handled outside the container by trained professionals."

"Next slide, please. This shot shows a container with Russian markings. It did not evidence any radiological signature. Upon further investigation, it appears to be high yield explosives and sophisticated triggering devices. It is believed that these triggering devices and this explosive material were of high enough quality that they could be used to construct a triggering explosion for an atomic bomb." The generals took some time whispering among themselves before settling back down and looking at Tony.

"Most disturbing of all was the last item we found. Next slide, please. The small, briefcase sized box with Korean markings was shown on the screen. "This box was a strong alpha emitter. Upon examination, this box was found to contain several kilograms of highly enriched Uranium 235 – enriched enough to form the core of an atomic bomb. The container and associated paperwork seem to indicate that this was sold by Korea to Iran as part of its nuclear weapons research program. With this material, and the triggering devices from Russia, al Raqman had the makings for, and was in the process of constructing, an atomic weapon. Interrogations indicate that, if possible, an American city was to be the target of this device. However, it is possible that they would need to have used it closer to home. Israel, Egypt, Turkey or Saudi Arabia have all been mentioned as potential targets."

The generals again proceeded to lean back and talk amongst themselves. Tony waited until they slowed down before putting his hand up and saying, "Gentlemen, we have only two more slides to go. Next slide please." This slide showed several documents spread out over a table. "These documents seem to indicate that these items were shipped through Syria with the knowledge of at least some members of your current regime, in exchange for a great deal of money. We have copies of these documents for you. Sergeant Patterson." Master Sergeant Patterson moved forward and handed a manila folder to each member of the Syrian delegation. "I think you will find these documents unambiguous," Tony added.

"Final slide, please. Colonel Hansen." The final slide showed only the word "Conclusions" at the top. Colonel Hansen stood and waited until he had the full attention of everyone in the room before he began. "Gentlemen, I am going to report the following conclusions to my superiors upon my return to base." As he spoke, Robert hit a button and each bullet comment appeared on cue.

"First, there is not a doubt that al Raqman's organization intended to conduct further nuclear attacks against the west. Second, we are certain that he acquired this material, and the Boston material, from Iran. Third, we are certain that Russia supplied atomic weapons grade components to the Iranians who in turn provided those to al Raqman. Fourth, the North Koreans supplied fissionable material to the Iranians who then turned at least some of that material over to al Raqman. Finally, we have evidence that at least some members of the current Syrian regime have direct involvement in all of the above transactions."

He paused while they looked over the list.

"All of these taken together very likely mean that a state of war, either declared or undeclared, may exist between our governments in the very near future. You are in danger of being associated with some very unpopular regimes, including your current leadership. Do you have any questions for me or my team at this time?"

General Barat asked, "What assurance do we have that what you are sharing with us is true?"

Colonel Hansen said, "If you know our country well enough you know we have a long tradition, sometimes much to our chagrin, of having a free press. At this time, please feel free to question our reporter guests as to their opinions."

General Barat turned and faced the two reporters and said, "I am anxious to hear your thoughts."

Rahib looked worried and nervous. Finally, he said, "Your honor, I am convinced that what they have laid out is the truth. If it is a hoax, it is one that I am unsure how they could pull off. There were too many small things that even they could not have anticipated. As difficult as it is for me to believe this is true, I intend to report to the world much of what you have heard from Colonel Hansen. Linda?"

Linda nodded. "I agree. I feel a bit of a pawn in this, but the U.S. military seems to be playing this straight. My report will be much like Rahib's.

"When do you anticipate going to press?" LTG Barat asked.

Colonel Hansen said, "We will release them to report their stories – Rahib in print and on air, and Linda online and on air, within three days from today."

General Barat and his compatriots huddled with their heads together and whispered sharply back and forth. Among the American delegation, only Rahib seemed to be able to follow anything about their chatter. He whispered in a voice loud enough for Tony to hear that they were discussing whether this would give them enough time. LTG Barat looked up from the group, without separating from it, and asked "What of al Raqman? Did you find him?"

"No, there was no sign of him. Do you have any idea where he might be, General?"

"Our last intelligence indicated that he was at the camp. He could not have had much warning or you would never have found the material. He cannot be far away."

"Our thoughts exactly, but short of occupying the Bekka Valley with ground troops, we will be hard pressed to find him," opined Colonel Hansen.

"Trust me, in few days there will be many people looking for him. Some to honor him as a prophet, but more to hunt him like a dog," added LTG Barat.

After another minute, the Syrian delegation sat back and appeared to have come to some sort of resolution. LTG Barat said, "Colonel, thank you for your information. We have much to do here in Syria to bring those responsible for these crimes to justice. We will set the groundwork, but your announcement of your findings will serve as the trigger for us to move. We are confident we can be ready. Good luck in your travels. We hope that you and your troops arrive home safely. We also hope that the situation in Korea is resolved peacefully and quickly."

Tony's hair stood on end. The last word he had received before the communication blackout was that John's unit had arrived in Korea safe and sound and was about done with assuming the border security mission from their active duty counterparts. "What situation in Korea?" he asked.

LTG Barat replied, "This must have begun after you had started your mission. My apologies. The North Koreans are shelling across the border and seem to be massing troops. Many believe they are preparing to attack south."

"On what provocation, sir? Have they said?"

"They have announced that they were attacked by several South Korean missiles and that the South Korean Army and the Americans have crossed the border in several areas. They have not produced any independent evidence of those claims and the Americans and South Koreans are denying them vigorously."

Tony said, "My son is serving in Korea. Any word on casualties?"

"None, but the reporting seems to indicate that the bombardment is such that there will surely be many. May Allah watch over your son."

"Thank you, sir."

The group members made their way back to the waiting helicopters. They were quiet, alone with their thoughts. Colonel Hansen walked next to Tony and said, "My son is a fighter pilot in Korea. I share your concern. Hopefully, cooler heads will prevail. The news channels must be crazy right now – what a time to be away from Fox News!"

"You said it, sir. I have it on almost constantly at home. It is a fixture in our house."

They packed into the helicopters in much the same way they had before. The exceptions were that Rahib joined them in their helicopter – he wanted to spend some time with Linda comparing notes. Similarly, Robert switched choppers to commiserate with Mark. Finally, Major Rodriquez joined Tony's group on the second helicopter to talk to Major Gears about the whole experience. The helicopters lifted off and flew straight and steady toward the west. As they did so, Tony thought to himself that he was quickly flying out of danger while danger was heading for John at full speed. All in all, he would have preferred the danger heading for him.

He leaned back and found himself falling asleep. He realized that it had been nearly 30 hours since he had slept much more than a catnap. He decided to try to catch a few winks. Even the noise of the helicopter wasn't enough to keep him awake.

Tony awoke when the helicopter dropped like a car going over a cliff. He looked around in alarm and noticed that everyone else looked calm. He realized that this was the return to nap of the earth flying. "Back into the Bekka Valley," he thought to himself. "Yea though I walk in the valley of death I will fear no evil...." He settled down to 'enjoy' the ride.

* * * *

Linda looked across the helicopter to where Lt. Col. Cooper was sitting. He looked confident and relaxed. There was something about him that she had liked from the moment she met him. He didn't carry himself like so many of the other military officers she had met. "Must be the National Guard influence," she thought to herself. Gears reminded her more and more of the stereotypical military man – fit, self assured, confident to the point of arrogance. However, watching Cooper these last couple of days, especially in the building clearing, she realized that he had a strength that was totally different from what Gears and his type valued. He knew what he knew, but also seemed to know that he didn't know everything. She had trouble describing exactly what she was thinking.

She realized that, although not classically a handsome man, there was something about him that appealed to her. He had looked at her a few times and it was obvious that he appreciated what he saw, although he hadn't done anything that could in any way, shape, or form be considered inappropriate. In fact, the only thing he had done that could conceivably be on the edge of obvious was when he had breathed in her perfume when she had passed him in the hall. *Did men not realize that we women know when they do things like that?* she thought to herself.

She shook herself out of her wasted thought process and concentrated back on the moment. What a story she was sitting on! She set her mind to thinking how best to package the story for the biggest bang. *Certainly a special report on the evening news; followed by much follow-up. Maybe Sunday morning's Late Edition? Larry King? Anderson Cooper? Maybe even go outside of the network?* Her mind raced with the possibilities. Next to her, Rahib looked to be lost in similar thoughts, although with a much more sorrowful expression. She wondered if his face reflected sadness for what looked to be another round of misery that seemed in store for the Arab world.

"Wars may be fought with weapons but they are won by men."

- General George Patton Jr.

CHAPTER THIRTEEN

Southern Bekka Valley, Lebanon
June 15, 4:50 pm (1450 GMT)

Akim Albazi was feeling old. He had farmed this land in the valley for thirty years, and hadn't picked up a gun in anger since the Israeli invasion in the eighties. Even then, he had had no cause to use it. The Jews had not penetrated this far into the valley. Now, he went about his daily business with a rifle again strapped around his shoulder and back. He had heard the rumors of helicopters, invasions, and the Jews coming across the border. He would do what he could to protect this land, as little as that might be. He had cleaned and oiled the rifle. It was, of all things, an old U.S. Army M1 Garand. It shot clean and true. He was surprised during his little test fire that his hands still seemed to know the weapon and that he could still hit almost anything he aimed at. He had always had a talent for shooting, a talent evidently not much diminished by age. If only the same thing could be said of his back. He decided to try a couple of more test shots, just for fun. He positioned himself on the ridge up above his farm. The ridge protruded out from the valley, producing a natural choke point for any forces approaching. He often thought it would make for a natural defensive position. Similar ridges projected out from the valley walls throughout the valley.

While he prepared his weapon, he thought he heard the sound of something mechanical approaching from the south. Looking that direction, he saw what appeared to be two birds flying low down the valley. As he watched them, he realized that they weren't birds – they continued to grow as they got closer and the sound of rotors became pronounced. The Jews with their helicopters, he realized. They appeared to be headed straight for him. He dropped behind the rock he had been intending to use to steady his aim and prepared to fire at a real target. The helicopters continued to fly straight for him, so low in the valley that it appeared that they would run into the spot on the ridge where he lay. He watched them come closer and closer and realized that he would indeed have a shot or two before they passed. He lined up his shot on the first helicopter. Once he thought it was in range, he squeezed the trigger. At first there was no reaction. Then the first helicopter pitched and swayed slightly before straightening itself back into level flight. He squeezed off another round, not sure if he hit the helicopter or not. Finally, as the pair of helicopters swept over him, he squeezed off one more round toward the lead bird. As with his second shot, he saw no immediate effect.

His pulse was racing and he realized that he was short of breath. As the sound of the helicopters faded, he accepted that he must have failed. No matter. Allah would remember that he had tried, and wasn't that the key? The helicopters disappeared behind the next ridge to the north.

In the cockpit of the lead helicopter, Major Mike Seransky flew with a practiced hand. He had been a lead pilot on the bird for two years. He was eager for his next promotion and the assignment to a regular squadron that would keep him home more. His son and daughter were getting to the age where they noticed him gone, and his wife was tired of the single parenting that comes with having a husband in the Special Forces. He was confident that he would get a squadron command that would keep him home more – he secretly even hoped for cargo helicopters. He had had all of the gung ho combat experience he would ever need.

Major Seransky barely felt the bullet as it passed through the front of his throat and out the back of his neck, slicing nearly completely through his spinal cord and laying waste to his 2nd and 3rd vertebrate. He ceased to feel his legs and arms. His hands dropped from the stick and cyclic like dead weights. He wondered if he was having a stroke, until he noticed the neat hole in the Plexiglas canopy right in front of him. His inner ear felt the helicopter start to drop and spin slightly, but he was powerless to do anything about it. He was relieved when his copilot – a young Captain named Richards, clamped down on his controls and reasserted his will on the aircraft. "Nice," Mike thought to himself, "just like we trained." He turned to say a nice word to the young officer, a movement that caused a shard of vertebrate to sever the rest of his spinal cord and to puncture the lining of his brain. His head slumped, the words of praise unspoken.

"Shit!" yelled Captain Richards. He had seen the hole appear in the windshield in front of Major Seransky but had heard nothing. A full second or two seemed to pass before he felt the helicopter begin to go out of control. With a fixed wing aircraft, letting go of the controls basically gives you level flight. On a helicopter, it was just the opposite. Letting go of the controls was the quickest way to ensure that it went out of control. As was standard for nap of the earth flying, Richards had been shadowing the pilot on the controls so the action of grabbing them was thankfully quick. The passengers very likely had not noticed a thing. Only he and the crew chief realized that they had come perilously close to dying. He glanced over to Major Mike and saw his head drop to an impossible angle. "Fuck." He called over the intercom and the dual channel to the other helicopter. "Major Seransky's been shot. I think he's dead!"

Colonel Hansen came on the intercom and asked, "Anything we can do – should I have one of the medics come forward?"

"No sir, it's too late and all it would do is make flying this thing even harder."

The pilot of the second aircraft asked, "Any damage to the bird?"

"Hang on." Captain Richards tentatively worked the controls, noting that things didn't feel quite right, and said, "I'm getting some weird resistance to changes in pitch. Any chance you can come up next to me and take a look to see if you can see anything?"

"Will do. Keep it slow and steady."

The second helicopter came up next to the first so that the pilot, copilot and crew chief could look over the first bird. The crew chief called out something like "There's a hell of a wobble in the …"

Before he could finish his sentence, the entire blade assembly of the first helicopter fell – or rather flew - apart. The helicopter, minus any lift, fell like a rock, 200 feet toward the valley floor below.

Tony listened in horror as his headphones carried the sound of the conversation that was so abruptly cut off. Captain Richards still had his radio mic triggered and thus it broadcast his screams all of the way down to the ground. Even more terrifying was the silence that followed when his screams ended. Tony leaned out the open side door and saw the fuselage hit the ground. It was obvious to him that there could be no survivors.

Parts of the separating rotor assembly had struck their bird as well. Their pilot and copilot started yelling out status readings, none of them good. "Fuel pressure dropping to zero! Hydraulic pressure going to zero! Set her down, set her down!" The pilot struggled to control the dying bird. He switched his radar to the Guard frequency and started calling out, "Mayday! Mayday! Flight 106, both birds down, both birds down!" He repeated that phrase again and again while he struggled against the dead controls. The engine noise died; an ominous sound in a helicopter. The helicopter was losing altitude quickly. "Autorotate! Autorotate!" the copilot yelled.

"I have no stick!" the pilot yelled back. The helicopter wasn't quite in a freefall, but it was close to it. At the last minute, the pilot was able to generate some lift from the still rapidly spinning rotor. The tail struck a small rise as the helicopter came in; pitching the front of the helicopter down so that the nose of the aircraft buried itself into the ground as it struck. The pilot and copilot were killed instantly as the nose of the aircraft collapsed into the ground. The passengers were strapped in and suffered less than the crew. The crew chief was not belted into a seat; he had only a strap affixed which was intended to keep him from falling out when the aircraft was in flight while giving him nearly complete freedom of movement. He was thrown violently into the front of the aircraft. Afterward, they realized that he had shattered both legs and his pelvis and suffered several internal injuries. The passengers were relatively intact except for a broken arm suffered by Master Sergeant Patterson. They all hung in their harnesses as the crashed copter slowly grew silent. After performing their individual self-assessments, they began to stir.

"Is everyone ok?" Tony yelled out. "Get yourself free and away from the chopper. Help your neighbor if they need it. Let's go! This thing could burn and we don't want to be on it if it does."

Tony got himself worked free from his restraints and helped Linda with her straps. Rahib extracted himself. Tony crawled out of the partially collapsed doorframe and then stood, bumped and bruised but upright, on shaking legs. He looked back to make sure that the others were coming. He found Master Sergeant Patterson crawling out awkwardly, with one arm cradling his other, from the other side of the helicopter. Major Rodriquez and Major Gears followed him out. "Take the civilians up there," he said, pointing to an outcrop of rock on the edge of the valley floor. He then worked his way around to the front. He saw that there was nothing that could be done for the pilots. The cockpit of the helicopter had been flattened, crushing the pair who had fought until the last seconds to save the lives of their passengers.

He worked his way to the crew chief's door and peered in. The crew chief was crumpled like a broken doll, but was still awake; moaning gently. "Chief, can you hear me? I'm going to get you out of there," Tony called.

He crawled in through the door and grabbed the man under his armpits. Backing out of the door, he pulled the crew chief behind him. Every bump and knock along the way elicited a cry of pain from the man. "Sorry chief. We'll get you something for the pain once we have you away from the bird." The chief nodded through clenched lips and eyes that were squeezed shut. It was then that Tony noticed smoke starting to rise from the cockpit area. He realized that he needed to hustle. He tried to back faster, and the crew chief, having seen the smoke, made fewer noises, probably worried that his cries might slow Tony down. Tony pulled him about fifty feet before collapsing onto the gravelly valley floor. He saw Corporal Gonzales jogging toward him.

"How can I help, Sir?" he asked.

"We need to get everything we can off that bird before it goes up completely. Food, water and medicine are the priorities. Weapons as well if you can find them."

Corporal Gonzales headed to the bird, watching the smoke with dread as he crawled back into the fuselage. Tony saw him begin to throw items out of the open doors and decided to go help him. As he did, he saw Linda and Rahib head down as well.

"Get this stuff as far from the aircraft as you can, but also hustle back here to get more." He led the way by scooping up two medics bags and a case of MREs and heading for the outcrop. He saw the reporters start to gather items into their arms. As he reached the outcrop, he saw the reporters about thirty meters behind him loaded with a case of water and several packs. Major Rodriquez and Major Gears followed them, similarly loaded with water and weapons. Behind them, carrying his M-4 and a couple of more packs, came Corporal Gonzales. "That's it, sir. Not much."

Tony looked at the pile and said, "It will have to do."

The small group all looked at him, awaiting instructions. Tony realized that they all expected him to have a plan. He thought to himself that they must not realize who they were dealing with. Didn't they know he was just a glorified schoolteacher?

Realizing that there was no one else to do it, Tony mentally reconciled himself to the idea that he was in charge. He began by saying, "Our crew got a radio call out so hopefully someone in the world knows where we went down. The mission brief indicated that this was enemy country – the people around here are supportive of al Raqman. We must be at least twenty miles south of the training camp, but with the chief banged up we'll never make it that far on foot. On the other hand, the smoke from the helicopter will bring every Lebanese hillbilly running with guns. We need to get some separation from the crash site. Corporal Gonzales and Major Gears, use a couple of rifles and a parka to make a litter. The rest of us will repack these packs with essentials and leave the rest here. I want us to work our way toward that ridge jutting out from the valley just north of here. It looks like it might have some access to water while offering some cover and concealment."

"Sir. I'm not sure that's the best idea," Major Gears interjected. "Our best chance to get picked up is to stay near the bird. They taught us that in Escape and Evasion training."

"Major, I appreciate that fact, but there was no acknowledgment on the call our pilots got out. Our flight plan was classified Top Secret. There is a pretty good chance that no one on our side has any idea where we are. On the other hand, the smoke from the first chopper," he pointed at the column of smoke visible from the south, "and the smoke from our chopper will no doubt bring locals here. I think we need to get away from this spot. The intelligence was that the locals in this area are sympathetic to al Raqman."

"Sir, with all due respect, I disagree. I say that we stay put."

The rest of the team stood watching the interaction, unsure where to come down. Tony looked around the group, trying to get a feel for which way they were leaning.

"Major, I have taken your input under advisement. I stand by my decision. We are moving out."

Without question, the rest of them, even the civilians, started to do what he had directed. He went over to where Patterson sat and asked him if he could walk. Patterson said, "Hell sir, I can run if I have too. I just don't think I'll be much help shooting or carrying much of anything."

"Patterson, I'm just glad we don't have to carry you!"

Corporal Gonzales and Rahib tried out the improvised litter they had fastened for carrying the crew chief. They brought him from where Tony had dragged him to the outcropping where the others waited. He moaned as they set him down. Tony went through one of the medic's bags and found a self-injector of morphine. He pulled off the top cover and pressed it against the crew chief's thigh. Almost immediately, the man relaxed and looked like he was falling asleep.

"I'm afraid he might be going into shock, but there's not much we can do about that. Let's head for the hills," Tony said.

"Sir, I'm staying here," declared Major Gears. "Major Rodriquez is staying as well."

Tony looked at the two of them. Major Gears looked defiant, Major Rodriquez looked scared and indecisive. He said, "Look. I know we have a disagreement on this course of action. However, this is not a democracy. As ragtag as this group is, this is a military organization. My analysis tells me we need to get away from this site. I have taken your input and considered it. However, my decision stands. We're going."

"Sir. I know how rank works, but I'm telling you that based on my fifteen years of active duty experience as an infantry officer, along with all of the training I have gone through, staying here is the right decision. I know you outrank me, but I feel that I have more expertise on this. You're wrong, and nothing in the army code of conduct tells us we have to follow an order we feel is wrong."

Tony was amazed. He had never had an order so openly defied. "Look, Major. I know I'm right on this. Staying here is a mistake."

"With all due respect, Colonel, I don't believe you have the experience to make that judgment. The right thing, the by the book thing, is to stay here."

"Major. I am taking this group as far from this crash site as I can. If you want to stay, stay. But there will be consequences even if you turn out to be right. I hate to think about the consequences if you are wrong."

"Sir, I understand. I'm staying." Gears looked at Rodriquez. She looked far less sure, but she nodded as well and said, "Me, too."

The rest of them loaded up; even Patterson carried a pack slung over the shoulder of his good arm. They moved quickly but none too quietly toward the ridge that was their initial goal. The sun dipped below the western horizon while they hurried along. After what must have been the better part of a half-hour's hike, they reached the bottom of their target ridge. There they found a dry wadi almost tall enough to stand in. They gathered on the edge of the wadi and looked for the best path to follow to take them up the ridge beyond. As they gathered, they heard the distant sound of vehicles approaching from the south. The beams of headlamps careened wildly from what looked to be a pair of vehicles making their way cross-country toward the crash site. The delay could have meant that these vehicles had stopped at the first crash site before coming to theirs.

The small group hurried into the shelter of the wadi. Tony situated himself into a position where he could peak over the wadi rim and overwatch the crash site.

He saw a ragtag group of men, carrying rifles, moving around the crash site. In the dimming light, he saw a couple of the men crawl into the crashed helicopter. The bird was still smoking some, but the fire had never really gotten going. When the men crawled out, they reported to a tall man wearing a turban. His manner of dress was somewhat unusual for Lebanon. He looked to be calling out commands, accompanied by several hand motions; evidently he was the leader of the group. The group started to search around the crash site, moving farther and farther away from the helicopter. Rahib joined Tony. "What do you see?" he asked.

"They must have figured out that there were survivors. They are searching the area." They both watched the men wander around the desert valley floor. Finally, one yelled out and the others gathered around him. "Looks like they found the packs and the gear we left behind." It was becoming increasingly difficult to make anything out in the gathering darkness. Tony didn't think the searchers would be able to pick up their trail in this light, but he didn't want to take any chances. He said, "I hope Gears and Rodriquez saw them coming and cleared out of the area or else found a good spot to hole up. I can't imagine those men are the local search and rescue group. Let's get back with the others."

They made their way back to the group in the wadi. Tony looked to where the chief lay on his stretcher and saw that he looked pale and drawn, but otherwise quiet. Patterson had rigged a sling for his broken arm and seemed to be getting along better. He still could not do anything with his left arm, but his right arm was functional. Corporal Gonzales was the only fully able-bodied soldier beside Tony in the group, and he looked at Tony as if he expected him to know exactly what to do. Tony was a Lt. Col., after all. Tony wished that he felt the confidence inside that Corporal Gonzalez seemed to sense from his outward appearance. "Okay, here's the deal. What look to be bad guys have found the wreck and, if what Rahib and I think we saw is accurate, have discovered that there were survivors. I have a feeling that come morning they will be looking for us. We want to put as much distance between them and us as we can. We are going to head up to the top of this ridge. After we reach the top, we'll reevaluate and either keep moving or look for a place to hole up. Are there any questions?"

The rest looked at him, asking none. "O.K. Let's do it." Rahib and Corporal Gonzales again took up the litter. Tony led the way, searching in the fading light for the best path. He looked back to the crash site and in the falling darkness could see only a small patch of ground lit by the headlights of one of the small trucks that had carried the group of men there.

A few minutes later shots rang out from the darkness near where the helicopters had gone down. The group crouched behind whatever cover they could find, looking back at the wreck.

While they watched, they saw two figures wearing ACU being led into the pool of light formed by the beams. "Must be Gears and Rodriquez," Linda said.

The tall man with the turban approached the pair of figures. He stood in front of them, gesturing. The intervening kilometer kept any sound from reaching them, but from that distance it looked like the man was screaming at the pair of U.S. soldiers. They saw the man reach out and strike the shorter figure – evidently Major Rodriquez. Major Gears moved toward the man, but was struck by the butt of a rifle by one of the other locals. He dropped to his knees, staggered by the blow.

The tall man pointed at Gears. Two of his men brought the infantry Major to his feet and positioned him next to the smaller figure of Rodriquez. To Tony's horror, he watched as three of the group of locals formed what look to be a firing line, about 15 feet away from the pair of prisoners.

The turbaned man again stood in front of the pair of prisoners, gesturing angrily.

"Damnit. They aren't preparing to do what I think they are doing, are they?" asked Gonzales.

Before anyone could answer, the leader moved out of the line of fire between the captive pair and the small firing line. He raised his arm and waited a moment, and then two. The group watched in horror as he dropped his hand. Small flames appeared from the barrels of the rifles of the three men on the firing line. Gears and Rodriquez collapsed, their falling bodies intertwining in limp, strange twists. The three terrorists continued to fire into the bodies until their magazines went empty.

"Fuck me!" said Gonzales. Linda let out a small cry and buried her face in her hands. Rahib stared at the far off scene with a look of disbelief on his face.

Tony was stunned into silence, unsure what to feel or say. He was overwhelmed with the sense that he should have done more to bring the two Majors with them.

Patterson said, "Fuck! Fuck! That removes any doubt about whether these are bad guys. Why the hell would they shoot them?"

Tony said, his voice unsteady, "Damnit. Damnit! Why the hell didn't Gears listen? I've never wanted to be wrong more than I do right now. What should I have done?"

"Sir, should we have left them there? What ever happened to never leave a soldier behind?" Master Sergeant Patterson asked.

"I had the same thought, Sergeant, but couldn't figure out a way short of shooting Gears to get him to come. I certainly wasn't going to stay there."

Linda looked up, tears in her eyes. "Why would they shoot them?"

Rahib looked over at her and said, "Because they are animals. Nowhere in Islam is it allowed to murder prisoners."

The group stared at the distant scene, quiet, seeming to hope against hope that they would see something that would somehow show that what they had just seen happen had not really happened.

Finally, with resignation in his voice, Tony said, "There's nothing we can do about it now. Trust me, once we get out of this situation I will move heaven and earth to ensure that we get those bodies back to their families and that those men pay for what they did. For now, we need to get as much distance between us and that crash site as we can. There are enough clues there that they may figure out that there were more survivors. In fact, that may have been what they were trying to get out of those two. Let's go."

At the top of the ridge they found a trail network that led down into the valley below as well as up into the side hills. Tony scouted toward the hills and sent Corporal Gonzales to scout toward the valley. They established a fifteen-minute time limit and met back where they had left the group. Corporal Gonzales reported that he had found nothing. He reported that the trail seemed to drop toward the valley with no other obvious hiding places around. Tony had found more promising terrain; including many large boulders and half-caves where they should be able to find a place to hole up.

He led the group carefully into the hills, trying not to leave too much of a trail but having no idea in the dark if they succeeded in that attempt. When they came to what looked to be a good spot, Tony and Gonzales scouted off into a promising boulder field. They found a massive boulder that had fallen from a small cliff face at some point in history and was now sitting a few feet away from that same cliff face. By the dim light of the moon he saw that behind the boulder, at the base of the cliff, was a crevice that looked large enough for several people to crawl into. This looked like a spot that would keep them out of sight from anyone not standing directly outside of the crevice and also protect them from the hot sun of the day. Tony left Gonzales there, worked his way back to the group and said "I think we found a spot for us to hole up. Follow me."

They followed him into the boulder field. Once they reached the selected spot, they first worked the crew chief into a position that offered him the most comfort and protection. The others then situated themselves as best they could. Tony felt exhausted but knew that they needed someone to keep a watch. "Anyone not feeling tired?" he asked. From the looks he got back he realized that no one could possibly honestly answer yes to that inquiry. "O.K. I'll take first watch. I'm going to go back to the trail and walk further into the hills, making as many marks as I can. If they track us this far, I want them to keep going. I'll keep an eye out as best I can while I do that. Corporal Gonzales, get a quick nap in. I want you to relieve me in a couple of hours. Sergeant Patterson; same deal. A couple of hours after that and you have the watch. We'll come up with a more detailed watch schedule from there. Let's get rested up while we figure out our next move. Hopefully, the good guys are on their way to find us; they must know we are missing by now."

*   *   *   *

Linda turned over, trying to find the softest patch of rock she could. She was exhausted – the aerobics she did religiously hadn't seemed to have prepared her as well for tromping through the hills of Lebanon carrying an Army pack as she would have thought.

Around her she heard the others settling into position and falling asleep. The crew chief lay quietly, but his breathing did not sound quite right. She worried that he was going to need more medical attention than they could give him. She had heard Cooper as he gave his directions to the two soldiers he had remaining in his small command. She hoped that his walk through the hills would go smoothly. She couldn't imagine how he had the energy to go out for more walking.

The act of stopping and relaxing gave her mind the chance to catch up with the events of the afternoon and evening. She had trouble figuring out how this could end well. By hiding from the bad guys, weren't they effectively hiding from any would be rescuers as well? Theoretically they could come out of hiding if the good guys came around, but what if they didn't see them? On the other hand, Gears and Rodriquez had been available for rescue but also available for the bad guys to find. There didn't seem to be a good solution. She hoped that Tony found something in his trip that might help, but couldn't imagine what that might be.

She forced her brain to relax and rolled over again. Right about the time she had convinced herself that she would never be able to fall asleep, she did.

*   *   *   *

Tony worked his way back to the trail and after crouching for a few moments, listening as much as watching, satisfied himself that there was no one there. He began following the trail as it led farther into the hills to the east of the valley floor. The quarter moon had risen higher, giving him more light to work by. Of course, it gave anyone else out there more light as well, he realized. The trail moved fairly straight and true, less meandering than what he would have expected if it had been merely an animal trail. It also showed no signs of tapering off. He realized that it must lead to something. He slowed his pace and took more stops to listen and watch. The trail crested a small rise on the ridgeline and then dropped sharply to the left. He followed it cautiously. As he made his way along, he heard what sounded like a motor running. It was a steady hum, not like one would expect from a vehicle making its way along in this rugged terrain. He followed the trail a little farther and as he came around a bend he saw a light ahead, down in what looked to be a small box canyon. He stopped and crouched, watching and listening. Only then did he hear a sound from off the trail to his left.

He thought at first that it might be a wild animal of some sort, but then realized that he was hearing the sound of someone snoring. He almost laughed at the absurdity of that sound in this situation, but the realization that he probably did not want to awake the sleeping man cut the laugh off in his throat. He pulled his 9 mm pistol and moved toward the sound as quietly as he could. Just to the left and above the trail, he saw the outline of a man, slumped over onto his right side with his head back against a rock. He had what looked to be an AK-47 propped between his legs. Tony saw that the sleeping guard was situated in a location that allowed him to see the trail almost from where it had turned sharply to the left. If this man had not been asleep, he would have seen Tony's approach easily. Tony breathed, quietly, a sigh of relief. He also thought that if a guard was posted, there must be something of interest below. Of course, with a guard this relaxed, how important could that thing be? He decided to take a chance and try to find out. He continued down toward where he saw the light until he could make out what it was. What he saw was a small, fairly typical Bekka Valley farmhouse. The mud walls appeared standard, but the ceramic roof indicated that this was not an altogether poor farm. Still, it was small and non-descript nevertheless. The only thing that made this small house seem different from the scores of similar farmhouses they had seen during their flights into and out of the valley was its hidden location, the armed guard, the generator – he had realized that was the motor sound he had heard – and the large antenna located behind the house. Whoever lived here wanted, and had, contact with the outside world. As he watched, he realized that the horizon to the east was beginning to show a little light. He had been gone much longer than he anticipated. Then, he saw the front door of the farmhouse open and an armed man exit. The man stopped to light a cigarette and then started in Tony's direction. Tony realized that this might be the next shift for the guard and realized that if he intended to get out of there undetected, now was the time. He started back up the trail quickly but as quietly as he could. As he approached the guard location, he slowed and crept along. What he saw made him relax. The man continued to sleep, although he had shifted position and had stopped snoring. Tony crept by and then again picked up speed. Just as he rounded the sharp turn – just out of sight of the guard position – he heard yelling in Arabic. Evidently the replacement had found the night shift guard asleep and was upbraiding him. Tony could hear only one voice, which made him think that the night watchman must be answering very meekly, if at all. He didn't stay around to listen to the conversation – gibberish to him in any event. Instead, he hurried back to the site where he had left the others. When he left the trail, he tried to do so without leaving any marks from his passage. He was able to make it all of the way to the crevice entrance without incident. Only at the last minute did he hear Corporal Gonzales say "Colonel – is that you?"

"It's me, Gonzales."

"What did you find – you were gone a while."

"There's a farmhouse deeper into the hills that looks to have a generator and a radio. I looked around some; might be good to know for future reference."

"Did you see anyone there?"

"A couple of guards – one of whom was asleep. Must be something going on there. I don't think that most farms around here have guards, but I could be wrong. Who knows what goes on in Lebanon? Keep an eye out for anyone coming off the trail. Wake me if they do. When you get tired, wake Patterson. Don't fall asleep or I will shoot you." His smile assured the young Corporal that he was not entirely serious, but not such an assurance that the young man wanted to find out.

He crawled into the biggest open space he could find – not far from where Linda was curled up, and fell almost instantly asleep.

"War is cruelty. There's no use trying to reform it, the crueler it is the sooner it will be over."
-    William Tecumseh Sherman

CHAPTER FOURTEEN

Bekka Valley, Lebanon
June 16, 11:56 am (0956 GMT)

Tony awoke with a start, unsure for a moment where he was. Sergeant Patterson was gently shaking his arm. Tony groggily asked, "What is it? What time is it?"

"It's around 1200, sir. I think you should come take a look at the chief. He doesn't look good."

Tony was wide awake immediately. He crawled on hands and knees behind Patterson to where the crew chief lay. The chief actually had better color than he had the last time Tony had looked in on him. However, he moaned softly, apparently in great pain. "Is it his legs?" Tony asked.

"No sir, it's his stomach. Look." Patterson pulled back the blanket covering the crew chief's lower body. What Tony saw was deeply troubling. The man's stomach was swollen and deep blue and purple. "My guess, sir, is internal bleeding. I'm not an expert, but I worry that if he doesn't get help – and soon – he won't make it."

"Have we seen any movement since I've been out?"

"No, sir. A couple of fast moving fixed wing aircraft really high up, but they seemed to be on the way somewhere, not looking for us."

"How's your arm?"

"Hurts like a mother, sir, but next to him I feel very lucky," Patterson said, nodding toward the crew chief.

"Let me think for a second, Sergeant." Tony worked his way to the mouth of the crevice and got to a spot where he could stand and stretch. He then sat back down and tried to figure out their next step. Only one solution seemed to work, but he wasn't sure if they could pull it off. He moved to where he could see Corporal Gonzales. He threw a small rock so that it landed behind the young NCO. Gonzales turned his head toward the sound and in so doing caught sight of Tony waving him over. Looking around before moving, he jogged, crouched down, over to the team's hiding place.

"Haven't seen a thing, sir."

"The chief isn't doing well. We may need to call for help rather than just waiting and hoping."

"Sir, may I point out that we don't have a radio."

"You can, but I know that. However, we know that the farmhouse up the trail does."

"You think they would let us borrow it if we asked nice, Sir?"

"You are a funny man, Gonzales. I suspect that they might not be excited about the opportunity to help the U.S. Army on this one. We may have to use it without asking permission."

"Do you mean sneak in or assault in, sir?"

"Which do you prefer?"

"I've never been real good at sneaking, sir. On the other hand, there aren't many of us. Any feel for how many people there are at the farm?"

"Based on the size of the house, I would guess only four or five at the most," Tony surmised. "If we could get in close, the element of surprise might be enough to even the odds."

"Us two versus five – we would need some luck as well as surprise."

"Is it two or three? I wonder if Rahib would help us?" Tony asked, almost to himself. He said, "Let's talk this over as a group." He made his way back into the crevice, hearing Gonzales following behind.

"Listen up, please. I want to tell you about a plan I have in mind based on something I saw last night and the fact that we haven't seen any good guys beating the bushes for us. The chief may not last another day without treatment. We need to do something proactive rather than sitting around here waiting and hoping. Further up the trail there is a farmhouse. This farm appears to have radio equipment. We should be able to use that equipment to get word to U.S. forces to come and get us."

"Is the farmhouse occupied?" asked Linda.

"It is, by what appear to be several armed men."

"Then how are we going to get to the radio? Knock on the door?" she asked.

"Not likely that they would welcome us in. My thought is that we may need to shoot ourselves in. I scouted the route out yesterday. There's only one way in, but the guard watching it last night fell asleep. With any luck, he'll do the same thing tonight. If not, we'll have much less surprise than we may need. Rahib, the question for you is, would you like to join us on this trip and if so, will you fight with us or would that violate some sacred journalistic vow?"

"Colonel, I will fight with you. These people are insane. What they were hoping to do with that nuclear material is a crime against Allah. What they did to Gears and Rodriquez last night is a crime against Allah. If fighting with you gives us a better chance to get the word out to the world about what we saw, I will gladly fight."

"That's great to hear. We'll head out after dark tonight."

"Colonel ... Tony, what about me?" asked Linda.

"My thought was that we would leave you and Sergeant Patterson here with the crew chief."

"Patterson makes good sense to stay here, but I'm going with you. Remember, our rules of engagement were pretty clear that I could go along where I wanted."

"The rules of engagement didn't anticipate this situation. You are much safer back here."

"You sexist bastard," she said, but with no real venom in her voice. "You're taking Rahib. I can shoot, and I'm pretty good with bandages and first aid. Don't let this pleasant exterior fool you – I can hold my own."

"Are you willing to carry a weapon?"

"I can take a pistol. Not sure if I can hit anything with it but I'm willing to try. Mostly, I just want to see what kind of trouble you can get yourself into."

"Hell – you'd fill up a book if you followed me around long enough."

The only excitement the rest of the day was an old man with a loaded donkey who passed by in the early afternoon, headed for the farm in the hills. He passed by again later in the day, with the donkey empty.

"Must have been the supply run," mused Corporal Gonzales.

*   *   *   *

As darkness fell they prepared to move. They made for a ragtag group. Tony carried his 9mm in a holster and an M4 in his hands. Rahib followed with another M4. Linda followed him, clutching the crew chief's 9mm in her hand. Tony had given her a quick lesson on the weapon prior to their moving out. She had pleasantly surprised him by showing some comfort with the weapon. "Spent a couple of summers on an uncle's farm," she said, by way of explanation. Corporal Gonzales brought up the rear, also carrying an M4. Master Sergeant Patterson stayed behind to keep a watch over the crew chief. The chief had passed out late in the day and had not reawaken. He looked decidedly worse and seemed to have begun laboring for breath. Tony was sure that he would not live much longer without medical assistance.

They worked their way along the route Tony had taken the previous night. He found the way easier the second time, but the trip still took a couple of hours as they tried to stay as quiet as possible. As he approached the point where the trail took the sharp left – the place where the guard could see them – he halted the group. He had been thinking about how to approach this situation. He was tempted to try the same thing as last night, hoping that the guard was equally inattentive. However, he wasn't sure he could count on that. Next, he considered trying to work his way around the guard and sneaking up on him, but he didn't like his chances in the rough terrain off of the trail. Finally, he settled on what he decided would be the final plan.

"Rahib. I want you to come forward with me. We will walk on the trail in plain sight with our weapons slung. When the guard hails us, you will respond that we are lost and looking for a place to stay the night. Once we are close enough, we will jump him and try to disarm him without firing any shots. Then, we will bring forward the others and try to take the farmhouse. Any thoughts?"

In the dim light cast by the stars and the quarter moon that had just come up low on the horizon, Rahib looked like he had several. However, all he said was "O.K."

They slung their carbines and started down the trail. They tried to walk as if they hadn't a care in the world. Tony had left his helmet and body armor with the others so that his silhouette wouldn't give away his true identify. He felt naked without the gear and half expected them to be cut down by automatic rifle fire at any moment.

They got surprisingly close to the guard location before the man stepped from his hiding spot and called out what Tony could only assume was "Halt" in Arabic. The man had his gun leveled at their midsections.

Rahib greeted the man in Arabic. There followed an exchange wherein the man seemed to be expressing disbelief and doubt. Rahib spoke in reassuring tones. All the while, Tony and Rahib worked their way closer in as non-threatening a way as possible. Tony put his hands behind his head in what looked to be a surrender pose. Little did the guard know that this made him more threatening since he had hidden a knife in a sheath wrapped around his neck. The man glanced at him occasionally, but focused on Rahib since he was doing all of the talking. The man seemed to be telling them to go back the way they had come. Rahib took out his canteen and asked the man for some water. The man gestured in the negative; but also seemed to relax somewhat. Evidently thieves or troublemakers were not in the habit of asking for water. He again indicated no and motioned with his weapon for them to go. Rahib nodded in agreement. Tony realized that Rahib must have agreed to the man's request. Rahib put his hand out to shake the guard's hand. Perhaps by instinct, the man reached out his own, allowing his rifle to dip to the ground while his front hand was occupied reaching for Rahib's. Rahib grasped the guard's hand, not in a gesture of greeting but with a sharp, vicious jerk. The man stumbled forward, off-balance. Tony unsheathed the knife and brought in down toward the man's upper back. The blade penetrated only slightly before hitting bone and stopping. The man did not seem to have even noticed the blow, but instead continued to try to extradite himself from Rahib's grip while struggling to regain control of his rifle.

Tony realized that he had to act fast before the man came to his senses and yelled at the top of his lungs, an action that evidently hadn't occurred to him yet, thankfully. He stepped in close behind the guard, grabbed a handful of his hair, pulled his head back and thrust the knife into the front of the man's throat. This time, it penetrated easily, with a sickening feel of cut cartilage and spurting blood. The man dropped his rifle and brought his hands to his throat in an attempt to stop his life from flowing out. Rahib and Tony stepped back and watched and listened as the man rolled to the ground and made nauseating sounds of gurgling air and pumping blood. Tony felt warm liquid on his hands; then felt his stomach convulse. He turned away, dropped to his knees and heaved dryly. The few items from an MRE he had eaten that day made for very little volume for his stomach to reject, but it made a game attempt. By the time he stopped gagging, he turned and saw that the man had stopped moving. Rahib was also on his knees, and Tony realized that he had also been sick.

"Some heroes we are, just like the movies," Tony thought to himself. He regained his composure enough to get to his feet and said, "I'm going to get the others." He made his way back to the others and was challenged by Corporal Gonzales. "We can move forward. Let's go." He got his protective gear back on and then led the small group to a point just past where the guard lay. The moon had come up so the light was better, giving Linda and Gonzales the chance to visually reconstruct what must have happened. They gaped at the body as they made their way by. The group stopped once the small farmhouse was in full view.

Tony, attempting to sound confident, said, "I don't think we do anything subtle. My feel is that we head straight to the front door. I'll try the front door. If it is unlocked, I'll signal and we'll go. If it is locked, I'll put a burst into it and then Gonzales, you kick it in. I'll go left, Gonzales, you go right. Rahib, come in third and go straight. Clear the room as quickly as you can and then move on to any other rooms. If people resist, kill them. If not, cover and disarm them as best you can. Any questions?"

Gonzales looked like he was in shock. Rahib looked remarkably calm; evidently fully recovered from the fight with the guard. Linda said, "What should I do?"

"Cover our rear. Crouch down out of sight and make sure that no one comes in from the perimeter."

He looked each of the three in the eye in turn. They all gave short nods. With that, he turned toward the farmhouse. They followed close behind; not keeping as much distance between them as trained soldiers would have, but nevertheless moving quickly and fairly quietly. As they approached the farmhouse, they saw an old well head about thirty feet from the front door. Tony indicated to Linda that she should position herself behind that. She nodded and veered off, crouching behind it. The three men moved to the door, Tony and Gonzales to the left and Rahib to the right. They stopped and listened. No sound came from inside, but the warm glow of artificial light showed through a crack at the bottom of the door. The outside light that had glowed above the door the previous night was dark, but the same mechanical hum of the generator still sounded from behind the building. Everything seemed consistent with a quiet, rural farmhouse, late at night.

Tony reached for the doorknob; actually more of a latch he realized. He tried it and it seemed to move, somewhat noisily, but freely. He nodded to the others, took a deep breadth, said a little prayer, and pushed on the latch. The door started to move easily, but stopped after moving only about a quarter of an inch. Then, it halted as if it had hit a wall. The screech of the latch and the thud of an interior bar sounded, to the ears of the three men, like a sound that would wake the dead. Almost panicked, Tony stepped back and let out a long burst from his M4 in the vicinity of where he thought the bar must intersect the door. He then moved out of the way and Gonzales kicked the door mightily. It budged, but did not open. Gonzales next threw his shoulder into it. The sound of splintering wood gave hope, but the door still remained hung up. Almost desperate, Gonzales backed off and bulled toward the door like a charging fullback, something he had been back in high school in his small high school in Texas. The door fell in under the weight of his body and he tumbled in after it.

Falling probably saved Gonzales life. On the far side of the room a man crouched next to a tussled looking cot. As the door crashed in he let loose a burst from an AK-47. The first bullet passed inches over Gonzales's head and the following rounds passed even higher as the gun barrel worked upward in the manner typical of automatic weapons. Tony was not as lucky. As he jumped through the doorway and to the left, one of the rounds clipped his left shoulder, feeling for all the world like a tug on his sleeve. He barely noticed at the time, and as he dove down he let out a burst of his own at the center of mass of the crouched figure. The man fell backward as if he had slipped; he did not fly back like in the movies, Tony noted. However, despite it looking as if he had merely slipped, the gunman made no move to get back up.

Tony heard Rahib move into the room and to his right. As Rahib did so, another man stumbled in from a side room opposite the front door. He clutched a pistol. He aimed it at Gonzales, who was still trying to extricate himself from the splintered door. The man, who wore loose robes and had a long beard, squeezed off two rounds, both of which struck Gonzales in the torso just as he made his way to his feet. Gonzales fell backward onto the remains of the door, crashing heavily.

Tony moved to bring his M4 around but the barrel caught on the leg of an overturned chair, frustrating his efforts. He saw the man begin to swing his pistol in his direction. Rahib seemed stunned, looking at Gonzales and not at the bearded man. Tony struggled to regain control of his weapon and line up on the new target, any moment expecting to feel bullets penetrate his body. Just as he got his weapon into alignment he heard two pistol shots. He closed his eyes and expected to feel the heat and pain of rounds impacting, but felt nothing. A moment passed. He opened his eyes again just in time to see the bearded man slump to the ground. Looking to his right, he saw Linda standing in the doorway with the 9mm pistol that Tony had given her smoking in her hand.

Rahib looked even more stunned than he had before, glancing back and forth from Linda to the second fallen man. Tony called out to Rahib and Linda, "Check on Gonzales!" and headed for the doorway from which the second man had come. He burst in to find what looked to be a master bedroom. In front of a desk next to a large, low bed a man was bent over, screaming into a radio. He wore what looked to be a loose robe and did not appear to be armed. Tony raised his M4 and fired two rounds past the man, attempting to get him to drop the handset. The man leapt out of the way toward the bed. Tony called out "Don't move!" The man stopped moving and sat quietly on the edge of the bed. Tony called out, "Rahib, get in here!" He then moved to the radio and looked it over.

To his horror, he realized that one of the two rounds he had fired had penetrated the front of the radio casing. The dial that he was sure that he had seen glowing when he first entered the room was now dark. He kept glancing at the man sitting on the bed and saw that the man seemed to be content to sit and quietly watch him. Tony heard Rahib hustle in.

"How's Gonzales?" Tony asked.

"His body armor stopped one of the rounds but another penetrated his side. He is bleeding only a little but his left lung is collapsed. Linda is working on him."

"I'm afraid I shot the radio. Not sure if we can get it to work or not. Ask him if there are any other radios in here," Tony said, pointing at the man on the bed.

Rahib made no reply to that request; nor did he say anything to the man. After an uncomfortable period of time, Tony looked over to see what Rahib was doing. He saw Rahib staring, speechless, at the man on the bed.

"What's wrong, Rahib?"

Rahib continued to stare. The man stared right back at him, not saying a word. The exchange showed no sign of ending.

"Rahib, what's wrong?" Tony asked again.

Rahib slowly move his eyes to Tony and said, "Do you know who this man is, Tony?"

Tony turned to look at the man again and thought that he did indeed look familiar. "Who is he?"

Rahib said, "That is Sheik al Raqman."

Tony looked again at the man and realized with a start that Rahib might be right. "Ask him if that is who he is," he ordered.

Rahib let out a stream in Arabic. The man nodded, surprisingly confidently.

"That is him, Tony.'

"Holy shit." Tony's head was awhirl. He had no idea what the next step should be. "Ask him if he got a hold of anyone on the radio."

Rahib again shot out a stream of Arabic. The man answered calmly and apparently without any hesitation.

"He says that his men will be here for him shortly, Allah willing. He says that if we put down our weapons and convert to Islam here and now he will see that we are well treated."

"Tell him to kiss my ass."

Rahib turned to do so. Tony stopped him and said, "Never mind, no reason to get into a debate. Ask him if there are any other radios."

Rahib did so and passed back the reply that there were none.

Tony fiddled with the controls of the radio, feeling mocked by the neat hole in the middle of the front panel, but nothing he did would bring the radio back to life. He then started searching through the rest of the room, to no avail. The last place he looked was under the bed. He saw what looked to be, in the dim light, a large walkie-talkie. He reached down and only when he got it out did he realize that it was a satellite phone.

"Tell him he's a lying prick."

Rahib spoke a short, sharp string of words that sure sounded like they conveyed that feeling. The man answered back calmly. "He says you asked about another radio, not about a phone."

"Is he a terrorist or a lawyer? He knew what I meant."

He powered up the phone. One of his fellow soldiers in Afghanistan, one with more dollars than sense given the $5.00 per minute cost, had brought one of these, and later they had been issued them to communicate with convoys that went outside the base. Unfortunately, Tony could not remember how to use it except for making personal calls, nor did he know the number of any military members.

"Shit, who do I call? Do you have any ideas?"

"We could call my news bureau, but they have only junior staffers at this time of night," Rahib replied.

Tony thought more about it and decided to make the one call he knew how to make. After several pauses, clicks and hisses, he heard Rachel pick up with the apprehensive "Hello" of someone not recognizing the caller ID.

"Rachel, it's me, Tony."

"Tony, what's wrong? Is everything all right? Is it something about John?"

"Rachel, it's nothing about John, but right now I'm in a real bind and I need to try to get in touch with someone who can help."

"What's wrong? Are you hurt? Where are you?"

Almost as if her asking had triggered it, he felt his shoulder begin to throb. Looking over, he could trace where the bullet had furrowed his uniform and left shoulder. A surprising amount of blood had soaked his left side, especially surprising because he had forgotten about the wound entirely in the excitement of the moment.

"I'm fine. I'm in Lebanon – not sure where exactly. Rachel, I don't have much time. I need you to transfer me to Dave Powell – remember my Army buddy from Afghanistan? His number is in the address book."

"Of course I know Dave – we went to dinner at his house. He has the big house near Cincinnati. Three boys."

"That's him. Use three-way calling to get him on the line. His number should be in the address book."

He heard Rachel rummaging through the junk drawer and could picture the kitchen/dining room in his mind. She said, "Found it. I'm going to switch over to the other line and make the call. Hold on."

Tony waited for what must have been only moments but felt to be a very long time. Finally, he heard a click and Rachel said "Dave's on, Tony."

"Buddy, what's up?" Tony heard Dave say.

"Dave, I'm with a small team that survived a helicopter crash. We are stuck in a small farmhouse in the middle of Indian country. Can you transfer, using three way calling, this call to the Ohio Joint Forces Headquarter Joint Operation Center?"

"Shit, Tony. You are kidding me. Let me look up the number." Again, Tony heard rustling. "Let me put down the phone for a second, Tony. I have most of my guard stuff in my den."

Tony heard the phone being put down on a hard surface and then heard Dave tromp away. He was back quickly. "Got it. Rachel, you are going to need to get off so I can do this."

"Tony, are you okay? Tell me if you are okay!"

"Rachel, I'm fine. I'll call you back as soon as I can. In the meantime, I have to get someone here to pick us up. I love you, Rachel, but you have to get off."

"Tony, don't you get hurt. Call me back as soon as you can."

Tony could hear that she was near tears as she got off the line. Dave said, "I'll give it a go. Hang on."

The line went silent for a few moments. When Dave clicked back on he said, "Tony, the JOC is on the line."

"LT Hansel here, sir. What can I do for you."?

"Hansel, did you get promoted? What are you doing working there?"

"Yes sir, finally finished college and took my commission. Haven't found a real job yet so I'm working here for now."

"Great. Look Hansel. We're in deep shit here. I was on a chopper that crashed and I have a small group of survivors. We are in a farmhouse in Lebanon with a prisoner. I need an extraction. Pass me on to whomever you have as a contact at higher so we can get someone to come pick us up. "

"Damn, Sir. I can transfer you up to Guard Bureau. I've never done it but they showed me how. Anything we can do on this end, sir?"

"Not unless you can fly to Lebanon in the next few minutes. Transfer me up, Hansel."

"Lt. Col. Powell, when I transfer him you will be cut off."

"Alright, LT. Tony, take care of yourself. Call me back if there is anything you need.

"Thanks, Dave."

The line clicked and Hansel said, "Here goes, sir. Good luck."

*   *   *   *

Tony finally hung up. The battery symbol had been flashing and a tone sounding periodically for the last several minutes of the call. He had lost count of the times he had been transferred. All he knew was that he had ended up in the 18th Airborne Corps TOC with several people getting on and off the line. They had traced the call and pinpointed the location using the satellite feeds. They had scrambled fighters and an extraction team and promised that everything was on the way. As he was switched from location to location and person-to-person, he had made his way around the farmhouse, as much as he could while still watching al Raqman.

Al Raqman had not moved much at all. After several minutes of watching Tony talk into the phone, he positioned himself so that he was lying flat on the bed with his hands behind his head. Tony didn't think he was sleeping, because occasionally a few words of Arabic would escape his lips. Praying, Tony concluded.

Linda had patched up Gonzales as best she could. She had found some plastic wrap and had sealed the wound to his lung. He still wheezed like a buzz saw, but he had decent color in his face and nodded in the affirmative when she asked if he felt better.

Tony had sent Rahib out to the trail to keep a watch from the position the guard had occupied. He walked to the front door and was amazed that he saw the first signs of dawn on the eastern horizon. Where had the night gone? He sat, took out his canteen and took a long drink of water. He propped his arms on his knees and then rested his head on his arms. Just as he got himself finally comfortable, he heard a burst of gunfire from the direction of the trail. He jumped up and moved to the front door. He saw Rahib running full speed back toward the house. Tony opened the door to let him in and Rahib collapsed against the interior wall.

As Rahib struggled for breath, Tony asked, "What happened, what did you see?"

"A group of men, Arabs, making their way down the path. I think I got the lead one and they all hid. I ran back here to tell you."

"How many? What weapons were they carrying?"

"Looked like AK-47s. I think about fifteen men."

"Okay. I got through and the good guys are on the way. It will be a while, though. About fifteen minutes for the fast movers, a little longer for any helicopters."

"We don't have fifteen minutes."

"We do if we can get those guys to keep their heads down. Take a spot at the window and shoot anyone you can get a good shot at. Linda, watch al Raqman. I'm going to go out to see if I can encourage them to keep their heads down as well."

He made his way along the edge of the house, and after looking in the direction of the trail and seeing nothing, ran toward a ragged collection of rocks to the east of the house that looked promising in terms of cover and concealment. He settled himself in and arranged his M4 into a comfortable prone supported firing position. He hoped that when the group received fire from his direction in addition to the fire coming from the house that they would be confused and take some time figuring out what to do. *A little time is all we need.*

      *   *   *   *

Linda watched Tony head out the door and felt a sense of purpose rise up in her, juxtaposed over the sense of unreality she had been feeling since she had watched the three men bust through the front door. She had been on autopilot since that moment and was only just now coming to grips with what had happened and what she had done. She looked to where Rahib was settling into the best firing position he could find. He raised a curtain and broke out the lowest pane in a small front window. He looked over at her and she saw a look of near panic in his eyes. However, she also saw a reassuring look of determination. He nodded, acknowledging her glance, and then turned back to his preparations.

She turned back to Gonzales. He was conscious, struggling for breath. He was not bleeding much, but she could hear a small gurgling sound with every breath, originating from the wound in his side. Evidently, the small piece of plastic wrap she had used with the first bandage had slipped. She had watched enough TV to know that sealing the wound again would help him breath. She looked around the room for something larger that might work. Her eyes settled on a loaf of bread wrapped in plastic. She glanced through the doorway to the other room and saw that al Raqman was still lying with his hands behind his head. He looked relaxed, his eyes closed, although something about his manner told her that he wasn't asleep.

Satisfied that he was no immediate threat, she crossed the room and retrieved the loaf of bread. She quickly unwrapped it and threw the bread toward a corner of the room. She rubbed and flicked the plastic wrap to dislodge as many of the crumbs clinging to it as she could. With another quick glance at al Raqman, she bent down to Gonzalez. He watched her through pained and slightly panicked eyes. She lifted the combat bandage she had first applied to the wound, folded the plastic into a six inch by six inch square, placed it over the wound, and then reapplied the bandage, tying it tightly. Almost immediately, Gonzalez's breathing eased and the look of panic in his eyes dissipated. He let out a small sigh and breathed deeply experimentally. "That's a lot better," he said softly. "Thank you."

"Save your breath. You're going to be okay. Now, I'm going to move you into the back room so that I can keep an eye on our host back there. This is going to hurt."

He nodded understanding. She got behind him, reached under his armpits, and started pulling him. She could barely budge him, and the effort elicited a groan from Gonzalez. Rahib looked over and saw her struggling. He looked out the window quickly and, evidently seeing nothing, headed over. With his assistance and a few more small groans that Gonzalez was obviously trying to suppress, they muscled him into the back room and settled him into the corner of the room opposite the bed on which al Raqman rested. Al Raqman looked over when he heard the sounds of their efforts. His eyes showed no reaction.

"Thanks," Linda said to Rahib. He nodded and headed back toward his position by the small window located near the front door.

*   *   *   *

Just a couple of minutes after Tony got settled into position, he saw the first member of the group come into sight. The man moved warily along, off of, but paralleling, the main trail. Several others came into sight, trailing behind the first. Tony lined up his weapon and just as he was ready to try a shot, a rifle sounded from the main house. The men ducked down, apparently unhit. They began firing rounds toward the farmhouse.

Where they had gone to ground gave them good cover from the farmhouse. However, the second man to have come into sight had settled into a position where Tony could see his lower body projecting out from behind the large rock he was hiding behind. Tony lined up the M4, missing the longer feel of the M16 or the 30-30's he had used as a kid. He squeezed off a round and saw a puff of dirt rise up about 10 feet beyond the man. The man made no move. Apparently, he hadn't even realized he had been shot at. Tony lined up his sights again, took in and partially let out a breath, just as he had been taught on the rifle range, and let loose another round. A small spray of red erupted from the man's upper thigh. The man rolled into full sight, clutching his thigh. Tony squeezed off another round, and then another. The man continued to roll around, although he seemed to notice the shots and started to scramble toward his original hiding place. Tony squeezed off one more round. The man stopped moving and lay still.

Suddenly, the rocks around Tony were filled with the sound of impacting rounds. Shards of rock flew around him. The other members of the enemy squad had noticed the shots coming from the field of rocks and had let loose several volleys in his direction. He burrowed deeper behind his rock and the impacts subsided. He glanced around and was able to see several members of the enemy squad dashing forward from hiding place to hiding place. They did not appear to be as coordinated as professional soldiers, but they weren't rank amateurs either, he decided.

Tony rolled to another location and squeezed off another couple of rounds. He heard a few rounds coming from the farmhouse, headed outbound, as well. He didn't think that either he or Rahib had hit any of the bad guys, but they did at least go to ground. He could hear them calling out to one another, apparently in an attempt to coordinate their movements.

After a few moments, he saw several heads pop up and rounds started impacting all around him. He ducked down and from his hiding position he saw dust flying from rounds impacting the farmhouse as well. Peering around his rock, he saw several figures moving forward under the cover of the fire. Trying to stay as sheltered as he could, he squeezed off a few rounds. After the last round the bolt locked to the rear, indicating that the last round in the magazine had been fired.

"Too many video games – I hadn't even thought about ammo," he thought to himself. He burrowed behind the rock and dug into his cargo pockets for another magazine. He found one, but his quick search revealed that it was the only one he had.

"Have to watch my rounds, I guess," he said out loud, to no one in particular. He was feeling amazingly lonely here in his field of rocks and wished that he were back in the farmhouse. However, the bad guys had gotten close enough that making his way back there didn't look possible.

*   *   *   *

Linda checked to make sure that Gonzalez was in as comfortable a position as she could get him. She gave him a small drink out of her canteen; barely enough to wet his mouth. He nodded his thanks and then closed his eyes.

She looked over to al Raqman. She saw that he was watching her, a look of disapproval, or perhaps even disgust, on his face. She raised an eyebrow at him. "Something I can do for you?" His look of disgust deepened and he shook his head.

She realized that he had understood her words. "You understand English?" she asked. He looked at her without speaking and then shrugged his shoulders. She took this as an acknowledgment.

Her journalistic instincts kicked in to full gear. She realized that she had the opportunity to interview the most wanted man in the world. Her mind raced, sorting through the hundreds of questions she wanted to ask.

She settled on, "What goal did you hope to accomplish with your attack on Boston?"

She was somewhat surprised that he actually seemed to be formulating a response. Just as his face revealed that he was about to start speaking Rahib's weapon sounded from the front room, followed by what sounded like a curse in Arabic. The

177

sound of the weapon seemed louder than she remembered from the earlier fighting. Al Raqman showed the trace of a smile. "My men are coming," he said, in remarkably good English.

The sound of the incoming fire reached into the back room, a combination of thuds and zings as rounds slapped into and bounced off the mud and stone front of the house or the ceramic tiles of the roof.

Her mind registered the events, but she found herself distracted by the need to hear answers from her captive. She reached into her belt and retrieved the 9mm pistol from where she had stashed it when she was working on Gonzalez. She turned back to al Raqman and said, "You were about to tell me why you killed all of those innocent women and children in Boston. What goal was worth their deaths?"

He said, "Boston was a partial payback for what your country has done to our people for centuries. It was about letting your people know the pain my people have known at your hands."

"Those women and children caused your people pain? By what logic?"

"If not them personally then collectively through the actions of their leaders. In your supposed democratic system, aren't the leaders doing the will of the people?"

One part of her mind couldn't believe that she was debating philosophical issues while people were coming with the intent to kill her, but the other side of her brain couldn't pass on the opportunity. "But you must have wanted some reaction?"

"We want to be left alone," he answered.

"How is that working out for you? Did you get that reaction? Did you honestly believe our country would simply not respond?"

"Who knows with your crazy country? You fled from mosquito bites in Somalia in 1993 and Lebanon in 1983, but then stay in Vietnam and Iraq under huge losses. No sense can be made of what your country does. Now, you invade Lebanon and may set off a regional war. In the end, it will not matter. Allah willing, we will prevail in the end."

She heard the volume of the fire from outside pick up, although Rahib's firing seemed to be dropping off, if anything. She felt a decision click into place in her mind.

Hefting the 9mm pistol she had been holding without real thought in her right hand, she pulled the slide back enough to ensure that there was a round in the chamber. She dropped the magazine and saw that it looked to be almost full. Slamming it back into place, she looked to make sure that al Raqman was still watching her. Jerking her head toward the front of the house, she said, "If any of your friends make it in through that door I am going to put a bullet into your face. Then, I will take as many of them with me as I can.

The first look of doubt he had expressed crossed al Raqman's face. "It is forbidden to execute prisoners without a trial," he said, without real conviction.

She laughed ruefully and said, "Not if they are trying to escape." She checked on Gonzalez one more time and then settled herself into a position against a wall where she could watch the front door while covering al Raqman with her pistol. He looked at her with a wide range of emotions playing across his face. She thought she could see fear, disgust and acceptance, all at the same time. She heard a huge increase in volume of fire from outside; a far different sound from what had proceeded it. The air sounded like it was being ripped open. Almost simultaneously, she heard the roar of jet engines passing overhead.

The deafening sound passed, replaced by the sounds of small arms fire as before, although now at a substantially reduced volume. Next, her ears heard a disturbingly quiet but terrifying sound from the front room, almost like a melon accidentally dropped on a floor. Looking through the doorway into the front room, she saw Rahib sprawled out, his head a bloody misshapen mass. She felt bile rise in her throat. For a moment she thought she would pass out, Breathing deeply, feeling tears coming to her eyes, she slumped against the wall. Her hand holding the pistol swayed but stayed pointed in the general direction of al Raqman.

*　　　　　*　　　　　*　　　　　*

Tony chambered the first round of his last magazine and again peered from behind his rock. He saw that the group of men had split in two, with one group angling his direction and the other group angling toward the farmhouse. He saw one man expose himself fully and Tony squeezed off a round. The man dropped like a sack of potatoes and Tony felt a momentary rush. That moment was short lived as rounds again hit all around him. One hit so close that shards and dust from the rock next to him flew into his face, momentarily blinding him. He felt blood run down the side of his face, but felt no real pain.

He wiped it away as best he could and again moved into a firing position. The men were even closer, hiding, firing, moving and hiding again. He realized that there was probably no way he could stop them from overrunning his position and prepared himself with the thought that he would take as many of them with him as he could. He rolled quickly to another rock, with rounds impacting all around him as he did so. One round punched into his body armor and he felt the impact like the kick of a mule. His breath rushed out of him and he struggled for a few moments to get it back. As he lay on his back behind a rock, trying to gather himself again, he heard a buzz sound from the east. In an instant, the deadly looking cross-shaped body of an A-10, followed by another, flashed into view. The pilots stood the planes nearly on their sides as they circled, assessing the situation. Tony looked around his new rock and saw that the men who had been approaching him were now shooting at the airplanes instead.

"Might as well be shooting BB guns for what they are going to do to an A-10," he muttered. The A-10 was designed to be a tank killer and was probably the most survivable plane in the Air Force's inventory. The pilot sat in a titanium bathtub and the plane itself was notorious for surviving small arms and machine gun fires. Rumor was that, during the first Gulf War, one A-10 had made it back to its airbase missing over half of one wing.

The A-10's swooped down toward the valley and their main guns opened up. The massive 30mm rounds threw up large clouds of dust and stones. Tony saw one of the attackers who seemed to literally explode as a round made full impact with his torso. The others dropped and burrowed themselves into the ground as best they could. Even twenty meters from the beaten zone, Tony realized that he dare not move or the shrapnel would cut him down. After the planes swooped overhead, there was a momentary silence, punctuated only by the cries of one of the men who must have been terribly injured. Tony looked around and saw that the men who had been approaching him were either down or were running full tilt back toward the trail. He looked toward the farmhouse and saw that a group of five or six men continued to move toward it, firing as they did so. The A-10's had missed this group entirely. Tony saw that unless something happened immediately the farmhouse would be overrun.

Without much thought, he sprinted from his hiding place and ran toward the farmhouse and the group of men, yelling and firing. He saw one or two go down but the others turned toward him and started firing. He heard several rounds pass close by, but no rounds managed to find him. However, just as he reached the shelter of the side of the farmhouse wall, a round struck him straight on in the chest, again right on his front armor plate. He went down, the breath again out of him. He lay on the ground with his back against the cool adobe-like surface of the farmhouse and felt his energy and will to resist leave him. He brought his weapon around, unsteady. He saw that a couple of the men had cautiously maneuvered themselves around to where he was again in their line of sight. He lined up his weapon on one of them but when he pulled the trigger nothing happened. When he looked down, he saw that the bolt was again locked to the rear. He looked up to see the two men spot him and raise their rifles. For the second time that day, he prepared himself for the impact of rounds on his body. A great sense of fatigue overwhelmed him; a resignation to his fate.

Just as the men looked ready to fire, a great cloud of dust appeared around them and the men dropped to the ground. Only then did a zipping sound penetrate Tony's consciousness, along with the sound of rotors. He struggled to his feet and stumbled around to the front of the farmhouse. He saw two Chinook helicopters, with guns blazing out of their door gunner positions, settling into the field in front of the farmhouse. Troops poured out of them, starting even before the wheels hit the ground. Tony worked his way to the front of the farmhouse. Tripping over something as he entered, he fell through the door. He looked as he fell and realized that he had tripped over Rahib's outstretched legs. Rahib's lifeless eyes stared up at nothing. Apparently he had been shot late in the firefight, because Tony had heard rounds outbound from the farmhouse until only moments before he had been hit.

Linda, clutching her pistol, crouched just in his line of sight next to Gonzales in the next room. She held her pistol aimed at something out of sight. "Damn, I almost shot him. Are you okay?" she blurted.

"I'm fine. The cavalry's here. Put your weapon down or they're likely to shoot you. He took his own advice and moved into a seated position, weapon on the ground next to him. No sooner than he had done so, two very mean, very professional looking infantry types burst through the door. They quickly assessed the situation and yelled, "Clear." With that, several more people, thankfully some of them carrying aid bags, came in. A medic crouched beside him and said, "Sir, are you okay?"

"I'm fine. Work on the Corporal," Tony said, pointing at Gonzales.

The last person through the door came as a surprise.

"Dana, what the hell are you doing here?"

"Tony, are you okay?"

"Why does everyone keep asking me that?"

"You're covered in blood from a head wound."

"It's superficial, just bleeding like a son of a gun, I guess. Again, what are you doing here?"

"We were just getting ready to clear the objective area when the call came in. I was the highest ranking member still on the ground so I pulled rank and came along for the ride, on the justification that I could recognize you."

"I'm glad you can recognize me, but take a look in there and see if you recognize the gentleman in the other room."

Al Raqman was again sitting on the edge of the bed and for the first time looked troubled. Dana stared at him for a moment and then said, "Is that who I think it is? How did you find him?"

"A complete accident. I was looking for a radio and found him instead. We have a couple of wounded men holed up about a mile from here. Let's get loaded up, go get them and get out of here."

*   *   *   *

Near the village of Chigyong-dong, South Korea
June 16, 5:15 pm (0815 GMT)

John showed PVT Pho how to do the circuit integrity test. Pho seemed to have the process down and even seemed to understand what John meant when he talked about circuit continuity. The demolition charges and circuitry seemed to have weathered the rocket attack just fine.

The two young men stopped and sat on the edge of the bridge abutment. "Hard to believe we're here, isn't it Coop?" asked Pho.

John, in preparing his response, realized that he didn't know Pho's first name. He said, "Long way from Ohio. Do you think the North Koreans are really headed this way, Pho?"

"I don't know. I don't see how they could make it through the air strikes."

As if to reinforce this, they watched as a couple of what looked to be F16's streaked low overhead, headed north. They had seen many such pairs of fighters headed that same direction. Either none of them were making it back or else this valley was for northbound traffic only, because they had seen no jets heading south.

John hoped it was the latter. He said, "I wouldn't want to find out what being hit by those guys would be like. The rocket strike was bad enough."

"No doubt. I almost shit myself."

"You wouldn't be the first," John laughed. "Well, we better get back."

They stood and adjusted their gear. The body armor and the helmets were not yet something they were completely adjusted to, but they were feeling more and more comfortable in them every day. Just as they started to head back toward their positions, they heard the same whistle-like sound from the sky they had heard earlier.

"Get down!" John yelled, jumping toward the edge of the bridge abutment below where they had been sitting. Pho followed right behind and they lay close together as they sought to make themselves as small and invisible as possible.

This barrage was more intense than the previous one; something John had not realized was possible. He found himself edging closer and closer to panic, wanting to stand and run and run and run until the overwhelming noise was farther and farther behind him. Just as he felt himself giving in to the urge to run, the intensity of the bombardment seemed to subside. The last rounds coming in sounded very different from the earlier rounds. John at first thought the rounds might be duds. Then, he remembered reading somewhere that chemical rounds don't sound as loud as others. He realized that when he had left the bunker he had forgotten his mask.

"Hope that's not gas. I don't have my mask with me," he said. Pho said, "Neither do I."

The final mute-sounding rounds fell, followed by a remarkable silence.

John raised his head up over the edge of the bridge abutment. He saw that there were large chunks blown from the abutment façade. Smoking craters dotted the landscape. The tent and small hut were in ruins, although the Port-a-John looked remarkably intact.

He looked to where Sergeant Cody's position had been. He was shocked to see that there looked to be nothing remaining of the bunker that had housed the squad leader and his commo man. He began to trot over to see if there was anything he could do. When he was almost there, he was knocked down by a small explosion, but couldn't figure out what had caused it. As he picked himself up, he saw some tears in his uniform on the right side. He realized that blood was oozing from a couple of small wounds, but he seemed otherwise no worse for wear.

"What the heck?" he thought to himself. He decided that it must have been a piece of unexploded ordnance and moved on. He saw Lott and his team climbing from their bunker, looking around. As he arrived at the remains of the command bunker, he realized that there was nothing that could be done. It must have taken a direct hit from a large shell. He saw what must have been pieces of his squad leader and radioman, but there was nothing large enough left on which to do first aid.

He looked back to where Lott's team had emerged from their bunker. Beyond, he saw his small team exiting from theirs as well. Both teams looked thankfully intact.

He saw Lott headed toward him and started moving over to meet him. As John approached the Corporal, a small explosion went off at Lott's feet, throwing him up and to the side. Again, John saw no immediate cause. He froze, thinking intensely. Out of his peripheral vision, he saw Lott's team members heading toward their team leader.

"Freeze!" he yelled, neurons finally firing in rapid succession. The muted sound of the rounds at the end of the bombardment came to his mind.

"Mines! Those last rounds must have had scatterable mines! Stop moving!" he yelled.

He froze himself and began looking around at the ground around him. At first, he saw nothing. Then, an irregularly shaped object caught his eye. He bent down to examine it and realized that is was indeed a small mine. It had two long filaments trailing from it. They looked to be almost like fishing line, draped out haphazardly on either side of the small mine body. Each filament looked to be at least five feet long and had a small weight on each end, probably to help them spread out.

He stood carefully and called out, "The mines are gray and about three inches across. They have trigger wires that drape out around them. They are not very powerful, but they are dangerous, so move very, very carefully!"

The others looked at him, obviously terrified to move. John, watching the ground carefully, began picking his way toward where Lott had gone down. Lott was calling out in pain, still alive, but obviously hurt badly. The others watched John making his way slowly along. A couple of them stayed still, but John saw that one of them, he thought maybe Collins, was working his way over as well.

John and Collins arrived at Lott's location at about the same time. Lott had quieted and looked to have composed himself. His left foot was badly mangled and he lay on his back grasping his left knee with his hands so that his foot and ankle dangled without any weight on it.

The area of ground around him seemed clear, so Collins and John knelt down on either side of Lott. "Shit, what did I step on?" asked Lott.

"They dropped a scatterable anti-personnel minefield on us. It's not real dense and the mines aren't real big, but they will make it much harder for us to move around," John said.

Collins had a small medic bag with him. He took out a combat bandage and wrapped it around the ruined toes. "It's not bleeding much, Corporal. I don't think I'll put on a tourniquet. If I do you may loose the foot."

Lott nodded through clenched teeth. After he finished the dressing, Collins gave Lott an auto-injector of Morphine. "Should help take the edge off."

While Collins worked, John looked around, trying to figure out the next step.

Lott, obviously in less pain, said, "How's Sergeant Cody?"

John looked him in the eyes and said, "He's gone. So is Smithson and the radio. They took a direct hit from what must have been a 155 mm round."

"Shit. What are we going to do?"

"I guess we'll do what we were supposed to do. We need to keep an eye on this bridge and blow it if we have to, " John said.

"I understand that we were told not to blow it without orders. How will we get orders if we don't have a radio?"

John considered that for a second. "I guess we'll have to figure it out when the time comes. If North Korean tanks show up, I'm not waiting for orders. For right now, I'm going to move what's left of the squad to the south side of the bridge. That will get us out of the minefield and on the side away from the bad guys if we do have to blow that thing."

Lott nodded, although his eyes revealed that he was losing focus.

"Coop, he's going into shock. I better get his feet up and get him covered."

"Alright, Collins. I'm going to start getting everyone else to the other side."

John began the slow process of working his way over to the remaining squad members.

At 19 years old, he found himself the senior able-bodied member of the group. Corporal Lott was the ranking survivor, but with him out of commission the remaining squad members would look to John for guidance and orders. He had a clear plan for the next thirty minutes; get to the other side of the bridge and out of the minefield. After that, he had no idea what to do. Overhead, he saw another pair of American fighters heading north.

"They are in front of us, behind us, and we are flanked on both sides by an enemy that outnumbers us 29:1. They can't get away from us now!"
- Lewis B. "Chesty" Puller

CHAPTER FIFTEEN

Airborne over the Syrian/Jordanian Border
June 17, 11:15 am (0915 GMT)

The rest of the extraction had gone as smooth as silk. They had found Master Sergeant Patterson and the crew chief just where they had left them. The crew chief was unresponsive, but Tony felt confident that the U.S. medical system could save him. The helicopters were headed for the Iraqi Forward Operating Base as quickly as they could. Al Raqman sat next to him, with two very pissed off looking infantrymen covering his every move.

Tony was surprised when al Raqman leaned over and said, in only slightly accented English. "Will you get the $25 million dollar reward that is on my head?"

"I don't know. But if I do, I'll give it to the families of the people you have killed, you son of a bitch. Why didn't you tell me you spoke English back in the farmhouse?"

"You didn't ask. Besides, I expected my men to spirit me away so I thought that talking to you would just be a waste of time. Unfortunately, they failed in what should have been a simple matter."

"What were you doing in that farmhouse with so few men?"

"Ask your intelligence services. They had no idea where I was and expected to find me in a much larger, more defended position, so they weren't even looking in that direction. No one would have found me had you not stumbled in."

"Your luck sure failed you, then. Now you will have a chance to pay for your crimes."

"I have committed no crimes. What I did, I did for Allah. What you call my payment will be my reward. Killing me will only send me to paradise sooner rather than later."

"I don't want them to kill you. I want them to lock you up in a little, non-descript cell in the middle of Kansas. Once a year, they should publish your picture, looking frail, weak, short haired, clean shaven, powerless - to remind everyone that in reality you are nothing more than a murderer."

"We shall see. You have had your day and I will have mine." With that, al Raqman sat silent for the remainder of the trip.

Tony, shoulder and head throbbing under their combat dressings, leaned his head against the bulkhead and promptly fell asleep.

*   *   *   *

Linda sat and watched the interaction between Tony and al Raqman. They had evidently had a fairly cordial conversation, although the body language didn't indicate that they had reached any sort of agreement. Al Raqman saw her watching him and gave her a look that chilled her to the bone. She shuddered on the inside, but tried to keep her outward appearance nonplussed. Al Raqman finally turned away with a look of disgust on his face. She decided that her appearance, in western clothing with no headdress, must not be to his liking. Frankly, she hoped that was exactly what was the problem. He better get used to it, she concluded. Not many burqas where he was headed.

*   *   *   *

Near the village of Chigyong-dong, South Korea

CIVILIANS IN PEACE

June 16, 7:15 pm (1015 GMT)

John had set the remaining squad members up into two positions just to the south of the bridge. The process of extracting themselves and Corporal Lott from the minefield had been excruciating but successful.

The team members continued to expand and improve their new bunkers. John and Pho went back out and checked the circuitry and relocated the triggering circuit so that they could detonate the bridge from their new position. After that, they contemplated their next move.

No vehicle traffic had come down from either the South or the North since the last bombardment. Prior to that barrage, there had been a small but steady trickle of civilian vehicles heading south. Collins speculated that artillery delivered minefields must have closed the roads. John guessed that he was probably right. More than four hours had passed from the time of the barrage and they were still as cut off and alone as they had been.

As John walked from one position to another, more out of boredom than for any real purpose, he heard a vehicle approaching from the South. In a mild panic, his first thought was that it could be an enemy vehicle. He sprinted for the B Team bunker – it had been improved on enough that he had stopped mentally referring to it as a foxhole about an hour before. He got himself into the bunker and into a position to watch to the south just as an up-armored Hummer came into view. He watched it approach, realizing that the approach of an enemy vehicle from the south was extremely unlikely, especially an enemy in an American vehicle. Feeling somewhat foolish for having panicked, he climbed back out, telling the other guys to stay down while he checked out who was coming.

The vehicle driver saw him and angled the Hummer over to his position. As it rolled to a stop, the front passenger door opened and John recognized his Platoon Sergeant, SFC Williamson. He made his way over to the senior man, with a feeling of relief in his chest. Williamson seemed just as pleased to see him.

"Cooper! Thank God you guys are intact. We got the shit pounded out of us at bridge 8. The LT's dead and we haven't heard from Company since we got pounded. Where's Cody?"

"He's dead. So's Smithson. Our radio's gone as well. Corporal Lott stepped on a small mine – his left foot is in bad shape and we're treating him for shock."

"So who is senior here?"

"I guess I am, although that's a relative term. We have only PFCs and PVTs here. I moved us to the south side to get us out of the minefield and to give us a better chance to blow the bridge if we need to. Can you send us another radio and a new squad leader?

"Coop. You *are* the new squad leader. We haven't been able to raise 3rd squad either at bridge 6 north of you. I'm the only one from the platoon HQ. Staff Sergeant Clemens is still with us, but he is in charge of bridge 8. I'm afraid you are going to have to stay here at seven. I'm going to try to get up to bridge 6 and see what is going on.

"There's an AP minefield across that intersection ahead. Can the Hummer make it through those, Sergeant?"

"We already made it through one, although we had to replace a tire. I had thrown in an extra spare so I still have one more to go. Got to give it a try. I'm going to try a new tactic. Once I check on 3rd squad, I'll come back through. I'll take Lott back with me when I do – we have that little aid station still intact at bridge 8. Coop – you've done well here. Keep it up."

"We will. See you soon."

John watched the Hummer work its way across the bridge surface slowly. At the far side he saw it stop and Williamson get out again. Amazingly, Williamson climbed onto the hood with a

Squad Automatic Weapon and positioned himself into a decent prone supported firing position. Williamson then fired off a few test shots. Satisfied, he motioned for the driver to start forward. John watched as the vehicle inched forward. After about twenty meters, Williamson made a closed fist "Stop" sign and then let out a burst from the SAW. Two small secondary explosions sounded from about 15 meters in front of the vehicle. Williamson then motioned for the driver to move forward again. This process repeated itself several times until the vehicle was through the intersection. Satisfied that they were clear, Williamson again signaled for the driver to stop and climbed back into the passenger compartment. With that, the Hummer rounded a bend in the road and disappeared from sight.

"Williamson is one bad-ass NCO," said Root, who had climbed out with John's fellow team members to watch the process. "Of course, growing up in Cleveland, Korea is like a walk in the park for him."

The others nodded and chuckled softly at that observation.

"Sure wish I had thought of that back when we were stuck in the middle of those damn mines," John mused.

"Heck," said Campbell. "None of us thought of it either. Live and learn. Well, Coop. What do we do now?"

"Let's all huddle and figure that out." He waved over to the other team's position and motioned for them to gather around him.

*   *   *   *

John shifted himself into as comfortable a position as he could. The team brief had gone well. He had shared what he had learned from their Platoon Sergeant, which wasn't much, and the guidance that they were to hold fast until they were told otherwise. PFC Collins had reported that Lott was in a lot of pain and in and out of it, but that he seemed to be in no immediate danger. Finally, John established a watch schedule that had half of the men resting and the rest watching and continuing to work to improve their bunkers and to begin the construction of alternate positions. All in all, he felt that they were doing everything they could.

As darkness fell, not long after John had finally be able to get some sleep, they heard firing pick up again from the north. They could again see flashes and hear the thunder-like sound of what must be artillery. This time, they could also hear sharper cracks that sounded like direct fire weapons. Soon, all of the team members were awake and on edge.

"Sounds like a hell of a firefight near bridge 6. Sure wish Williamson would come back through," said Root.

"No doubt," John replied.

The firing from the north seemed to reach a crescendo and then dropped off quickly. The team members speculated on what that meant, but came up with no consensus. The optimists among then assumed it meant good news, the pessimists bad. While that debate dragged on, a pair of headlamps appeared from the north, coming around the bend in the road.

"Look's like HMMV lights," shouted Williams, much louder than necessary in the small bunker. As the vehicle approached the intersection, they expected it to slow. Instead, it continued to barrel toward them. About half way through the minefield, a small explosion erupted under its right front tire. The vehicle veered slightly to the right but continued to bull forward. It reached the relative safety of the bridge, right wheel rim sparking as it ground its way across the concrete surface. The vehicle pulled off of the south side and screeched to a halt next to their position.

John climbed out of the bunker, weapon at the ready, just as Williamson pulled himself out of the crazily tilted vehicle. Williamson looked at the ruined tire in disgust.

"What's going on at bridge 6, Sergeant?" John asked.

"Third squad is gone. The Koreans hit them with a barrage of light high explosive rounds and while the squad was hunkered down in their bunkers bulled across the bridge in tanks. We were about a kilometer south, changing a tire, when we saw the whole thing. I don't know whether the charges failed to go off or if they didn't get the chance to set them off, but the bridge is intact."

"What should we do?'

"I'm going to keep working south – as long as this rim holds out. Got to get word of this to Company or Battalion. You guys need to stay here. If you see tanks, or if a heavy bombardment starts, blow the bridge and head south."

"Can you take Lott, Sergeant?"

"We'll take him, Coop, but I don't know how far we'll get."

John motioned for Williams and Campbell to go get the Corporal. They hustled to do so. After he was loaded into the back of the Hummer, Williamson said "Good Luck," and headed south. The rim, with what rubber remained, ground into the asphalt but the vehicle was quickly up to a respectable speed and was soon out of sight. If possible, an even more oppressive sense of loneliness and vulnerability settled over the site.

"We can't be the northernmost American troops for real, can we?" asked Campbell. "We don't even have anti-tank weapons. Maybe we should bug out while we still can?"

"We have one huge anti-tank weapon," John replied, pointing at the bridge.

"Then let's blow it and go. We can't possibly hold here."

John thought for a second and then shook his head. "Our orders were clear. We need to delay blowing this bridge until the last possible second. If a counterattack were to appear, counting on this bridge, and we've blown it, it could ruin everything."

"What counterattack? We're getting our asses kicked from what I can see. Why should we stay around here for no reason?" countered Campbell.

"Because that's what we were ordered to do. We're not debating this."

"Why? Because Cody decided to make you a team leader we don't need to discuss things? You're not even the senior man here. Two of us have more time in grade than you."

"True enough, but being in the team leader position trumps time in grade. Even if it didn't, I wouldn't leave. We may very well need to blow this bridge, but I'm going to make sure that we do it at the right time based on the right events or orders."

Root and Williams watched the debate. John was confident that they would stick with him, but to make sure he turned to them and said "Any questions from you guys?"

"No, Sir," answered Root, who had gotten back from boot camp and Advanced Individual Training just before the unit mobilized and thus was still more prone to rote responses than the more senior soldiers. "No," replied Williams, with much less certainty.

"Good," said John. "Williams, go tell Team One what we are doing. And Root, don't call me Sir – I work for a living." John smiled to himself; he had always wanted to use that old line favored by Boot Camp Drill Sergeants everywhere and finally found himself with the opportunity. His moment of pleasure was short-lived, as the weight of their predicament very quickly returned to his shoulders. He nodded at the group. Williams scurried out to head for the other bunker. Root and Campbell returned to watching the northern approaches. John sat down heavily with his back to the earthen bunker wall, trying to think what else needed doing.

*　　　*　　　*　　　*

"Yes, commander," said Major Li, clicking off the mike. For what must have been the twentieth time that night, his Brigade commander had called to encourage them to move faster. In response, Major Li had moved his tank into the third position in the line of tanks. One of the reasons he was so much farther forward was that a good number of tanks, and their crews, had fallen prey to the vicious attacks from enemy aircraft. The other reason was that he had passed many, many tanks so that he could more clearly see the front and push the lead tanks to move as quickly as possible.

Enemy air strikes had initially been punishing, although they had dropped off considerably. Division had pushed forward mobile air defense units, and those fires seemed to be discouraging the enemy from the low bomb and missile runs they had tried early in the day. One helicopter assault force had been especially hard hit, with Li himself seeing at least six American Apaches shot from the sky.

Seizing the bridges had gone considerably better than he had imagined. After the first two bridges, held by South Korean forces, they had encountered no anti-tank fire. The method for seizing each bridge had settled into a familiar pattern. They would first mass their assault force of tanks just out of sight of a bridge; normally no more than a kilometer away. Next, an artillery barrage would go in, in hopes of cutting the bridge detonation lines or keeping the soldiers assigned to detonate the bridges too occupied, or too dead, to complete their task. Finally, the artillery would switch to all High Explosive rounds, devastating to infantry in the open but of almost no consequence to a tank except for a highly improbable direct hit. The tanks would rush forward and across the bridge, blasting anything that looked like it might conceal an anti-tank gunner or a sapper team assigned to blow the span.

"So far, so good," he thought to himself. Six bridges down, two to go. With luck, his Brigade would be done by morning, and the follow on forces could begin the push for Seoul.

He turned back to the task of arranging his forces for the assault on bridge number seven.

*   *   *   *

Campbell shook John's leg to bring him fully awake and reported that he heard what he thought to be tanks to the north. John listened, nodded and said he heard the same thing. He tested, for the fourth time in the last hour, the circuitry for the bridge charges and was satisfied that he still got green lights across the board. "Keep and eye out. I'll blow the bridge as soon as the first tank gets near it."

*   *   *   *

Li keyed the mike three times, the agreed upon signal for the artillery barrage to begin. Moments later, he heard the now familiar sound of large rounds passing overhead. Soon, blasts from the south penetrated his headphones. The forward observation team reported that the rounds were hitting precisely on target on the north end of the span and the area around the intersection. Their "refugee" scouts had given very specific information regarding the locations of the over watching forces, so Li felt good that they were making life hell for the U.S. forces down at this bridge.

The spotters directed one gun to shift its focus to the south of the bridge, to ensure that any soldiers trying to flee to the south would have a more difficult time of it. After several minutes, Li switched his indicator frequency to the battalion net and indicated that the assault force should move out. He then switched back to the command net so that he could give the artillery the lift and shift command when necessary.

*   *   *   *

John awoke as the first round whistled in. The blast was thunderous, but not as close as some of the last barrage had been. He moved to a position where he could see the bridge and saw that the rounds were hitting primarily to the north of the bridge, thankfully several hundred feet from where they were now. Occasionally a round would hit closer, but both of the new team bunkers seemed outside of the beaten zone.

"I'm going to blow the bridge," he announced, to no one in particular.

"Good. Blow the sonofabitch," replied Campbell. "Then, let's get out of here."

"I agree." John picked up the demolition initiation box. He keyed it on and waited for it to complete the self-test. The first row of lights began to turn green, but after the third light did so, the fourth started blinking red. Next, the fifth, sixth, seventh and eighth lights did the same thing.

"Shit. The wire must be cut after charge three."

"Who cares," said Campbell. "Blow what you have."

"It's not enough. Charges one through three won't bring it down."

The three other members of his small team looked at him, expecting more. "So what do we do now?" asked Root.

John struggled for an answer. Finally, he said, "I'll go find the break and reconnect it. Campbell, you keep watching this box. When you see it go all green, give me thirty seconds and then blow the bridge."

Campbell nodded, looking apprehensive. "What if the bad guys get here first?"

"Then blow what you have. I'll get out of the way as best I can. If the bridge blows, stay here. If it doesn't go down, bug out. I would head for the hills to the east, not to the south. We know the bad guys are heading that way. They probably won't send people into the hills to chase a few infantry soldiers."

The other three stared at him and nodded their understanding. John grabbed the small toolbelt that had come with the bridge demolition kit, adjusted his helmet and body armor, nodded at the rest, and climbed out of the bunker. As he did so, the noise level increased immensely. He crouched and ran for the bridge. On his way, he waved over to the Alpha Team bunker indicating that they should stay in place. He had no idea if they saw him or not.

When he reached the bridge, he worked his way along the east rail, feeling sure that the break in the wire must be there. The intensity of the fire around him seemed to increase. More rounds began hitting south of the bridge and down in the gorge below him. One particularly close round sent pieces of metal into the rail next to him. His head snapped to the side, evidently a piece of shrapnel had caught him on the Kevlar. He stopped and dropped to his knees, doing a quick self-assessment that led to the conclusion that he was fine. He felt a stinging in his right shoulder, but it didn't seem to be anything major. He crouched even lower as he made his way along. Once he passed where he knew charge three was, he reached out his hand and started to trace the wire with his fingers. Everything seemed fine until just before he reached charge number four. Suddenly, his fingers felt a ragged end to the wire. Again dropping to his knees, he craned his head to where he could see the wire. A piece of shrapnel had torn a two-inch gap in the wire. The wires on either end were cut as if from a massive pull rather than by a sharp instrument. John reached into his tool belt and brought out wire cutters and black electricians tape. As he did so, he heard a deep rumbling from the north. Rising up to look fully over the railing, he saw enemy tanks burst from the tree line to the north of the bridge. A couple of the tanks followed the road and made better time than the others. Most traveled cross-country, churning up mud from fields whose crops had only barely pushed through the topsoil in the early summer.

Frantic, John turned back to his task. He knew that if he didn't get this done quickly he was a dead man. Either the tank gunners would mow him down or Campbell would blow the bridge with him still on it. Neither possibility excited him. He pulled the wires to get enough slack to close the gap and to give him enough wire to work with. He quickly split the wires and used the stripping tool to give him bare ends to join. Almost feverishly, he spliced the wires and wrapped them in black tape as quickly as he could. Glancing again, he saw that the first tank had reached the intersection and had turned so that it was lined up on the bridge. John, realizing his time was out, ran as fast as he could toward the southern end. As he did so, large rounds from what must have been a coaxially mounted machine gun on the lead tank began pounding the bridge surface at his feet. He jigged left, but the railing stopped his leftward movement after only a meter. A great whoosh of air moved past his head and to his amazement he saw a main tank round explode a couple of hundred yards to his front.

Another trail of machine gun rounds started to kick up dirt to his right. He watched as the rounds slowly walked their way toward an intersection with his path. They showed no sign of slowing as they stitched ever closer. Desperate, still running full speed, he put a hand on the bridge rail and launched himself over it. He plunged into the darkness, not sure whether he was still over water or close enough to the bank that he would find rocks below. All he knew was that whatever he found couldn't be worse than the hot steel that was seeking out his body.

He felt the splash of water and then the jar of ground, in quick succession. He had been above the point where the river just met the bank and had splashed down in less than three feet of water. That had been enough, however, to cushion his fall enough that nothing seemed broken or sprained. He rolled onto his back on the bank, looking up at the bridge. As he did so, he saw the first tank rolling toward the middle of the bridge, firing in front of it indiscriminately. Just as it reached the middle, a great roar went up as the pre-placed charges, ready for so many years and now called to duty, went off one after another in almost indistinguishably small intervals. The pressure of the blasts crushed him down into the bank and pieces of concrete and steel began impacting all around him. With the air crushed out of him, he felt himself drop into unconsciousness.

   *   *   *   *

Major Li felt a quick sense of satisfaction as the lead tank rolled onto the bridge. He reached for the handset to tell the artillery to shift fires to the southern approaches to the bridge and to report the Brigade's latest success to the commander. Just as he keyed the mike, the lead tank rose up in the middle of the bridge. In fact, the whole bridge seemed to rise several dozen centimeters into the air, before beginning a fall that carried it past its original position and into the gap below. Li watched as the second tank in line tried in vain to stop its momentum. It too rolled off of the abutment and fell headfirst into the 20-meter gap. A deafening sound rolled over him. A sense of failure stayed behind after the sound passed him by. He brought the handset to his lips and gave the lift and shift command. He then toggled the radio to the secure command net and reported what had happened to his brigade commander.

"We will need the bridging equipment brought forward, Sir," he said, expecting a quick acknowledgement. Instead, what he got back was a long pause. "Li, there is no bridging equipment. The Americans targeted it once they found it. It is all gone."

Li waited for his brigade commander to continue, expecting guidance. The wait became a silence. Li finally keyed his mike and asked, "We can't bypass or ford here. What is your guidance, Sir."

Again after a long pause, his commander came on and said, "I will need to get guidance. Hold where you are."

Li acknowledged that and passed the word onto the lead battalion commander. In his mind, he pictured the line of tanks that was slowly bunching up behind him, stretching from his position north to the border. Scenes from the so-called "Highway of Death" from the first Gulf War appeared in his mind. If the American strike aircraft returned, they would find a similar target rich environment.

Li watched as the Battalion commander spread his tanks into a defensive arc; oriented to the south. The maneuver was well executed, but the best-executed defense in this battle was the same as a defeat. Li saw nothing to criticize, and ordered his own driver to move into a more concealed position.

* * * *

John slowly became aware of his surroundings. He realized that his feet and lower legs were draped into the water while his upper legs, torso, head and arms were spread askew on the riverbank. He waited until his eyes became more focused and then experimentally raised his head a few inches. Where the bridge had been he saw only night sky. Around him on the bank and sticking up from the water were several large sections of the bridge. The biggest pieces had fallen almost straight down, but large chunks, some rivaling the size of small refrigerators, had been thrown all around. Incredibly, no chunk of any size had come down on him. He lay his head down onto the bank again, quickly saying a short prayer of thanks. He had never been particularly religious, but had found himself becoming more so as he had gone through this mobilization and deployment. Nothing new about that, he imagined. He was sure that many other soldiers, perhaps even most, went through similar experiences.

He rolled over carefully, bringing his legs out of the water. He was sore almost everywhere, but everything seemed to work properly. He crawled a few meters up the bank, then stopped to rest and more fully develop his plan. He was sure that the bad guys had not gotten tanks across the river, but they could have troops across. He had been out of it for at least a couple of hours so who knew what had gone on since then? Would his team have bugged out? Were they still in their bunkers?

He contemplated these questions and then decided that he had better find out. He crawled the rest of the way up the bank. He then continued to crawl slowly to the area where he thought his B Team bunker should be. His eyes were well adjusted to the dark, and he soon thought he could make out the mound that was the top of the bunker. He whispered out "Campbell." No response came back. "Campbell!" he called louder. Finally, he called out in an almost everyday voice "Guys. Are you in there!"

"Coop? Is that you?" John heard. He wasn't sure who had responded.

"It's me. Who is this?"

"It's Root. Williams is in here with me."

"Where's Campbell?"

"He went to check on the other team after he blew the bridge. He hasn't been back since."

"I'm coming in. Don't shoot my ass."

John crawled the rest of the way and then dragged himself into the bunker through the left rear entrance. Root and Williams give him hugs, both tight enough to make John's body ache in protest.

"Where have you been?" asked Root.

"I was knocked out by the blast. What have you seen going on across the river?"

"Before it got too dark, we saw the Koreans moving into what looked like a defensive position. Nothing since then."

"What time is it?" asked John.

"4:00 a.m."

"Heck. I was out longer than I thought. Anything from the south?"

"Nothing. It's been very lonely out here."

"It always is at the tip of the spear. Why did you guys stick around?"

"Because you told us to before you headed out to the bridge," Williams replied, as if the answer should have been obvious.

"Do you think Campbell took off?" John asked.

Williams said, "I think so. Do you?"

"Don't know. I'm going to head over to A Team and see if they saw him, or if they are still there."

He stood slowly, with an audible groan. Root said, "I'll go, sir. You sit and rest up. I'll be right back."

"Thanks, Root. And stop calling me Sir."

*   *   *   *

Root returned and said that the other bunker was empty. "Those sonsofbitches," said Williams.

John agreed, but then added "We may need to do the same thing soon. Let's see what morning brings." They settled in, watching as the eastern horizon slowly brightened. Just as they could start to make out the shapes of tanks across the river, they heard the sounds of jets approaching from the south. Before they could visually spot the aircraft, huge explosions sounded from the north side of the bridge. They saw two of the more visible tanks burning, with pieces of debris raining down around them. Secondary explosions began to burst from the burning hulks as their ammunition cooked off.

Two jets flashed over, followed by two more. More explosions sounded from the North.

"I don't know about you guys, but I feel a lot less lonely," John said.

The other two nodded and exchanged small smiles.

*   *   *   *

Major Li watched as the tanks around him were destroyed one by one. He keyed his mike to report the air strike to higher, but got no reply. He tried the artillery Brigade frequency, but they reported back that they couldn't reach their higher headquarters either.

He switched back to Brigade radio net and again got no reply. Reluctantly, he jumped up to the Division net, something he was not allowed to do in most situations. When he got to the division frequency, he heard frantic reports but could hear no sign of anyone in control or with a grasp of the situation. He decided against adding to the confusion. Instead, he continued to drop to the Brigade net from time to time, returning to the division net only when he had assured himself that the Brigade net remained silent.

He had just made the switch for what must have been the twentieth time when his gunner yelled out "Fast movers approaching."

Li looked up to ensure that the hatch over his head was sealed. Satisfied, he leaned back in his seat. He had just decided to try to formulate a prayer, something he had seen his grandmother do in his youth, when the 500 lb bomb struck the front of the turret and turned itself and much of the front of the tank into molten metal. He died before he had made much progress in his journey away from the state religion of atheism.

"We don't accomplish anything in this world alone ... and whatever happens is the result of the whole tapestry of one's life and all the weavings of individual threads from one to another that creates something."

- Sandra Day O'Connor

CHAPTER SIXTEEN

Balad Air Base, Iraq
June 18, 9:20 am (0620 GMT)

Tony felt amazingly better after a good night's sleep in a real bed, a shower and a change into a fresh uniform. The bag of saline solution that they had given him had replaced some of the fluid volume he had lost over the last couple of days and had no doubt helped as well. His shoulder was well dressed, and his head had taken only a couple of small stitches. Out of vanity, he had pulled off the bulky bandage they had used to cover his head wound. After shaving, he looked at himself in the mirror and thought he looked fairly normal, if somewhat beaten up. He decided that he was ready to face the day.

A guard was posted outside of his room. He asked why and the young man said, "To let people know when you are on your way. They have a debriefing scheduled for you, set to begin as soon as you are ready. We're to head over to the JOC right away."

"Son, you are never going to get very far in this man's Army if you are too literal, or not literal enough. They said that we should go over as soon as I am ready. However, I am not ready. I need a soda and something to eat. Let's head over to the chow hall first."

"Sir, I think they want you right away."

"Corporal, what rank was the person who told you that?"

"Sir, he was my squad leader."

"Then I outrank him, do I not? Walk with me and tell me about yourself."

Tony quizzed the young man on his life, his schooling, and his plans for the future as they made their way to the chow hall. They sat briefly while Tony drank two Diet Cokes and ate a hot dog. "Have you seen CNN or Fox News, Corporal? What's going on in the outside world? Especially Korea"

"A bunch of countries are pissed at us for invading Lebanon. A bunch are quiet. Only a few have come out and said that they support what we've done. The U.S. media is howling about how we missed al Raqman the same way we missed Osama bin Laden. Overall, about what you would expect, sir."

"That's a pretty good synopsis, corporal. You keep up on the news pretty well. Have you considered becoming an officer?"

"Sir, I've banked almost every dollar I've earned during my time here. I am planning on going to college on the Army's dime and then getting as far away from the Army as I can."

"That's too bad. The Army needs some officers who have had enlisted experience. They make better decisions."

"Did you have enlisted time, sir?"

"A little. Not much, but enough to make a difference in my opinion. What is the word on Korea, Corporal?"

"The North is still shelling in several locations. They moved some forces into the south but have stopped. Some serious fighting – we seem to be pounding them from the air. No change in the last couple of days."

"Any reports of U.S. casualties? My son is there."

"None yet, sir. Probably will be, I would guess."

They sat silently as Tony pondered that response.

"What is this debriefing about, if I can ask, sir?"

"I could tell you, but I would have to kill you. Watch the news in the next day or two and I think you will know. Well, we better get over there."

When they reached the Joint Operations Center, the corporal led Tony to an out of the way conference room. As he was led in, the room grew quiet. Tony was shocked to see General David Petreus, the Centcom Commander, and LTG Lloyd Austin, the 18th Airborne Corp commander, as well as the 101st Airborne Commander.

LTG Lloyd Austin came over and wrapped Tony's normal size hand in his giant hand and said, "Tony, it is a pleasure to see you again. I remember you from Afghanistan when you headed up the construction on the new JOC at Bagram Airbase. We expected you a while ago."

"Sorry sir, if I had known who was waiting I would have hustled much more."

"No matter, you earned a little time. Damn, Tony. I thought you were pretty good in Afghanistan, but this was impressive. I'm going to introduce you around the table and then I want you to tell us the story from the beginning."

LTG Austin led Tony to a spot at the head of the table and introduced him as an old comrade in arms from Afghanistan. Tony smiled to himself, because from what he remembered Austin had spent about half the time they interacted in Afghanistan pissed at him because the JOC project was taking so long to complete. Gen Petreus and the 101st Airborne commander both shook his hand.

"Give it to us from the time you arrived at the objective, Colonel," directed General Petreus. Tony did so, leaving out a lot of details but hitting the broad strokes.

When he recounted the crash, he asked if the crash sites had been secured and the bodies recovered.

"They have. You were right. There were no survivors on the first chopper and the two pilots on your chopper were both killed in the crash. Majors Gears and Rodriquez were both mutilated pretty badly. Hell of a price to pay for not listening to you."

"Sir, I feel horrible for not asking this sooner, but how are the crew chief we carried out and Corporal Gonzales from my team?"

"The crew chief is still in serious condition and is enroute to Germany. He is expected to survive but he has serious internal injuries. Corporal Gonzales suffered a wound to his left chest. The bullet was slowed by his vest but penetrated his left lung. The CNN reporter's treatment on the spot saved his life. He's actually sitting up and eager to get out of bed. We hope to have him at the news conference."

"What news conference, General?

"Colonel, assuming that there are no surprises in the rest of your story, we are going to have a news conference in about 45 minutes announcing all of this to the world. You are going to be the featured attraction at this news conference. Do you have any problem with that timeline?" asked General Petreus.

"No sir. I think it is vital that Corporal Gonzales be there. Further, I think that it would be a good thing to have Linda, Miss Rogers, there to tell her story, if she is willing."

The General directed one of his staff members to go see about getting Corporal Gonzales there. He turned back to Tony and said, "We have extended the invitation to Ms. Rogers and she has agreed to speak after we give our presentation. Now quickly, tell us about what happened after the crash landing."

Tony proceeded to do so, interrupted by questions only a couple of times. He got a few laughs as he went through the string of calls it took to get to somebody who could arrange for someone to come and rescue them. At the end, he looked around the room and asked if there were any questions. LTG Austin asked, "Tony, you left out some details about a few things that we have heard from others. Did you lead the clearing of a building at Objective Calf in which you brought down a suicide bomber with your 9mm?"

"Hell sir, I got lucky with one shot, I missed with the others. Something must have gone wrong with his device or we would all have been dead."

"I'll take that as a yes. Did you take the guard at the farmhouse out with your bayonet?"

"Sir, it wasn't anything heroic like. Rahib Bretawi was the hero. He held the guy while I knifed him from behind."

"Did you lead the assault into the house that resulted in the capture of al Raqman? You used the term 'we' in your narrative."

"Corporal Gonzales, Rahib and I did that together."

"Did you leave the farmhouse so that you could distract the enemy, so that they would be delayed while you waited for friendly forces to arrive?"

"Sir, I thought I could bring some echeloned fires on them. I wanted to keep them pinned down as long as I could. Again, I did what you would have done in my place, nothing more."

General Petreus interrupted and said, "I think the point that General Austin is trying to make is that you did a hell of a job. It is my intention to put you in for the Congressional Medal of Honor, Colonel. If the President and Congress concur, you would be the first National Guardsman to be awarded that medal since the Korean War."

"Sir, with all due respect, I think that is overkill. I did what any of us would have done. The guys with me are the ones who deserve the recognition, especially those who won't be going home to their families."

"They will be recognized as well, although as the senior member there you will need to help us on writing out those narratives," replied LTG Austin. "Anything else we need to know, or you need to know, for that matter, before we hold the press conference?"

"Will we be announcing the nuclear material and/or the capture of al Raqman at this?" Tony asked.

"We won't be announcing anything; you will," replied General Petreus. "We have the podium set up so that you, Corporal Gonzales, Master Sergeant Patterson, Ms. Roberts and I are on the stage. You will spend most of the time briefing the situation. I want you to do it in a timeline narrative similar to what you did here. I will chime in as needed but this is your show. You are representing us in this. I don't want this coming through my press guy or through others. Your story is powerful and the world needs to hear it from you."

"Sir, again with all due respect, I think you are overstating my part in this. Mark and Robert were the brains behind the Syria mission. Colonel Hansen led the team. The pilots kept us alive at the cost of their own lives. The reporters saved us by being willing to choose sides and to get involved. I'm not comfortable overplaying my involvement in this."

"That's the beauty of the Army, Colonel," replied GEN Petreus. "You do what you are told to do when you are told to do it. Any questions, Colonel?" The general looked stern but a touch of a smile at the edge of his mouth gave the truth away that he wasn't really that upset.

"A couple of things, sir. Have all of the families of the soldiers wounded or killed been notified?"

"They have. You can use names."

"How about the CIA involvement?

"No. That is not to be made public. You are to maintain the military cover of Major Anderson and Captain Palmer."

"Okay, sir. I'm ready."

As they gathered in the side hallway, Tony first saw Corporal Gonzales. Incredibly, he was up on crutches. They hugged and exchanged greetings like old friends. Tony asked about the crutches and the young NCO explained that he couldn't support any of the weight of his torso. "They brought me over in a wheelchair, but I refuse to not be on my feet for my international television debut, Sir." Tony saw that even the slightest turn or bend was excruciating for the young man. By resting his weight on the crutches, Gonzales could indeed stay upright, but just barely. Next, Tony shook hands with Master Sergeant Patterson, his arm in a cast and a sling but otherwise looking fit. At that moment, Linda joined them. Tony gave her a hug as well. Linda pulled him aside and said, "You are the man of the hour. You saved us all."

"From what I remember, you are the one who took out a guy who was about to scatter my brains all over a wall."

"About that. You need to downplay my involvement, and the involvement of Rahib, for a couple of reasons. First, I won't be able to work again as a credible journalist if the word gets out that I did what I did. Second, it will make my views on this seem less credible if it becomes apparent that I so clearly took sides."

"But that's crazy. If you and Rahib hadn't done what you did, we would all be dead."

"It might be crazy, but that is how the game is played. You will ruin my career if you let out too many details. I will write a book on this someday, and maybe then I'll give some details, but for now please leave me out of this as much as you can."

"O.K. I'll do what I can. However, I'm not great at lying."

"You are not really lying. You are omitting."

"Oh yeah, Linda. Does your husband ever buy that?"

"I don't have a husband. How about you? Are you married, Tony?" she asked in a tone of voice and with a look in her eyes that gave Tony a momentary rush.

213

He gathered himself and said, "I am. Happily. And she's waiting at home with my daughter."

Linda smiled, "That's too bad. You know we women are supposed to have a thing for guys in uniform." Tony was surprised and a little amazed to see that she really did look disappointed.

"Yeah, but you have to remember that I don't wear this uniform much. Back home, I'm an overweight, middle-aged, married high school teacher. Not much excitement in that," Tony laughed.

"I don't know. A lack of excitement might be nice for a while. Oh well, you'll have to point me in the direction of one of these officers who isn't married."

"Would you settle for unhappily married? I know a couple of those."

They laughed and exchanged a hug before turning to make their way back to the group. General Petreus joined them and they were led into the large conference room. Cameras, lights and microphones pointed toward them as they made their way in. Tony recognized the logos of what looked to be every major American network and a few international ones as well. They made their way forward as still cameras snapped and buzzed, flashes nearly blinding them. When they were all on stage, something that took a little time because Corporal Gonzales required a great deal of assistance, Tony noticed that Linda hung back and to the side, creating a small but very noticeable distance from the group of soldiers.

General Petreus started with a brief statement that did not give many details other than to introduce the others on the podium with him. He stated that there would be a couple of announcements of worldwide importance. He gave the networks warning that if they were not carrying this news conference live, their audiences would miss out on a couple of very important items. With that, the execs at NBC and ABC decided to cut into the early morning news programs, much to the dismay of the talent on those high budget shows. The head of the news division at CBS decided to hold off for a while. He would be looking for work by the end of the week. The cable news channels were already carrying this event live. The presence of General Petreus alone was enough for them.

The general turned the microphone over to Tony. Tony nervously started into his narrative, gathering steam as he went on. He again skipped many of the details, but otherwise left out nothing he felt was important. He tried to spread out credit where credit was due as often as he could. He was especially complementary of the assault troops from the 101st Airborne and the engineers from the 112th Engineer Battalion, Ohio Army National Guard. When he talked about the nuclear material they had found, General Petreus interrupted him. He had arranged for several still photos of the canisters to be displayed on a looping PowerPoint presentation. Further, he had a packet of analysis passed out to every attendee. He assured them that the analysis confirmed the original field analysis conducted at the objective. With that, the General turned the microphone back over to Tony. Several reporters tried to interrupt with questions, but the General held up a finger, stared them down and said, "We'll take some questions at the end."

Tony picked up the narrative with the flight to Syria. He left out the names of those in attendance on the Syrian side, but played up the role of Colonel Hansen. He tried to say as many of the names of the American members of the delegation as he could and talk about their individual contributions. He did this as his way of trying to honor their service and their sacrifice. He worked to protect the identities of Robert and Mark, talking about them in the same manner as he did the other members of the team. He knew their real roles might come out at some point, but he didn't intend for those details to come from him.

The audience sat spellbound as he described the crash and subsequent events leading up to the fight at the farmhouse. He left out the details of the disagreement between him and the two active duty Majors, only saying that they had decided to stay with the wreckage in an attempt to link up with U.S. forces. He paused when it came time to reveal that capture of al Raqman. He turned to GEN Petreus who leaned over and said, "You tell them, and then we'll show some pictures."

There was a gasp when he revealed that they realized that the one survivor of the farmhouse occupants was Sheik al Raqman. Too late, CBS joined the news conference in progress. General Petreus stepped forward and called for another set of looped pictures, first showing al Raqman as he looked in file photos, and then showing photos of him in captivity, including photos of him receiving a medical exam in a manner that reminded Tony of Saddam Hussein. Like Saddam, and so many Hollywood stars upon their arrest, al Raqman looked like hell in the photos. Tony realized that they must have selected the least flattering shots they had to work with.

He took only a few more lines to complete his description of the rest of their time in the farmhouse, concluding with the fact that the A-10 pilots had killed or slowed enough of the bad guys that they were able to hold out for those few extra minutes until the helicopters arrived and killed or chased off the rest of the attackers. He mentioned Dana Maguire by name as having led the rescue mission. He concluded with the rescue of Master Sergeant Patterson and the crew chief and gave a review of the medical status of his team. He was momentarily nonplussed when he realized that he didn't even know the crew chief's name or rank, but Master Sergeant Patterson, who had spent the better part of a day caring for the man, chimed in with that information.

"Were you injured, Colonel?" yelled a reporter from the front row.

Tony looked at General Petreus who nodded that it was okay to answer.

"I guess this is as good a time as any to answer some questions," Tony said. "I suffered two very superficial wounds – one to my left shoulder and a couple of stitches to my head."

General Petreus stepped forward and motioned for another slide. On the screen was a shot of Tony as he was led from the helicopter after it had landed at the Forward Operating Base. The photo showed him with more of his body covered with blood than not. "Colonel Cooper received a bullet wound to his left shoulder. Further, he received a shrapnel wound to his scalp that led to a great deal of blood loss. Neither wound was life threatening, but don't let him fool you. They were in one hell of a fight. He also took at least two direct hits to his body armor. He has some impressive bruises as proof of those. Further, Colonel Cooper left out several details about his actions in this operation that I will fill you in on at a later time. It is my intention to recommend him for the Congressional Medal of Honor and his men for awards of great distinction as well."

The hands of almost every reporter shot up. The questions ranged from specifics about the nuclear material recovered to details about where al Raqman would be held and the charges he would face. General Petreus answered most of these; with many of his answers being "I don't want to go into the details of that at this time."

Visibly tiring of answering questions, he announced that the team had included two respected international reporters to provide an objective view of the operation and the items found. Unfortunately, Rahib had not survived the operation but he wanted to turn the microphone over to CNN reporter Linda

Rogers so that she could share her observations regarding the findings.

Linda made a very brief statement that basically mirrored what Tony had covered. She concluded with two items. First, she said, "I have no doubt that al Raqman and his organization, with the direct involvement of Iran and North Korea, and the indirect involvement of Syria and Russia, intended to construct several more dirty bombs and at least one atomic weapon to attack Middle Eastern and Western targets. The actions of U.S. forces in this case saved the world from horrific terrorist attacks." She concluded by saying, "I support what General Petreus recounted regarding Lt. Col. Cooper's actions. He and his men displayed the finest qualities of American soldiers. Not bad for a bunch of National Guardsmen. My prayers go out to those families whose loved ones will not be rejoining them after this operation." Her voice broke at the end of that sentence, but she continued. "Know that they died in service to their country and in service to the world. Finally, my thoughts go out to the family of Rahib Bretawi. He was also a hero in this situation, and he also paid the ultimate sacrifice."

Tony found himself with tears in his eyes, and several others seemed to be having the same problem. Hands again shot up, but this time the General cut them off by saying "That's all for today. We'll hold our standard briefing at 0800 local tomorrow." Questions rang out but he and his staff herded the group out of the room, down the hall, and into a small, quiet conference room.

"Nice job, everyone. I'll have my Public Information Officer handle the rest of these – not because you didn't do well but because you did everything you needed to. He can handle the rest."

"What's next for the rest of us, sir? Tony asked.

As he asked, the general's Chief of Staff hurried into the room and whispered into the general's ear. The general listened intently, nodding as he did so.

"I've just been told that the Syrians are announcing a change in leadership in their country. Assad is enroute to Iran, seeking asylum. The new leadership is announcing that Syria will end all support for Hezbollah and Hamas due to the ties those groups had to al Raqman's organization. Iran is crying ignorance about this whole situation. The President is about to announce that he will authorize the use of tactical nuclear weapons against troop formations in North Korea if they don't end their operation and demobilize their forces. Their move to the south has been stopped in the valleys in any event and our air forces are pounding their formations. I wouldn't be surprised if they sued for peace at any moment.

"You and the 112th are being fast tracked for redeployment home. The operation here is all but over. We've halted the assault into the Bekka – the government of Lebanon has asked for UN occupation. In fact, I have authorized the 112th to bring their wounded and dead home with them, as opposed to having those soldiers shipped back separately. The National Guard Bureau has asked to be given free hand in arranging for your transportation and reception home and they will be granted that."

"What will happen to al Raqman, sir?" Tony asked.

"He will be shipped to Guantanamo Bay."

"How tight is our evidence against him, sir?"

"Airtight. Why?"

"Why get him caught up in all the debate about Guantanamo Bay? Ship him to Leavenworth, give him a strong legal team, try him and convict him. Sentence him to life in prison with no contact with the outside world. That's what I would do, sir."

General Petreus asked, "Do you realize, Tony, that I had the same feedback for our civilian leadership? I was told that they would take my input under advisement."

"That's what I tell soldiers when I am going to ignore their advice, General."

"Me too. Good to know some things are the same all over. Nice job, Colonel. You did good."

"Thanks, sir. Damn shame about the men we aren't bringing home with us."

"It always is, Tony. It always is."

"War is always a matter of doing evil in the hope that good may come of it."
> - Sir Basil H. Liddel-Hart

CHAPTER SEVENTEEN

Balad Air Base, Iraq
June 29, 12:30 pm (0930 GMT)

The staff and commanders gathered around the table and waited for the arrival of Lt. Col. Maguire.

"Do you think he will have a flight date?" asked Captain Cristal, to no one in particular.

"Yes, but rumor has it that we need to leave a rear detachment behind. I volunteer you, Mike," said Matt Giardi.

"Hell, Colonel Cooper. If you hadn't got us caught up in all of this with al Raqman, we could have been home already," added Joe Bortello.

"Sorry, Joe. I should have thought of that and just let him go. Sorry for messing with your schedule," Tony retorted.

"I'm not arguing that you should have let him go. Couldn't you have just shot him?" Joe laughed.

"The thought occurred to me, trust me," Tony laughed. At that moment, Dana Maguire entered the room and the men grew silent.

"Guys, looks like we are finally done with debriefings, writing reports, interviews, and the like. We have received our movement order. We are going to Kuwait for two days of outprocessing, leaving tomorrow. We are then flying to Dix for three days of demobilization there. Finally, we are being flown to Columbus for a consolidated Battalion welcome home ceremony on July 4th at Nationwide Arena. This is one of the quickest demobs I have ever heard of."

"Sir, can we tell our families this timeline?" asked Captain Rosen.

"Normally the answer to that is no. In this case, National Guard Bureau has announced this already so the answer is yes."

"Any rear detachment?" Matt Giardi asked. "Cristal has volunteered to run that."

Dana did not see the look that Mike Cristal gave Giardi. Taking the information as legitimate, he said, "Mike, that's very generous of you. The answer to that question would normally be yes, but NGB wants this unit to go home together, so they are assigning another unit to take care of the stuff our rear detachment would do."

"Always glad to help, sir," said Mike Cristal, sticking his tongue out at Giardi. Again, Dana missed it all.

"A lot to do before we go. Let's get all of our stuff packed and the stuff we got in country turned in."

With that, the staff and commanders went out to share the good news.

"Tony, hold up," called Dana. "Have you heard from John?"

"I have – I actually talked to him yesterday. He is okay – picked up a little shrapnel in an artillery barrage – nothing too serious, actually sounds a lot like what I got. His squad lost some men. He said it was a long story. Can't wait to hear it. He said they might be flying him home for our welcome home ceremony."

"Are they flying him home due to his injury or is his whole unit coming home?"

"Neither one. I get the impression that he is being flown home as part of the whole welcome home ceremony brouhaha."

"Smells of special privilege, Tony. You heroes always get stuff like that."

"I would just have rather skipped it all, thank you very much."

"Too late for that. For all of us. Well, we better get ourselves packed up."

*　　　　　*　　　　　*　　　　　*

Atlanta, Georgia
June 30, 5:55 pm (2255 GMT)

"Linda Rogers. Thank you for joining us and sharing your fascinating story."

"Linda smiled and said, "My pleasure, Larry. Thanks for having me."

Turning away from her and looking directly into the camera, Larry King, in his rich baritone, continued, "And please join us tomorrow when our guests will be Susan Sarandan and Tim Robbins discussing their efforts aimed at mobilizing school children in an effort to save the polar bear population from the devastation being wrought by global warming."

Once the red light on the front camera went off, Linda stood while a technician removed her wireless microphone. She shook Larry's hand, but noticed that he returned the handshake in a perfunctory manner. However, on the way out of the studio, several crewmembers stopped her to shake hands and thank her for what she had done.

The full story of her involvement had indeed become public knowledge after Corporal Gonzalez had appeared on Fox's "The O'Reilly Factor." Corporal Gonzalez had made her out to be a combination of Florence Nightingale and Audie Murphy.

Her reporting on the mission had indeed placed her on a whirlwind tour of shows and interviews. The reception she had experienced today was not atypical. Her journalistic friends had become somewhat standoffish. She wasn't exactly shunned, but her friends seemed to treat her with a sense of distrust. The more liberal of her friends seemed to exhibit this to a higher degree. As someone who had always considered herself a liberal democrat, she was dismayed at this reaction. On the other hand, members of the general public had embraced her in a way she had never experienced.

She couldn't shake the feeling that her career at CNN was simultaneously soaring yet headed for an invisible brick wall. Her thoughts turned to the envelope sitting on her table at home. The envelope contained a job offer from the head of Fox's News Division. "Chief Correspondent for Military Affairs and Homeland Security." Two months ago, she would have discounted the idea of being considered for such a position laughable, and dismissed the thought of taking it out of hand. However, her experience in Lebanon had changed her view on the military. Further, her reception at Fox had been qualitatively different, indeed much better, than her reception at CNN. Finally, the money offered represented a significant increase.

Fox News? she thought to herself. A part of her felt like she would be selling her soul. On the other hand, she had always had a bit of a crush on Neil Cavuto...

"National Guard (and Reserve) soldiers, as you know, give up their jobs, their time with their family, make sacrifices to make sure this country is safe."
- Congressman Todd Tiahrt

CHAPTER EIGHTEEN

Columbus, OH
July 4, 1:00 pm (1800 GMT)

The crowd rose to its feet and began a thunderous ovation as the soldiers of the 112th Engr Battalion began to march down the aisles to begin the welcome home ceremony. The Ohio National Guard Band played an appropriate march that was drowned out by the crowd. Tony looked for Rachel and Julie and spotted them sitting with David Rosen's wife, Megan. Megan was holding David's new daughter, born in late June. Julie was waving a small American flag and smiling broadly. Rachel was searching the soldiers, not having spotted Tony at the lead of the second column.

As in the going away ceremony, Tony led half of the troops up one aisle and Dana led the other half up the other. Unlike the going away ceremony, this ceremony was being held in the capital city of Columbus at the Nationwide Arena, home of the Columbus Blue Jackets NHL team and involved the entire battalion, not like the individual company going away ceremonies they had done on their way out. The Governor, both Senators and many, many other VIPs filled the small stage set up in one end of the arena floor. As Tony and Dana reached the point where the troops would be seated, they peeled off and made their way to the stage. The CSM and Joe Bortello took their places and ensured that the troops got seated as quickly as could be done with 450 soldiers, a few of whom were still sporting injuries.

Tony and Dana met at the side of the stage and made their way to their assigned seats. Only after all of the troops were seated did the crowd begin to quiet. Tony looked around the arena and saw that while the crowd did not fill every seat, it came fairly close. The exploits of the 112th had been fodder for the local and national news media and the public seemed eager to celebrate a unit's successes after the years of ambiguity regarding the conflicts in Afghanistan and Iraq. Dana leaned over to Tony and said, "This could be painful. I hope that every VIP isn't given a chance to speak."

"Look around you, Dana. If people are worried about global warming, I think we have pinpointed a potential source of lots of hot air."

As it turned out, the speeches were indeed held to a minimum. Major General Kambic, the Adjutant General of the Ohio National Guard and Governor Secrest gave the only speeches, mercifully short, before the awards portion of the program began. It was then that the crowd, and the troops, received a shock. Governor Secrest, at the end of his remarks, introduced a special guest. He asked that the crowd rise to welcome their featured speaker and the person who would be handing out the awards. With that, he introduced the President of the United States, President Clark.

*   *   *   *

John stood in the wings, watching from a position where he could see the podium but not the crowd. He was amazed at the rapid changes his life had undergone. After a day watching jets flying over, a column of 8th Army tanks had approached their position from the South. A Major, John never got his name, had assumed command of the southern portion of the bridge site and sent John back toward where the survivors of his battalion were gathering. Before he tasked John with taking his three-man team back, the Major had him and his two teammates write out narratives about the events that had occurred. He told the three of them that they had made a huge difference. A similar event had stopped the North Koreans in the parallel valley to the west. Between those two events, the invasion of the south was over. He had said that all that was left was for the North's leaders to decide how many more of its men and equipment they wanted to lose before surrendering.

John, Root and Williams were welcomed back at their battalion like prodigal sons. The battalion commander, a college professor in civilian life and the Command Sergeant Major, a warehouse supervisor, had come over personally to hug them and to tell them that so far they were the northernmost survivors of the Battalion. The three of them were again asked to write out narratives, something they were rapidly tiring of. Finally, they were among the first of the Ohio Guardsmen to be sent to the large airbase near Seoul. There they got all of the amenities of life they had grown accustomed to at home: showers, beds with sheets, hot food.

John was called to the 8th Army Headquarters where he was further tasked with writing out a narrative and was subjected to a more formal debriefing. Finally, he was sent back to his platoon, which was down to fifteen members. Out of 31 platoon members, ten were listed as missing, five were confirmed killed, three were seriously wounded, including Corporal Lott, and thirteen were present and fit for duty. Of those thirteen, three were under investigation for dereliction of duty and were confined to quarters. The remaining ten had been assigned duty that consisted mostly of resting, relaxing, and writing reports.

Orders for John to return home had come through on July 1.
At a small going away ceremony, he was shocked when the
Division commander appeared and promoted him to Corporal.
The Commander also announced that John was being sent home
to take part in the welcome home ceremony for his father's unit.
The troops had by now heard all about the events in Lebanon and
a ragged cheer, which quickly gained strength, went up.

Finally, ten thousand air miles and three days later, he found
himself standing in the wings, with only the guidance that he
would be called out when the time was right. He listened to the
proceedings, nervously awaiting his cue.

Did they just introduce the President?!

*　　　　　*　　　　　*　　　　　*

The crowd went wild. The President had made several trips to
Columbus as a candidate but always with much fanfare and
disruption of air and freeway traffic. Tony couldn't imagine how
they had managed to keep this visit a secret.

President Clark waited for the exact moment when the energy
and noise of the ovation began to die on its own and then gestured
for silence – a trick he had learned on the campaign trail that
made it look as if he had the crowd in the palm of his hand. He
looked around at the guests on the stage, nodding at faces he
recognized. He then launched into his prepared remarks. He
talked about the 112th representing the best of what this nation had
to offer. He talked about the role of the National Guard. He
talked, movingly, about the soldiers the 112th had lost in the
operation, asking their family members in attendance to stand and
be recognized by the crowd. Finally, he talked about the
difference the unit had made in making the world safer.

He next began with the awards. He announced that every
soldier would be given a Global War on Terrorism medal, which
was standard. He also announced that the unit, and every soldier

in it, was receiving a Presidential Unit Citation, which was not standard. He then listed the awards that had been granted to soldiers of the Battalion, including 15 Purple Hearts, 35 Meritorious Service Medals, 16 Bronze Stars, 12 with "V" devices showing valor. Then, he said, that they had a couple of other awards they wanted to give out.

He and MG Kambic took a position and a Sergeant Major with a State of Ohio Headquarters patch on his shoulder stepped to the microphone and called out "Lt. Col. Dana Maguire, post." Dana stood and marched to a position in front of the President and saluted. The President returned the salute in a fashion not at all bad for a civilian. The Sergeant Major then said "Attention to Orders." With that, all military members in attendance stood at attention, as did all of the VIPs on stage. Tony looked out and saw that many of the older male guests in the crowd, probably veterans he guessed, also stood. The Sergeant Major then continued, "The Silver Star is herby awarded to Lt. Col. Dana M. Maguire, Ohio Army National Guard, for valorous service in ..."

Tony listened to the text of the citation and felt it was right on. It talked first about Dana's role in leading his troops into a hostile objective. The bulk of the citation dealt with the rescue mission, adding some details that Tony hadn't even known before, namely that Dana had had to push the issue of using the infantry's helicopters to effect a rescue – Tony learned later that the infantry had wanted to pass the job on to Special Forces Command in northern Israel. Doing so would have taken another fifteen to twenty minutes, time that would have made all of the difference in terms of how this had all worked out.

At the end of the narrative, President Clark pinned the medal to Dana's chest and had him turn to face the crowd for an incredible round of applause. He then motioned for Dana to fall in next to MG Kambic. When he was in position, the Sergeant Major then called out "Corporal Cooper, Post!"

Tony twitched and took a half step to begin to follow in Dana's footsteps. He stopped when he realized that the Sergeant Major had said Corporal, not Colonel. He saw some motion out of the corner of his eye, from the stage wings. There marched John, sporting Corporal stripes. Tony watched John post himself in front of the President and render a hand salute. Again, he was impressed with the President's return salute.

The Sergeant Major said "Attention to Orders" and proceeded to read a Silver Star citation. Tony was shocked. He realized that John hadn't been lying when he said he had some details to cover. The citation talked about how John had assumed control of his formation after a devastating artillery bombardment that had killed his squad leader and injured his fellow team leader. It went on to talk about his actions in blowing a bridge just as North Korean tanks were rushing across it. Finally, the citation narrative talked about his battlefield promotion to Corporal. Tony was amazed by what he heard, and felt his chest swelling with pride. The President pinned the medal on John's chest, and had him turn to face the audience. A round of applause nearly matching that given to Dana rose from the audience. MG Kambic motioned for John to stand next to Lt. Col. Maguire on the stage.

Once John had positioned himself, the Sergeant Major called out "Lt. Col. Tony Cooper, post!" Tony moved forward and performed the same process of reporting to the commander-in-chief as the other two had done. The President then motioned for him to stay in position and moved to the microphone. The Sergeant Major stepped back to make room for the Commander in Chief.

The President said, "I have never before had occasion to present one of these next awards before. Many presidents go their whole term without giving one. This is the first of these awards to be presented to a National Guardsman in over fifty years. It is well deserved, and a deep honor for me to do this."

With that, he repositioned himself in front of Tony and the Sergeant Major began again. "Attention to Orders. The Congressional Medal of Honor is awarded to Lt. Col. Tony Cooper, for exceptional valor ..."

Tony listened to the citation, still feeling that while what was said in the narrative wasn't exactly wrong, it was presented in a way that made what he had done sound much more impressive than what he remembered. He wondered if that was always the case. He had done what he was sure many, if not most, of the people on this stage or in the group of men and women in uniform seated on the main floor would have done in the same situation.

As the Sergeant Major finished reading the citation, President Clark removed a medal hanging from a blue star-covered ribbon from a box held by a waiting aide and latched the ribbon behind Tony's neck. He then shook Tony's hand, as did MG Kambic and Dana. He then motioned for Tony to turn around. The crowd broke out in thunderous applause. Tony felt a strange mix of embarrassment and pride. He searched the audience and again found Rachel and Julie. They both looked to be crying and smiling at the same time. He made a half smile back and gave a half wave. MG Kambic saw the motion, stepped from around Tony's back, and motioned for Rachel and Julie to come forward. They did so, nearly running up the stairs. As they reached him, Tony spread his arms and gathered them both into a bear hug. John joined them. The crowd cheered even louder. President Clark moved in and briefly joined in the hug. He then moved to the podium and, again sensing when the crowd was ready, waved for silence. He turned to Tony and said, "Colonel Cooper, I would like you to come forward and give a few remarks. You are a national hero, and I want you to have a chance to have the microphone." He stepped back, and waved Tony forward.

Tony reluctantly broke free of Rachel, John and Julie's embrace, and motioned for them to come to stand by him. He had not formally prepared any remarks, but he had thought a little about what he would say if he was called on to do so. He decided to start with the old standby of thanking everyone he could think of, starting with the President, the Governor, the Senators, the Generals, the families and most importantly, his fellow soldiers, for being there that day and for all of their support. He then said, "I'm not sure that I deserve this award today, but I am positive that those who didn't come home with us deserve it." The crowd rose to their feet and gave a round of applause that was both vigorous yet mournful at the same time. Tony continued as the crowd retook their seats, "I'm not sure that I deserve this award, but I am positive that the families of those soldiers deserve it." He gestured to occupants of the row that had been designated for the families of the following soldiers. The families stood hesitantly. The crowd again rose to their feet, given an even longer and more respectful round of applause. Again, Tony waited until the crowd settled in. "I'm not sure that I deserve this recognition, but I'm positive that the soldiers seated before us deserve it. I'm not comfortable being singled out for this recognition, for I know that so many of the soldiers, and sailors, airmen and marines who serve now or who have served since the beginning of this country are just as, or more, deserving. All we did," motioning to Dana and himself and the soldiers in the front rows, "was to carry on a tradition and do the best we could, just as all of those American fighting men, and increasingly women, who came before us did. Nothing more; nothing less. That's all we can ask from any soldier; active duty, reserve or National Guardsman!" He yelled out those last words and the troops before him cheered and again rose to their feet, led by General Kambic. Tony stepped away from the microphone and took Rachel and Julie by the hands. He led them toward the side of the stage, stopping only for a handshake with Dana that turned into a hug. John trailed behind. Tony spotted a door in the wings, and led his family toward that. They slipped out the side door, and again he gathered them in his arms.

"Are you supposed to leave, Dad?" asked Julie.

"What are they going to do, send me to Lebanon?" he joked. He said, "They can finish without me. We'll rejoin the troops when they dismiss. There's a reception in the lobby and plaza afterward for everyone to reunite with their families and say their goodbyes. We just got a head start. Now, let's talk about what we are going to do the rest of this summer. I got some time in the sand, but there wasn't much in the way of ocean. We should hit the beach. John, any requests?"

*   *   *   *

Linda watched Tony leave the stage with his family, again feeling a slight pang of loss, something she had no real reason to feel. She turned back to the ceremony as it worked through the last few acts.

The President had handled the whole situation magnificently. He had made sure that the story in the papers would prominently link him to the heroes of the short conflict. That reflected honor would, she was sure he hoped, translate to an even higher favorability rating and thus votes next election. Of course, those who remembered history might remember that Bush the Senior had similarly ridden high after the first Gulf War but had ended his only term after receiving the lowest percentage of the vote of any sitting presidential candidate.

She was scheduled for an interview with President Clark later that afternoon, on Air Force One headed back toward Washington. "Talk about basking in reflected glory," she thought to herself. If she hadn't gotten caught up in the Lebanon mess, she would very likely have gone another twenty years without getting an interview with a sitting president.

"Oh well. Might as well seize on the opportunity while I can," she thought to herself. She wondered if she should ask about the George H. W. Bush comparison. She decided to keep the question in reserve in case the interview didn't seem to be going anywhere.

*   *   *   *

Tony and Rachel finally returned home after 8:00 p.m. Tony felt that they had shaken every hand in the city at some point during the reception. He spent a few minutes petting Misty and just walking around his house with a new appreciation. John was going out with friends and was due for dinner the next night. Julie was staying over at a friend's house, to give Tony and Rachel some time alone.

Tony realized that Rachel had disappeared. He worked his way upstairs and found her lying across their bed in what was obviously a new teddy. Candlelight and soft music accented the effect. Rachel said, "I realized that I didn't send you off how a soldier should be sent off, so I thought the least I could do is welcome you home appropriately."

Tony smiled; but said nothing. He bent down, kissed her deeply and then settled down next to her. He positioned himself into a place where he could look her in the eyes. "I'll have to go away more often," he said.

"Never again," she said. "You've done your part. You have to get out."

"We'll see," he said, in that tone that she appeared to recognize as meaning "let's talk about it later, but don't count on it." At the moment, that seemed to be enough for her.

"The Nation that makes a great distinction between its scholars and its warriors will have its thinking done by cowards and its fighting done by fools."
    - Thucydides

EPILOGUE

Arlington Heights High School
September 9, 10:50 am (1550 GMT)

"Look, Brandon. You either do these Saturday detentions or I will have to suspend you. No Homecoming Dance, no attendance at football games, eventually, no graduation if it comes to that. You will ruin the rest of your high school career over a couple of stupid Saturday Schools. Do you understand?" Tony was uncharacteristically blunt with the young man. He had spent a good deal of time with this particular student over the past four years. He had hoped that Brandon would have matured during that time, but the growth had been slow and not very steady. Despite everything, Tony really liked the kid. He was the classic lovable Dennis the Menace character updated for the millennia, with long hair, baggy pants and a black T-shirt.

"But Mr. Cooper. It's not fair. I never should have gotten in trouble in the first place. The teacher had it in for me."

"Look, Brandon. Mr. Phillips gave you a lunch detention because he thought you were disrespectful. I don't really care what happened. Mr. Phillips is well within his rights to give you a lunch detention. The reason you are up to two Saturday Schools has nothing to do with Mr. Phillips. You have them because you have been disrespectful to me by not following the rules. Do you get it? This has nothing to do with the original offense, it has to do with you not doing what you are supposed to do."

"But Mr. Cooper. I still don't think it's fair."

"Nowhere is it written down that life must be fair. Now get back to class. You still need to pass English if you want to graduate." Tony wrote the details of time and location on Brandon's hall pass. Brandon said, "Thanks Mr. Cooper" and headed out the door. He was always polite; one of the reasons Tony hadn't suspended him more often.

He turned to file the paperwork into Brandon's thick file. As he finished that task, his phone rang. "Arlington Heights High School. This is Mr. Cooper. Can I help you?"

"Yes. I heard that you've been checking out all of the high school girls in a lecherous manner. I want to know to whom I should submit a formal complaint."

"Dana, you son of a bitch. Are you still up there stealing the taxpayers money?"

"Waste, fraud and abuse – those are my middle names. Seriously, how are you, Tony?"

"I'm good, thanks to you. Back into the routine. How about you?"

"Can't complain. I'm heading out to a Board of Health meeting regarding a pool variance. Exciting stuff."

"Hell. I got you beat. In the Army I can get 500 guys to do exactly what I tell them to do. Here, I can't get Brandon Roberts to go to his Saturday School detention. Life is strange."

"What are you doing about your next National Guard assignment, Tony?"

"I don't think there is one. It might make sense for me to retire. I'm almost radioactive. Would you want me on your staff?"

"You know I would. However, I understand what you mean. Who wants to play second fiddle to someone with your background? What are you going to do?"

"I'm toying with retiring," Tony answered.

"Hell. Don't do that. Let me talk to the ATAG. There may be a slot at Regional Training Institute that would be perfect for you."

"Both Battalion Commanders are brand new down there."

Dana said, "The RTI commander job is opening up. Hodge is retiring."

"That's a full Colonel slot. Hell, I'm a junior Lt. Col."

"They make exceptions from time to time. I suspect you would be one of those cases."

"That would make me even more radioactive."

"Probably, but you'd be a radioactive full Colonel," Dana laughed. "How's John doing at West Point?"

"Good. He made it through Beast Barracks no problem – he said that after boot camp it was really a joke. He seems to be hanging in academically"

"I had always heard that the children of Medal of Honor winners got automatic acceptance to the military academies, but I never knew whether it was true. What a chance for him, Tony."

"Julie is starting to think about the Air Force Academy. I think she would be a good officer. She's a better student than John ever was."

"How's Rachel about that?"

"Pissed, but also resigned to it. I think she realizes that she married into the military and she can't do much about it. The smartest thing I ever did was to get married in uniform. Whenever she gets too mad, I remind her."

"Tony, you talk a good game, but we know the truth. Without her, you'd be a chronically underemployed drunk. She's the best thing that ever happened to you."

"You're right, Dana. I think I'll get some flowers on the way home tonight. She's been through a lot."

"Hell, that phone call from Lebanon alone probably took years off her life."

"Can I take this chance to thank you again for rescuing my ass, Dana?"

Dana laughed lightly. "Hell, I couldn't let you die there. Rachel would have killed me."

"Probably so. Plus, I would have haunted you forever."

There was a long pause. Tony waited for Dana to say something. He had the impression there was more to the phone call. Finally, he said, " Dana, Is there anything else on your mind?"

"Tony, do you ever feel that what we are doing now is a waste of time? I can't get excited about what I do. And I can't forget those three young men I had responsibility for who didn't come back to their families."

"Dana, what about the 450 you did bring back, including me? What about the fact that the world is hopefully a little safer now than it was before? The whole point of what we did was to get back to here and to let everyone else have as normal a life as possible. Enjoy your girls, enjoy Lisa. Those three we didn't bring back to Ohio, those twelve who didn't come back from my flight; they would want us to carry on. They signed up knowing that they might pay the ultimate sacrifice. If you hadn't made it back, would you want the rest of us to carry on or would you want us to fall apart? You are a fine city planner. Your city is a better place to live because of what you do. I 'd like to believe that this high school is a better place to be because of what I do. A few kids each year make it through who might not have otherwise. Those are good things. We need to decide whether we are going to honor the memories of those who didn't make it back by going on with what we do or dishonor it by letting it screw us up permanently."

Dana didn't reply immediately. Finally, he said, "Intellectually, I know you are right. I just can't seem to shake this."

"Call into Wright Patterson. Use those veteran services they keep telling us about. The Veteran's Assistance Program is just for this. Rachel and I used a referral from them a couple of times last month and saw a counselor, just to help us to talk things out. I highly recommend it."

"You did? How'd it go?"

"It went OK. Not a magic bullet, but it made a real difference."

"I probably will. I don't know," said Dana.

"Besides, I hear that they have designated you as the next Brigade Commander. You are going to have a good chance to make general. You can influence the training of the next generation of guardsmen. In addition to those lives you saved in Iraq, you can save lives through the training and the work of the NCOs and officers you and your team will train for the next time the phone rings. Besides, someone has to make sure the garbage in Dublin gets picked up on time!

"Yeah, that's all I do. And all you do is hand out tardy slips," Dana laughed. "Hey, I better get back to the excitement that is my life. If we don't get this pool variance my entire capital budget is going to have to be changed."

"Good luck, Dana. Let's get together for lunch sometime soon."

"We will, Tony. I'll call you. Although, let's make it a happy hour. I could use a drink."

"Sounds good, Dana. Take care of yourself."

"You too, Tony. Think about the RTI position. We'll talk about that soon. And thanks for listening."

After he hung up, Tony spent some time thinking about the call. Dana had articulated something he had been thinking about for a while. He imagined that veterans around the world, throughout time, had experienced the same thoughts. After facing life and death, good and evil, how does one turn back to the mundane details of everyday life? Tony was reminded of a quote. General Washington had articulated it well, at the beginning of the experiment that would become America. "I am a soldier so that my son can be a farmer so that his son can be an artist."

What Washington's quote did not explain was how a single individual could make the transition from soldier to farmer – or city planner or teacher. *Oh well,* he thought to himself. *Millions have figured it out before us and millions more will figure it out in the future.* Despite Washington's wish, the world would always have a use for soldiers in addition to its need for farmers and artists.

He turned back to his computer and called up the Student Information System search function to look up the work phone number for Brandon's mother. *Right now, what the world needs is for this kid to graduate high school. Might as well try to get some support from home.* He found the demographics info page and punched in Brandon's mom's number into his phone.

Civilians In Peace Order Form

Use this convenient order form to order additional copies
of
Civilians In Peace

Please Print:

Name_____

Address_____

City_____ **State**_____

Zip_____

Phone(**)**_____

____ copies of book @ $10.99 each $_____
Postage and handling @ $2.99 per book $_____
OH residents add 6.75% tax $_____
Total amount enclosed $_____

Make checks and money orders payable to: A.S.I.

Send order to: Civilians In Peace
4166 Ashmore Rd. • Columbus, OH 43220
or visit www.civiliansinpeace.com